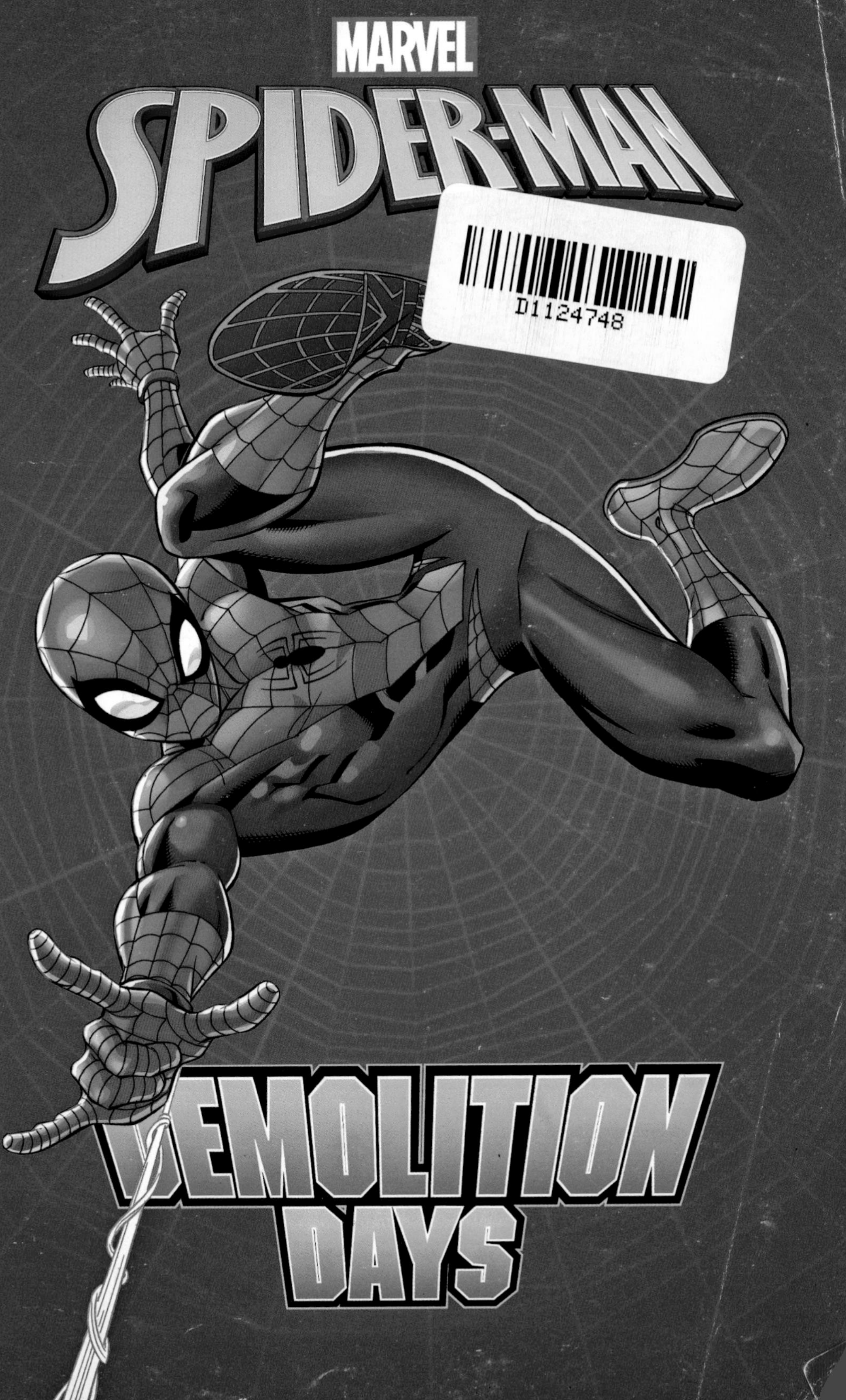
MARVEL
SPIDER-MAN
DEMOLITION
DAYS

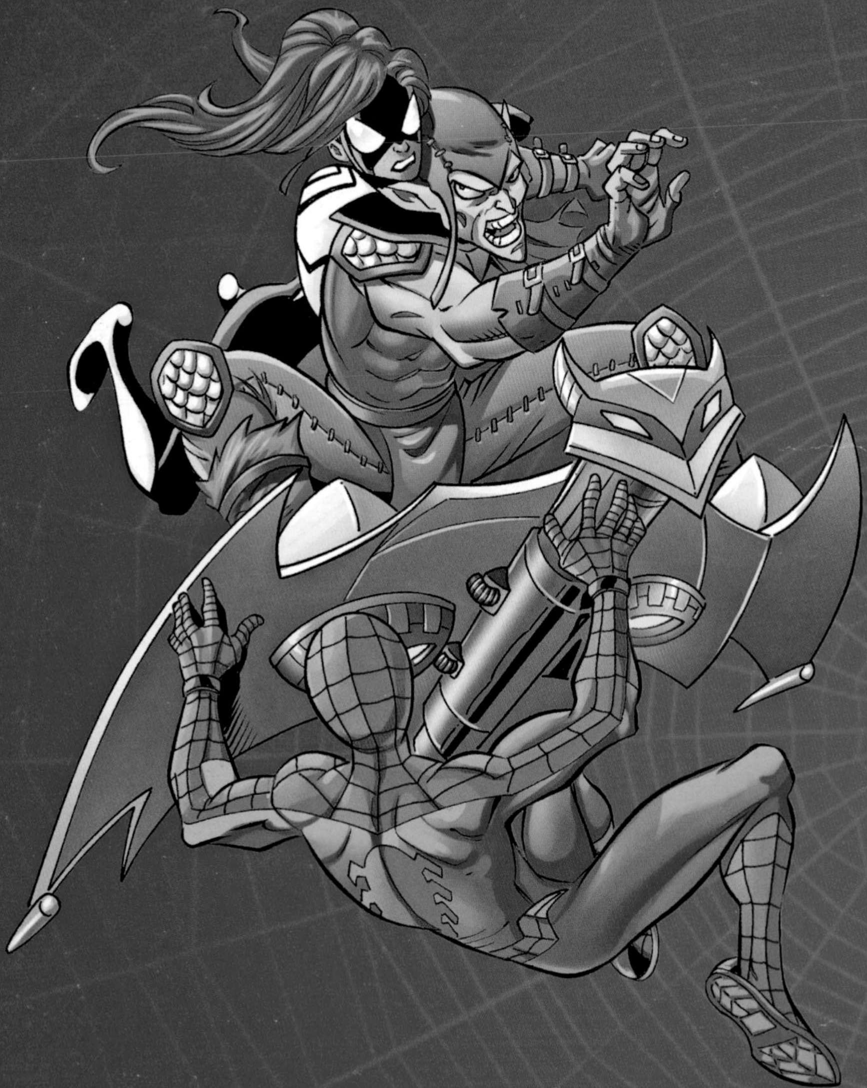

SPIDER-MAN CREATED BY **STAN LEE** & **STEVE DITKO**

COLLECTION EDITOR **JENNIFER GRÜNWALD** • ASSISTANT EDITOR **CAITLIN O'CONNELL**
ASSOCIATE MANAGING EDITOR **KATERI WOODY** • EDITOR, SPECIAL PROJECTS **MARK D. BEAZLEY**
VP PRODUCTION & SPECIAL PROJECTS **JEFF YOUNGQUIST** • SVP PRINT, SALES & MARKETING **DAVID GABRIEL**
BOOK DESIGNER **JAY BOWEN**

EDITOR IN CHIEF **C.B. CEBULSKI** • CHIEF CREATIVE OFFICER **JOE QUESADA**
PRESIDENT **DAN BUCKLEY** • EXECUTIVE PRODUCER **ALAN FINE**

SPIDER-MAN: DEMOLITION DAYS. First printing 2018. ISBN 978-1-302-91283-3. Published by MARVEL WORLDWIDE, INC., a subsidiary of MARVEL ENTERTAINMENT, LLC. OFFICE OF PUBLICATION: 135 West 50th Street, New York, NY 10020. **Printed in the U.S.A.** DAN BUCKLEY, President, Marvel Entertainment; JOHN NEE, Publisher; JOE QUESADA, Chief Creative Officer; TOM BREVOORT, SVP of Publishing; DAVID BOGART, SVP of Business Affairs & Operations, Publishing & Partnership; DAVID GABRIEL, SVP of Sales & Marketing, Publishing; JEFF YOUNGQUIST, VP of Production & Special Projects; DAN CARR, Executive Director of Publishing Technology; ALEX MORALES, Director of Publishing Operations; DAN EDINGTON, Managing Editor; SUSAN CRESPI, Production Manager; STAN LEE, Chairman Emeritus. For information regarding advertising in Marvel Comics or on Marvel.com, please contact Vit DeBellis, Custom Solutions & Integrated Advertising Manager, at vdebellis@marvel.com. For Marvel subscription inquiries, please call 888-511-5480. **Manufactured between 10/19/2018 and 11/20/2018 by SHERIDAN, CHELSEA, MI, USA.**

10 9 8 7 6 5 4 3 2 1

MARVEL

SPIDER-MAN

DEMOLITION DAYS

BRIAN SMITH & **IVAN COHEN**
WRITERS

RON LIM & **J.L. GILES**
PENCILERS

**WALDEN WONG, KEITH CHAMPAGNE,
ROBERTO POGGI** & **J.L. GILES**
INKERS

CARLOS LOPEZ & **CHRIS SOTOMAYOR**
COLORISTS

VC's JOE SABINO
LETTERER

KATHERINE BROWN
ASSISTANT EDITOR

DARREN SANCHEZ
EDITOR/PROJECT MANAGER

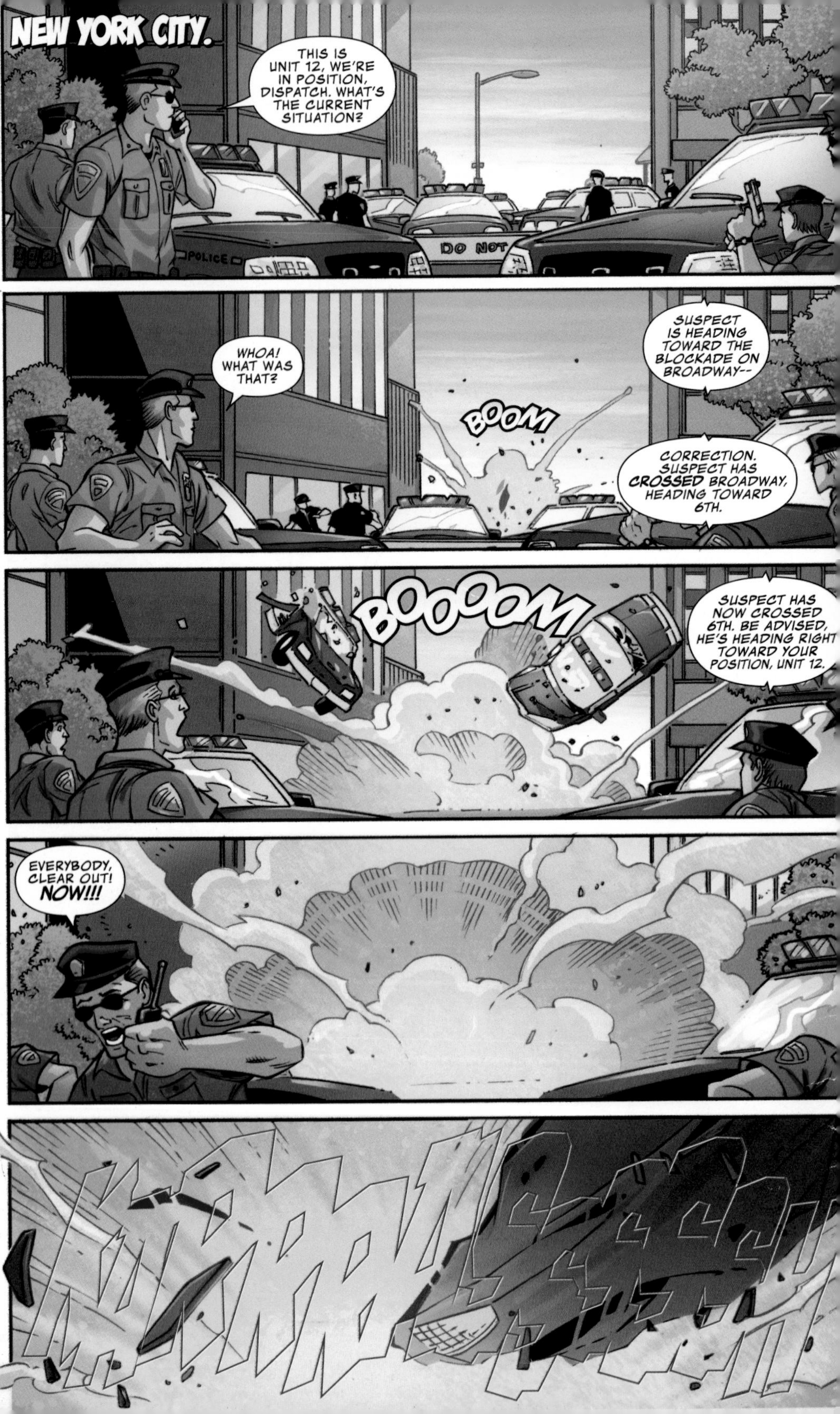
NEW YORK CITY.
THIS IS UNIT 12, WE'RE IN POSITION, DISPATCH. WHAT'S THE CURRENT SITUATION?
POLICE
DO NOT
SUSPECT IS HEADING TOWARD THE BLOCKADE ON BROADWAY--
WHOA! WHAT WAS THAT?
BOOM
CORRECTION. SUSPECT HAS CROSSED BROADWAY, HEADING TOWARD 6TH.
BOOOOM
SUSPECT HAS NOW CROSSED 6TH. BE ADVISED, HE'S HEADING RIGHT TOWARD YOUR POSITION, UNIT 12.
EVERYBODY, CLEAR OUT! NOW!!!

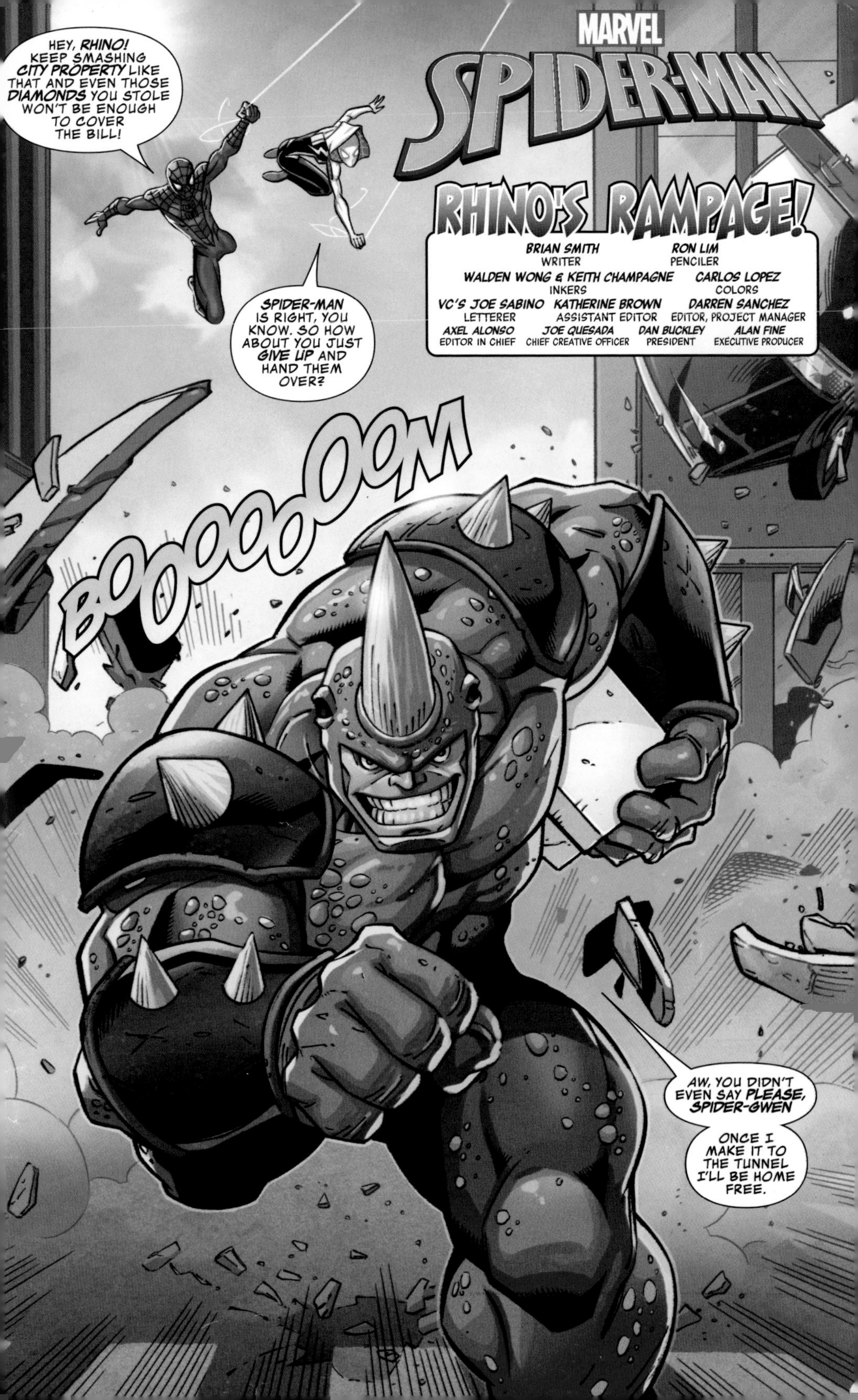
HEY, RHINO! KEEP SMASHING CITY PROPERTY LIKE THAT AND EVEN THOSE DIAMONDS YOU STOLE WON'T BE ENOUGH TO COVER THE BILL!
MARVEL
SPIDER-MAN
RHINO'S RAMPAGE!
BRIAN SMITH WRITER
RON LIM PENCILER
WALDEN WONG & KEITH CHAMPAGNE INKERS
CARLOS LOPEZ COLORS
VC'S JOE SABINO LETTERER
KATHERINE BROWN ASSISTANT EDITOR
DARREN SANCHEZ EDITOR, PROJECT MANAGER
AXEL ALONSO EDITOR IN CHIEF
JOE QUESADA CHIEF CREATIVE OFFICER
DAN BUCKLEY PRESIDENT
ALAN FINE EXECUTIVE PRODUCER
SPIDER-MAN IS RIGHT, YOU KNOW. SO HOW ABOUT YOU JUST GIVE UP AND HAND THEM OVER?
BOOOOOOOM
AW, YOU DIDN'T EVEN SAY PLEASE, SPIDER-GWEN
ONCE I MAKE IT TO THE TUNNEL I'LL BE HOME FREE.

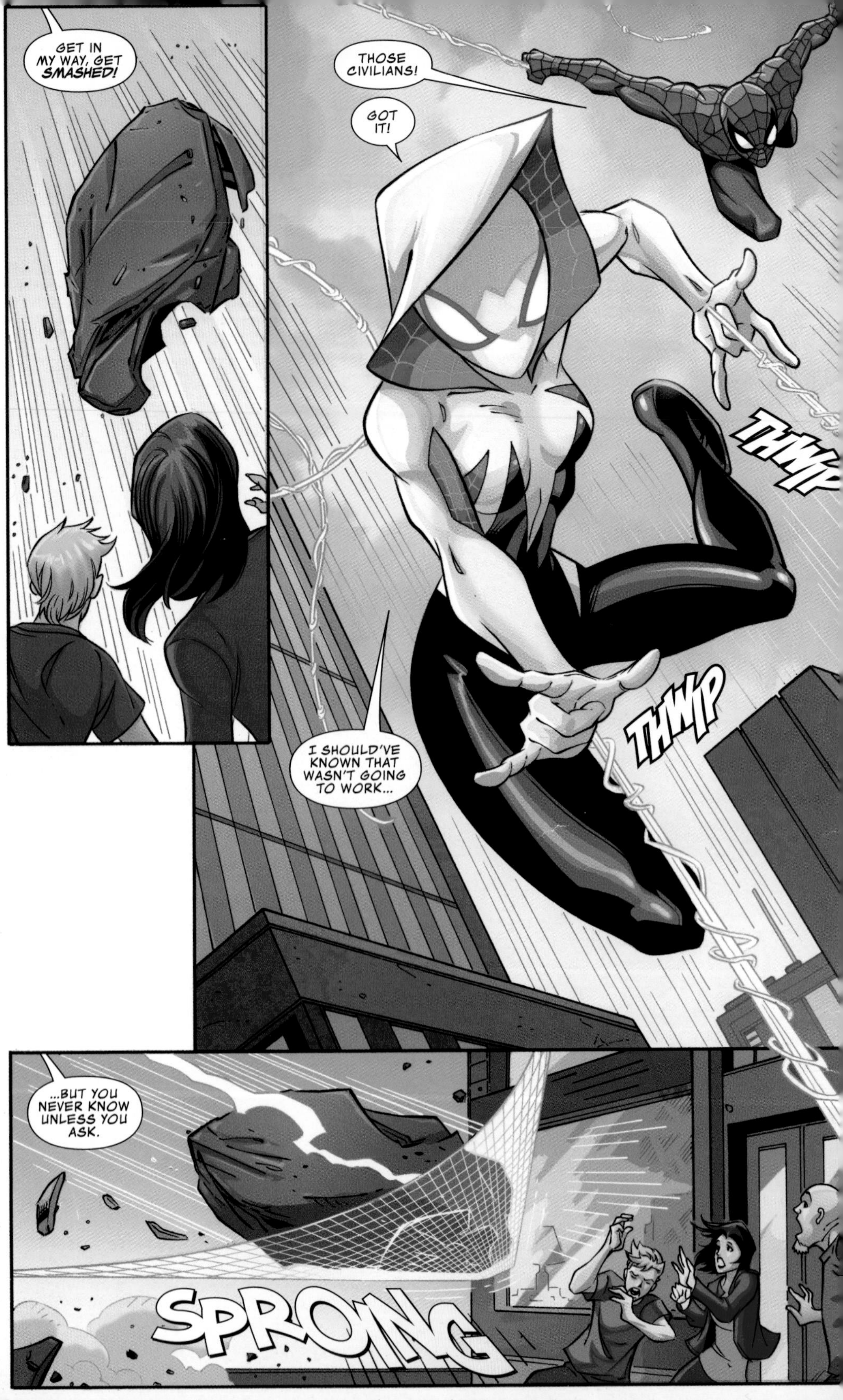
GET IN MY WAY, GET *SMASHED!*
THOSE CIVILIANS!
GOT IT!
THWIP
THWIP
I SHOULD'VE KNOWN THAT WASN'T GOING TO WORK...
...BUT YOU NEVER KNOW UNLESS YOU ASK.
SPRONG

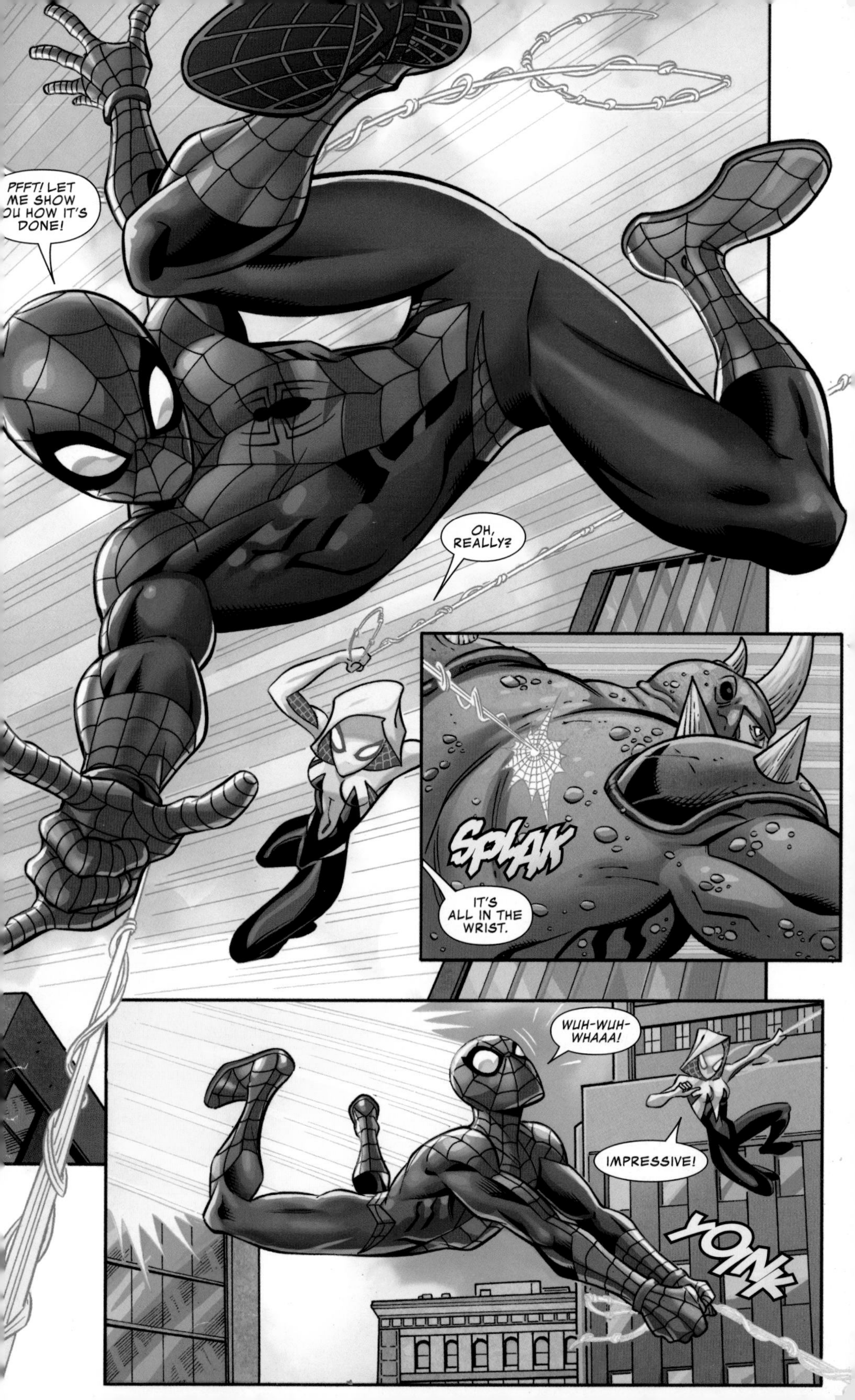
PFFT! LET ME SHOW OU HOW IT'S DONE!
OH, REALLY?
SPLAK
IT'S ALL IN THE WRIST.
WUH-WUH-WHAAA!
IMPRESSIVE!
YOINK

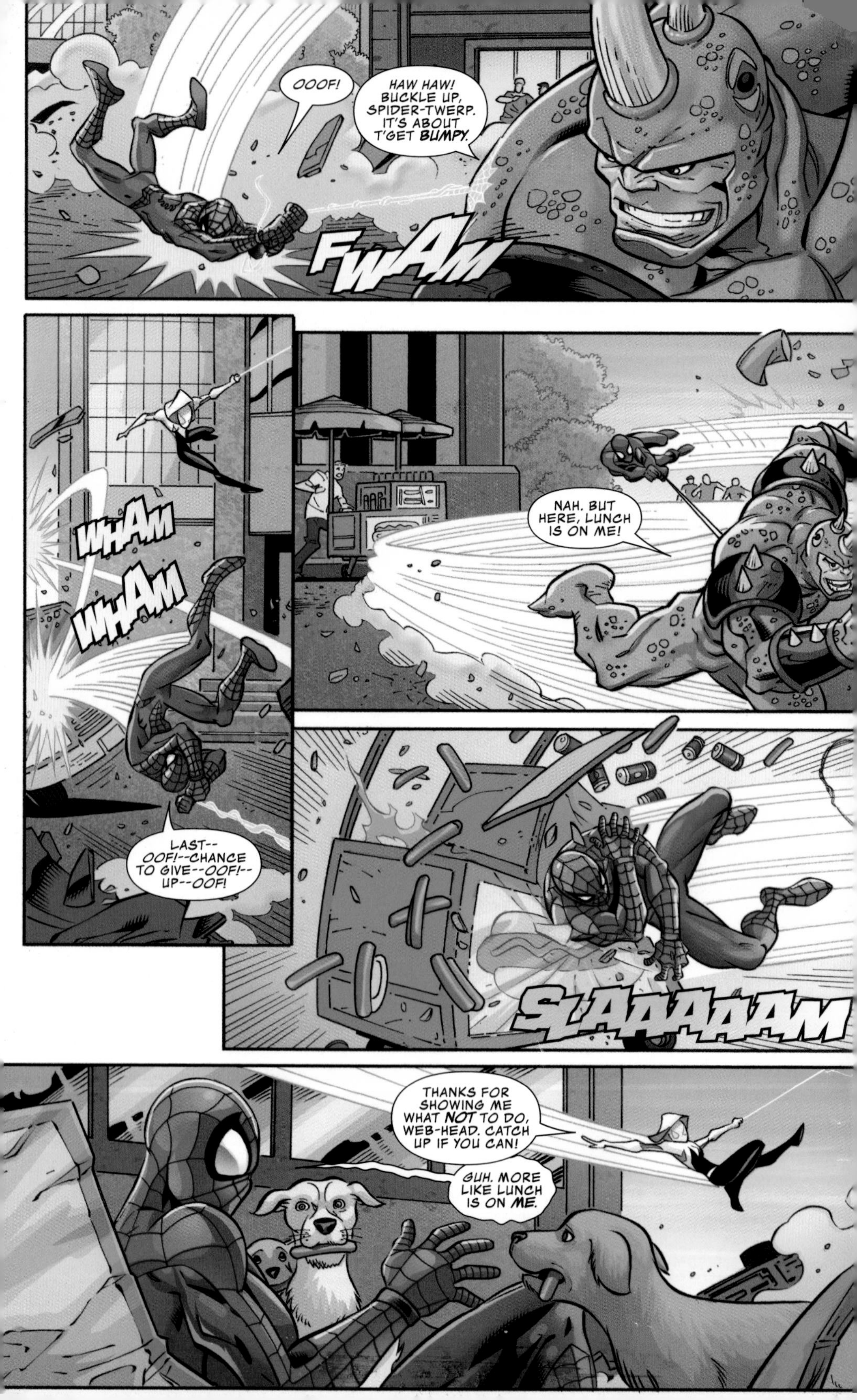
OOOF!
HAW HAW! BUCKLE UP, SPIDER-TWERP. IT'S ABOUT T'GET BUMPY.
FWAM
WHAM
WHAM
LAST-- OOF!--CHANCE TO GIVE--OOF!-- UP--OOF!
NAH. BUT HERE, LUNCH IS ON ME!
SLAAAAAAM
THANKS FOR SHOWING ME WHAT NOT TO DO, WEB-HEAD. CATCH UP IF YOU CAN!
GUH. MORE LIKE LUNCH IS ON ME.

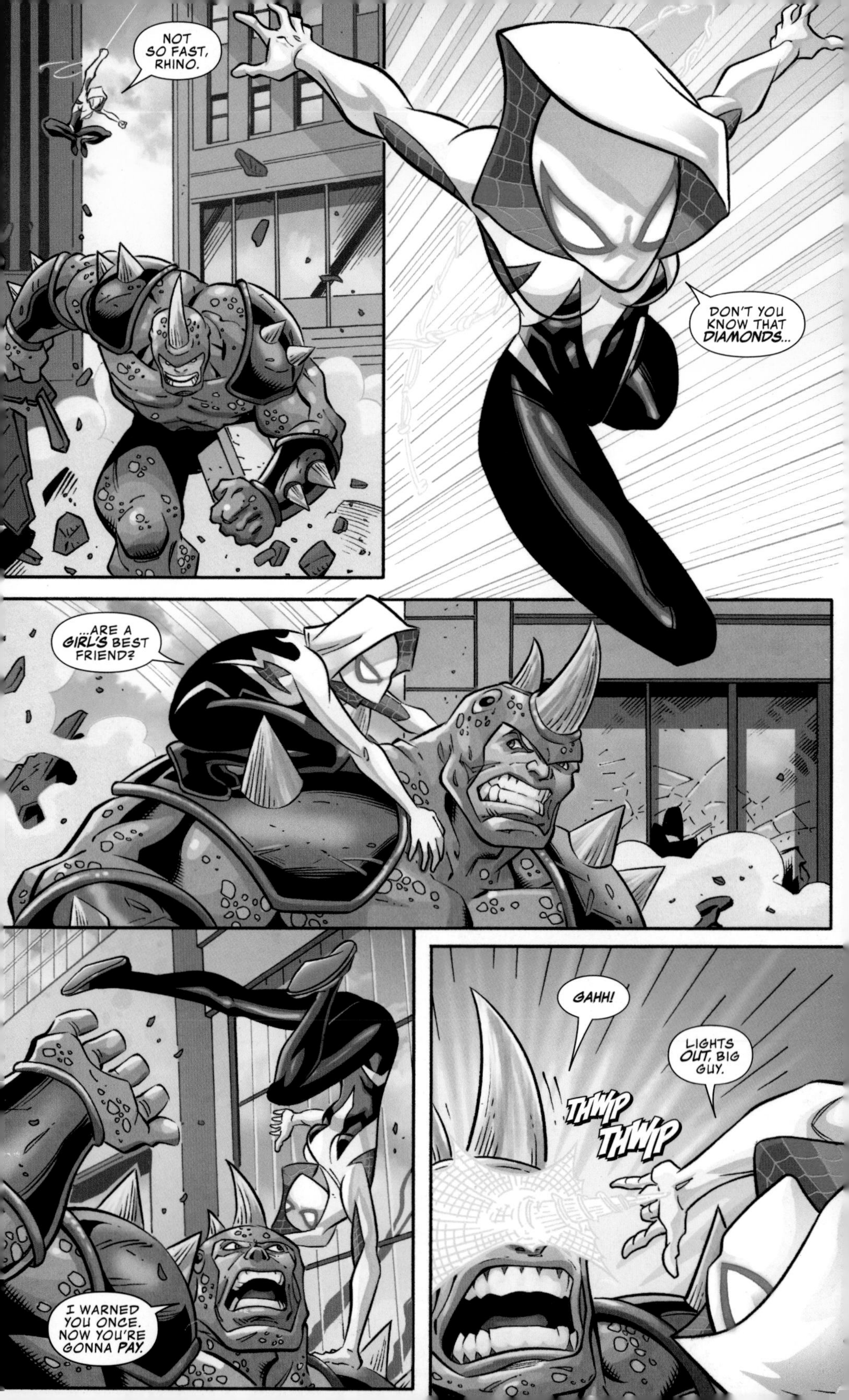
NOT SO FAST, RHINO.
DON'T YOU KNOW THAT DIAMONDS...
...ARE A GIRL'S BEST FRIEND?
I WARNED YOU ONCE. NOW YOU'RE GONNA PAY.
GAHH!
LIGHTS OUT, BIG GUY.
THWIP
THWIP

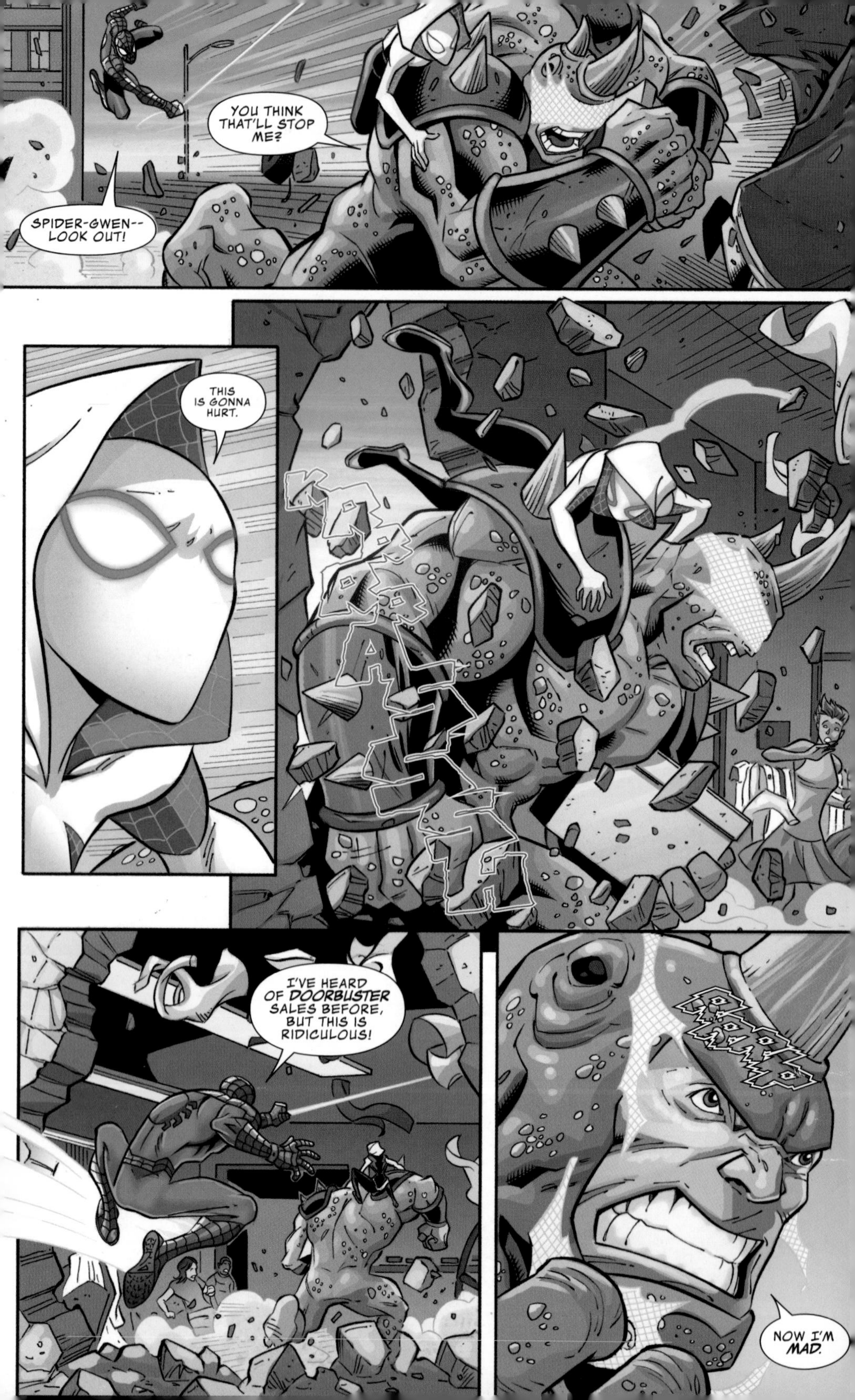
SPIDER-GWEN-- LOOK OUT!
YOU THINK THAT'LL STOP ME?
THIS IS GONNA HURT.
I'VE HEARD OF DOORBUSTER SALES BEFORE, BUT THIS IS RIDICULOUS!
NOW I'M MAD.

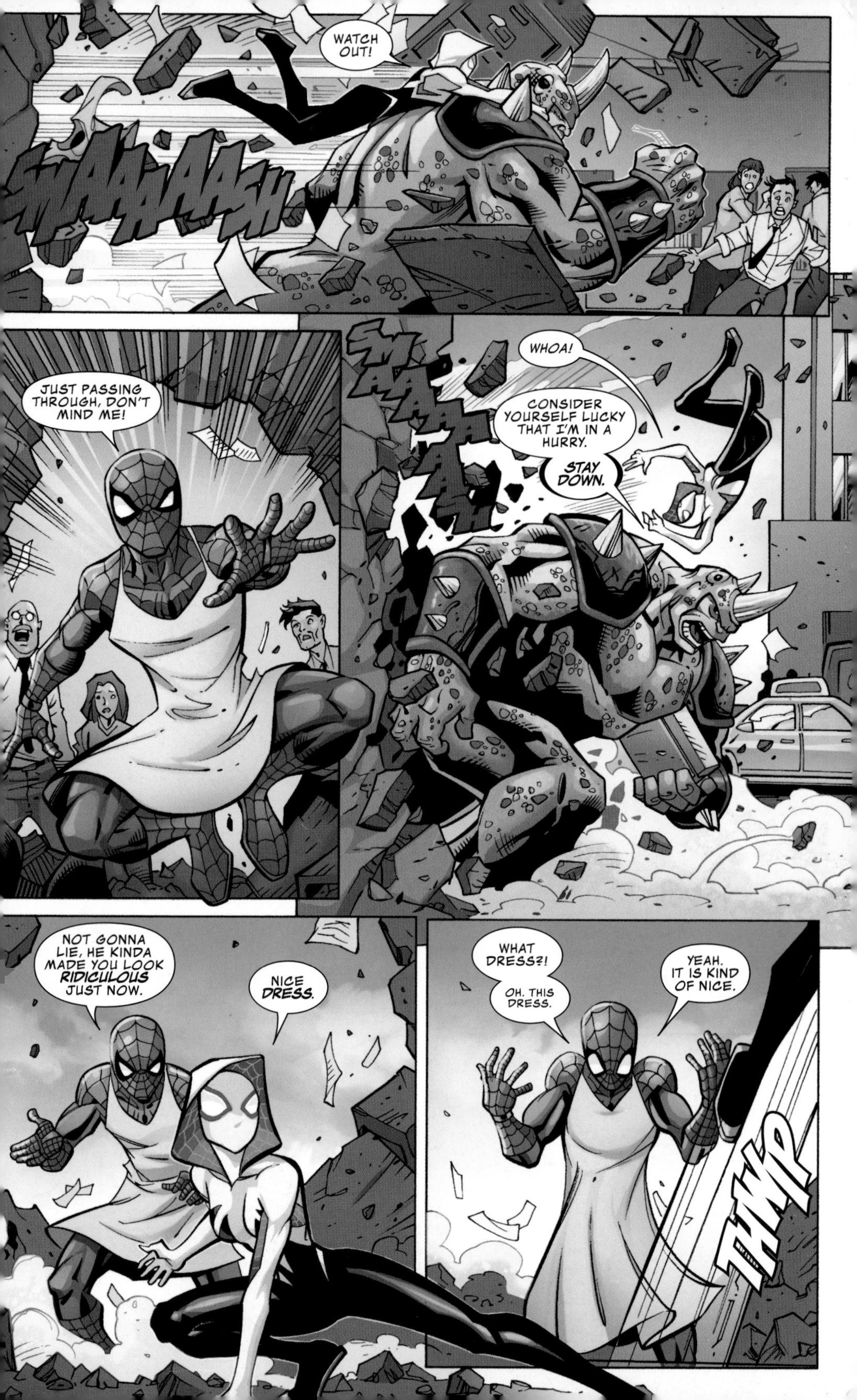
WATCH OUT!
SHWAAAAAASH
JUST PASSING THROUGH, DON'T MIND ME!
SMAAAAAAAASH
WHOA!
CONSIDER YOURSELF LUCKY THAT I'M IN A HURRY.
STAY DOWN.
NOT GONNA LIE, HE KINDA MADE YOU LOOK RIDICULOUS JUST NOW.
NICE DRESS.
WHAT DRESS?!
OH. THIS DRESS.
YEAH. IT IS KIND OF NICE.
THWIP

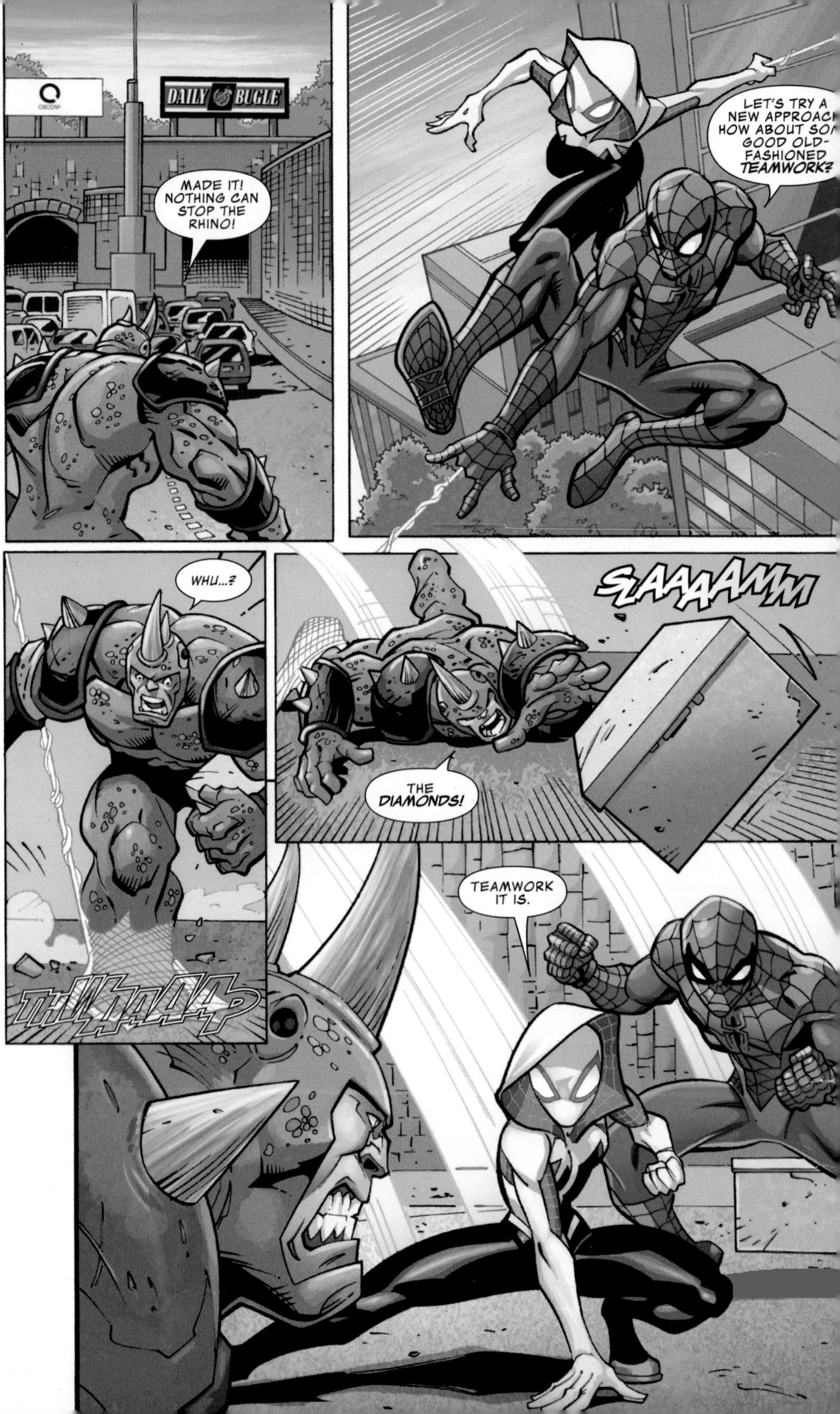
OSCORP
DAILY BUGLE
MADE IT! NOTHING CAN STOP THE RHINO!
LET'S TRY A NEW APPROAC HOW ABOUT SO GOOD OLD-FASHIONED TEAMWORK?
WHU...?
THWAAP
SLAAAAMM
THE DIAMONDS!
TEAMWORK IT IS.

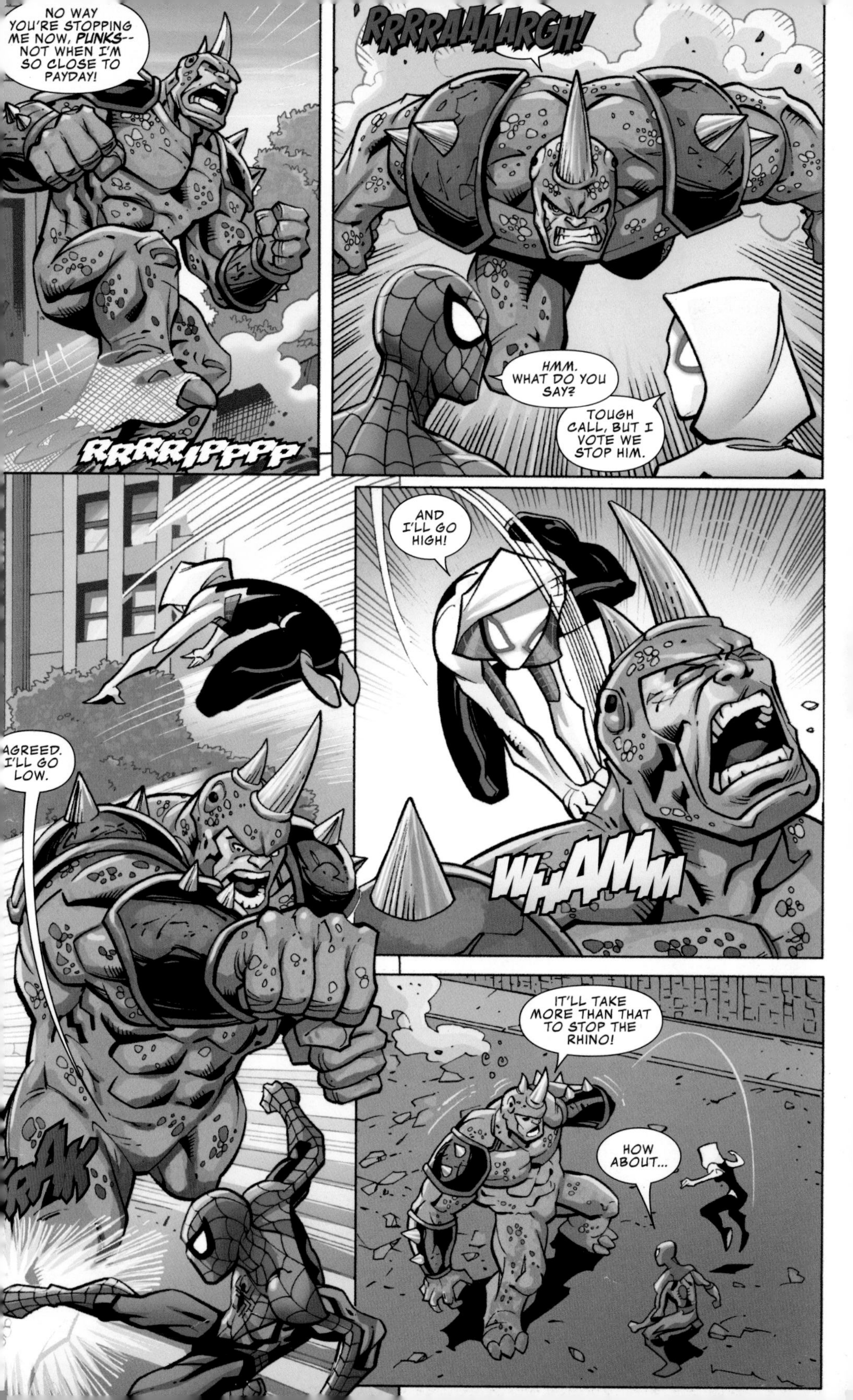

NO WAY YOU'RE STOPPING ME NOW, **PUNKS**-- NOT WHEN I'M SO CLOSE TO PAYDAY!
RRRRIPPPP
RRRRAAAAARGH!
HMM. WHAT DO YOU SAY?
TOUGH CALL, BUT I VOTE WE STOP HIM.
AGREED. I'LL GO LOW.
AND I'LL GO HIGH!
WHAMM
IT'LL TAKE MORE THAN THAT TO STOP THE RHINO!
HOW ABOUT...

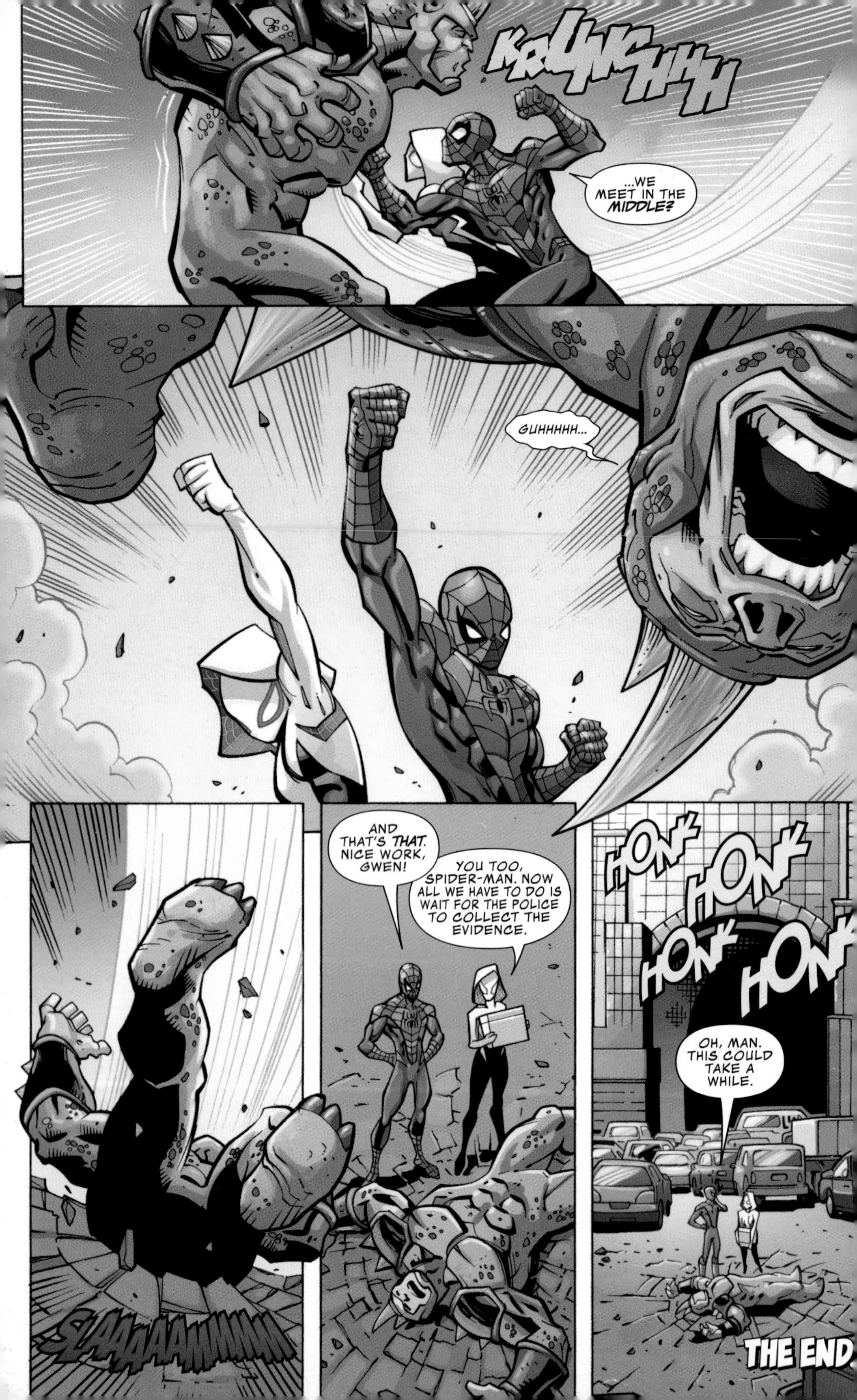
KRUNCHHHH
...WE MEET IN THE MIDDLE?
GUHHHHHH...
SLAAAAMMMM
AND THAT'S THAT. NICE WORK, GWEN!
YOU TOO, SPIDER-MAN. NOW ALL WE HAVE TO DO IS WAIT FOR THE POLICE TO COLLECT THE EVIDENCE.
HONK HONK HONK HONK
OH, MAN. THIS COULD TAKE A WHILE.
THE END.

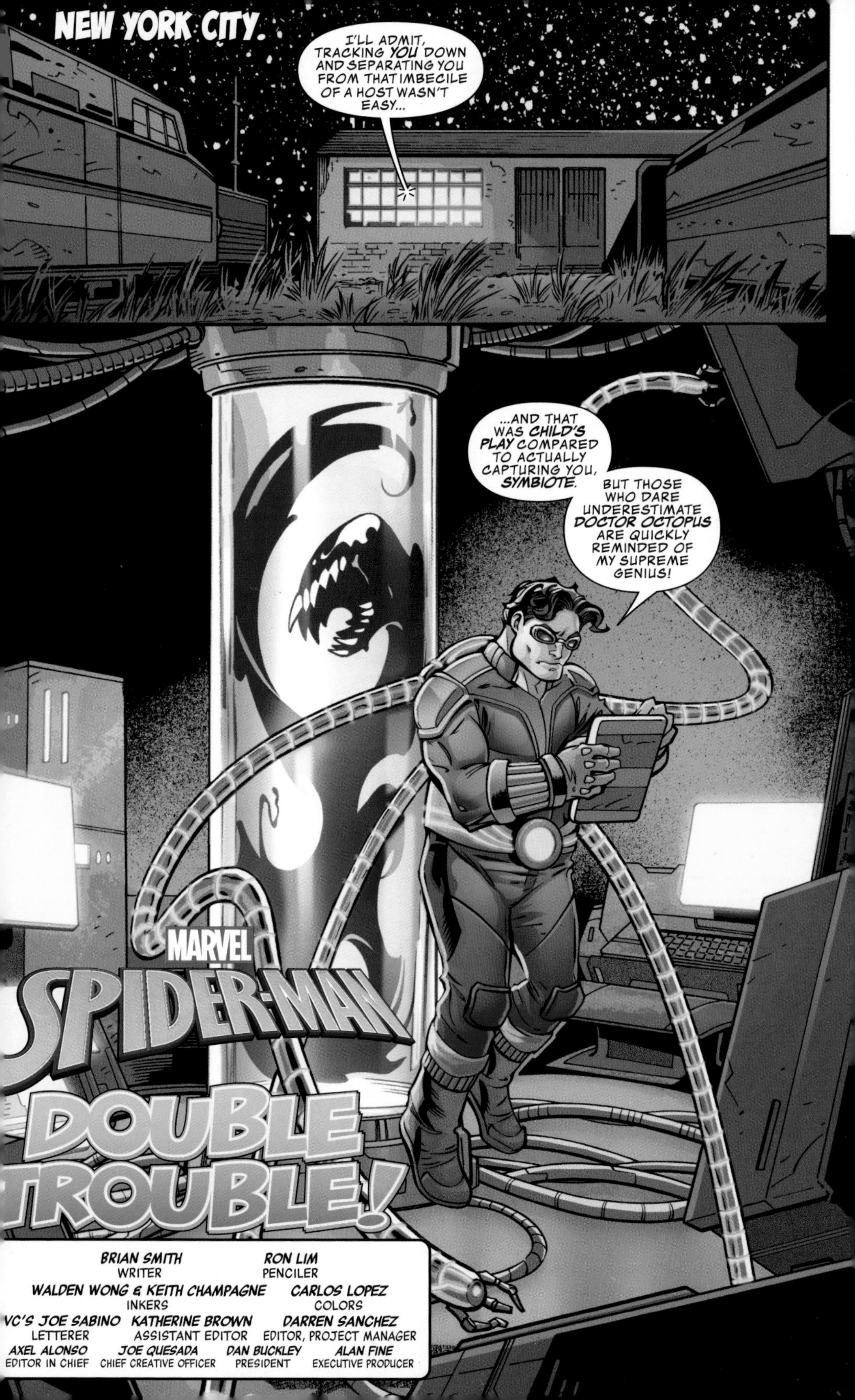
NEW YORK CITY
I'LL ADMIT, TRACKING YOU DOWN AND SEPARATING YOU FROM THAT IMBECILE OF A HOST WASN'T EASY...
...AND THAT WAS CHILD'S PLAY COMPARED TO ACTUALLY CAPTURING YOU, SYMBIOTE.
BUT THOSE WHO DARE UNDERESTIMATE DOCTOR OCTOPUS ARE QUICKLY REMINDED OF MY SUPREME GENIUS!
MARVEL SPIDER-MAN
DOUBLE TROUBLE!
BRIAN SMITH WRITER
RON LIM PENCILER
WALDEN WONG & KEITH CHAMPAGNE INKERS
CARLOS LOPEZ COLORS
VC'S JOE SABINO LETTERER
KATHERINE BROWN ASSISTANT EDITOR
DARREN SANCHEZ EDITOR, PROJECT MANAGER
AXEL ALONSO EDITOR IN CHIEF
JOE QUESADA CHIEF CREATIVE OFFICER
DAN BUCKLEY PRESIDENT
ALAN FINE EXECUTIVE PRODUCER

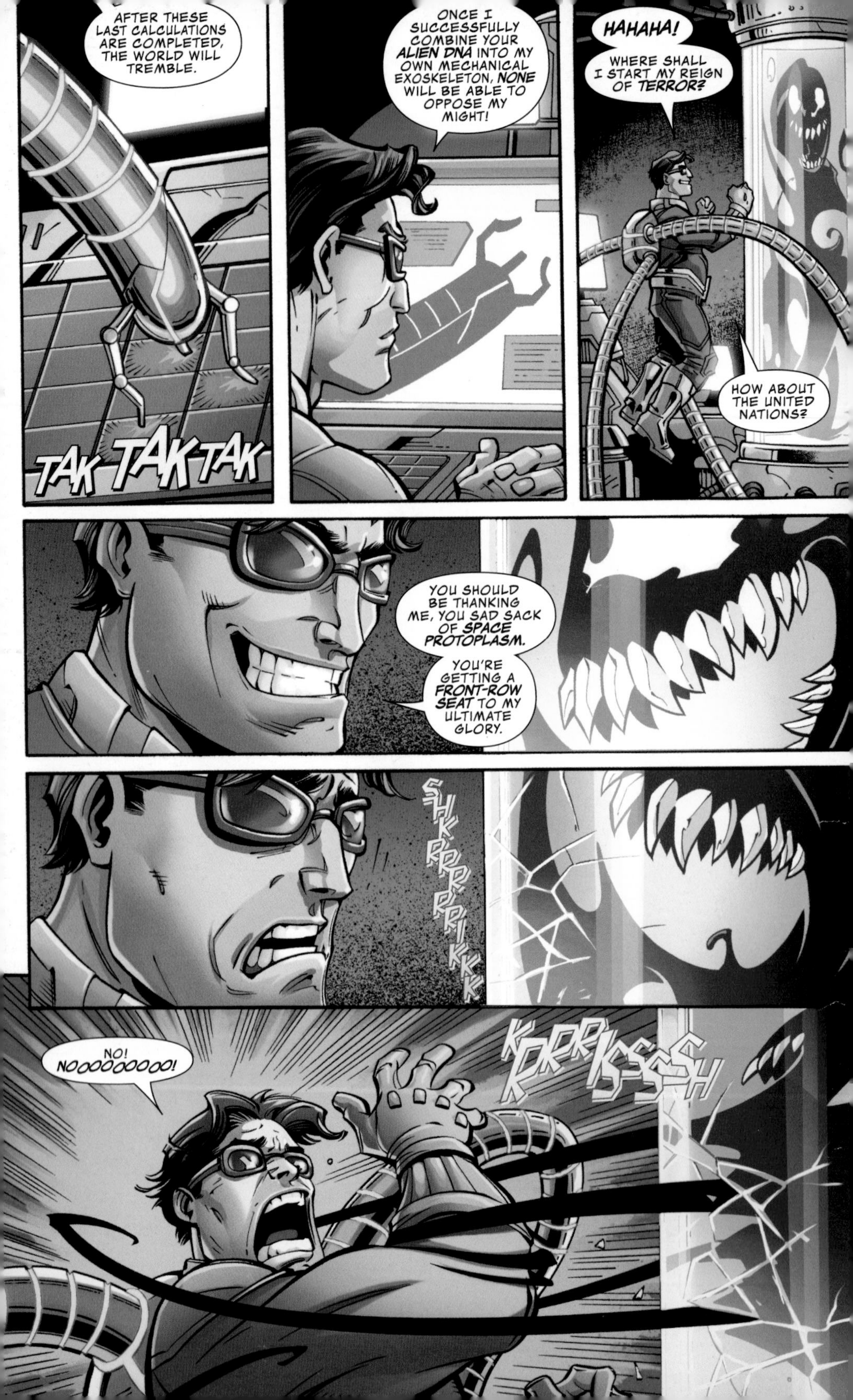
AFTER THESE LAST CALCULATIONS ARE COMPLETED, THE WORLD WILL TREMBLE.
TAK TAK TAK
ONCE I SUCCESSFULLY COMBINE YOUR ALIEN DNA INTO MY OWN MECHANICAL EXOSKELETON, NONE WILL BE ABLE TO OPPOSE MY MIGHT!
HAHAHA!
WHERE SHALL I START MY REIGN OF TERROR?
HOW ABOUT THE UNITED NATIONS?
YOU SHOULD BE THANKING ME, YOU SAD SACK OF SPACE PROTOPLASM.
YOU'RE GETTING A FRONT-ROW SEAT TO MY ULTIMATE GLORY.
SHKRRRRIKKK
NO! NOOOOOOOOO!
KRRRKSSSH

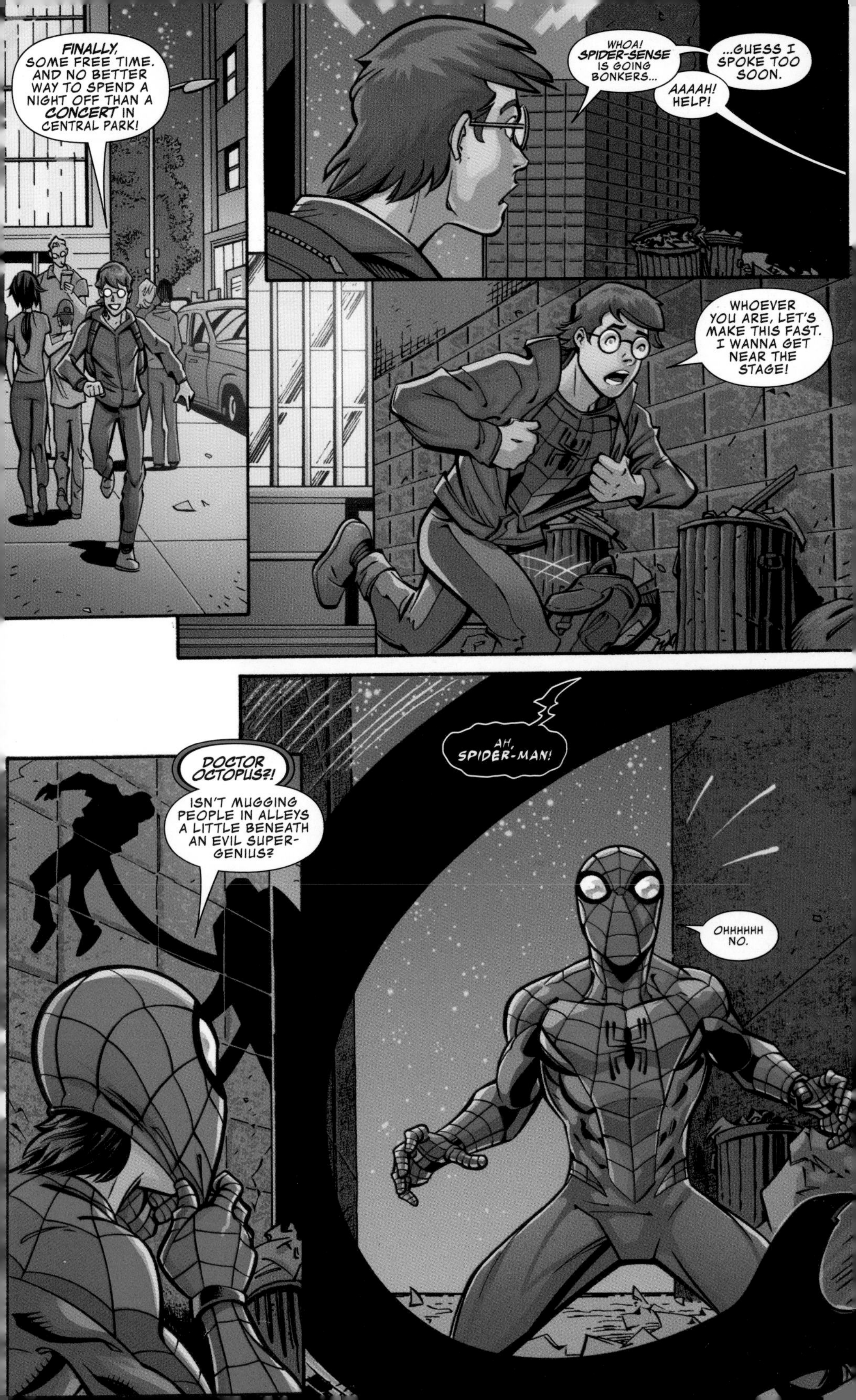
FINALLY, SOME FREE TIME. AND NO BETTER WAY TO SPEND A NIGHT OFF THAN A CONCERT IN CENTRAL PARK!
WHOA! SPIDER-SENSE IS GOING BONKERS...
...GUESS I SPOKE TOO SOON.
AAAAH! HELP!
WHOEVER YOU ARE, LET'S MAKE THIS FAST. I WANNA GET NEAR THE STAGE!
AH, SPIDER-MAN!
DOCTOR OCTOPUS?!
ISN'T MUGGING PEOPLE IN ALLEYS A LITTLE BENEATH AN EVIL SUPER-GENIUS?
OHHHHHH NO.

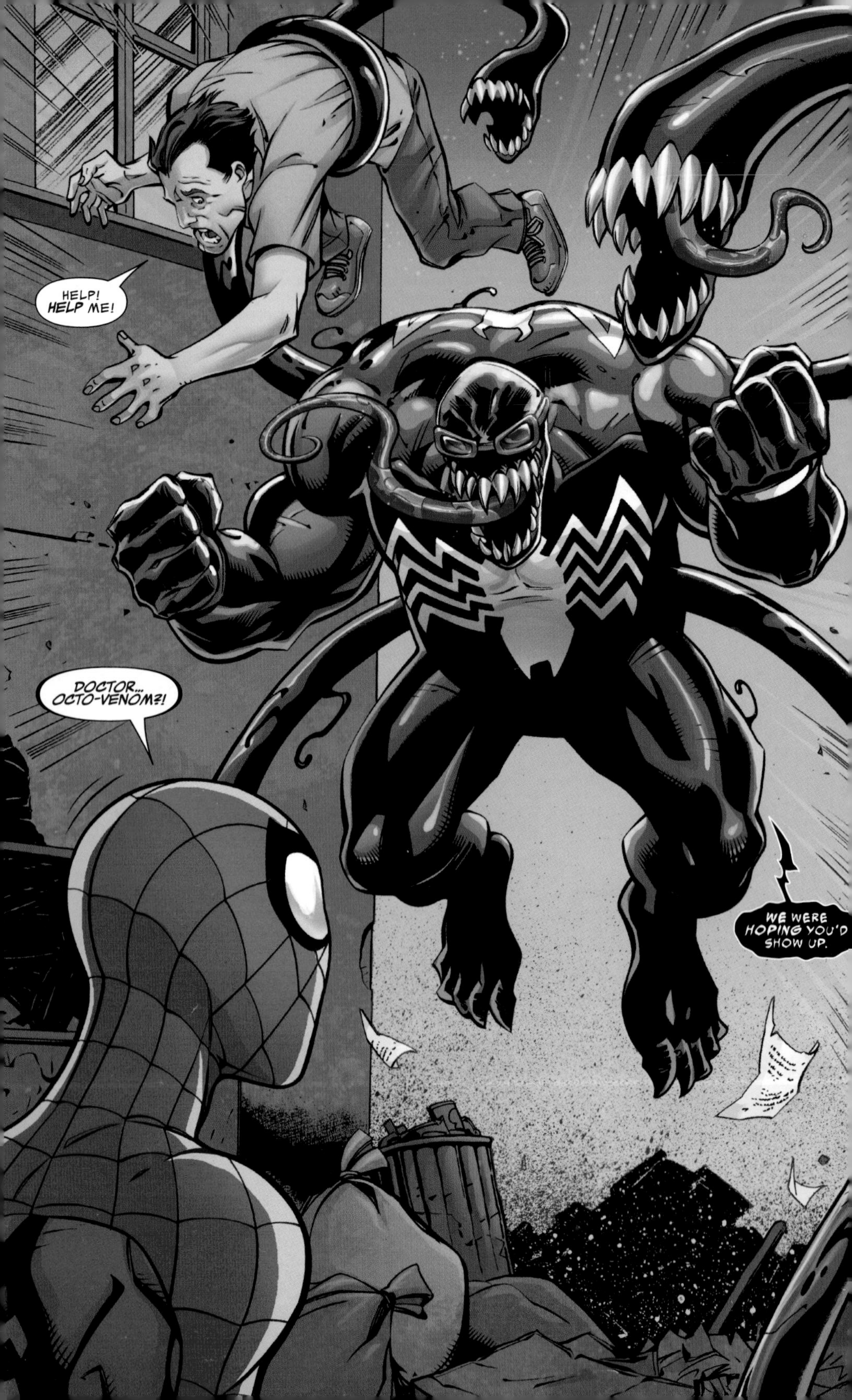
HELP! HELP ME!
DOCTOR... OCTO-VENOM?!
WE WERE HOPING YOU'D SHOW UP.

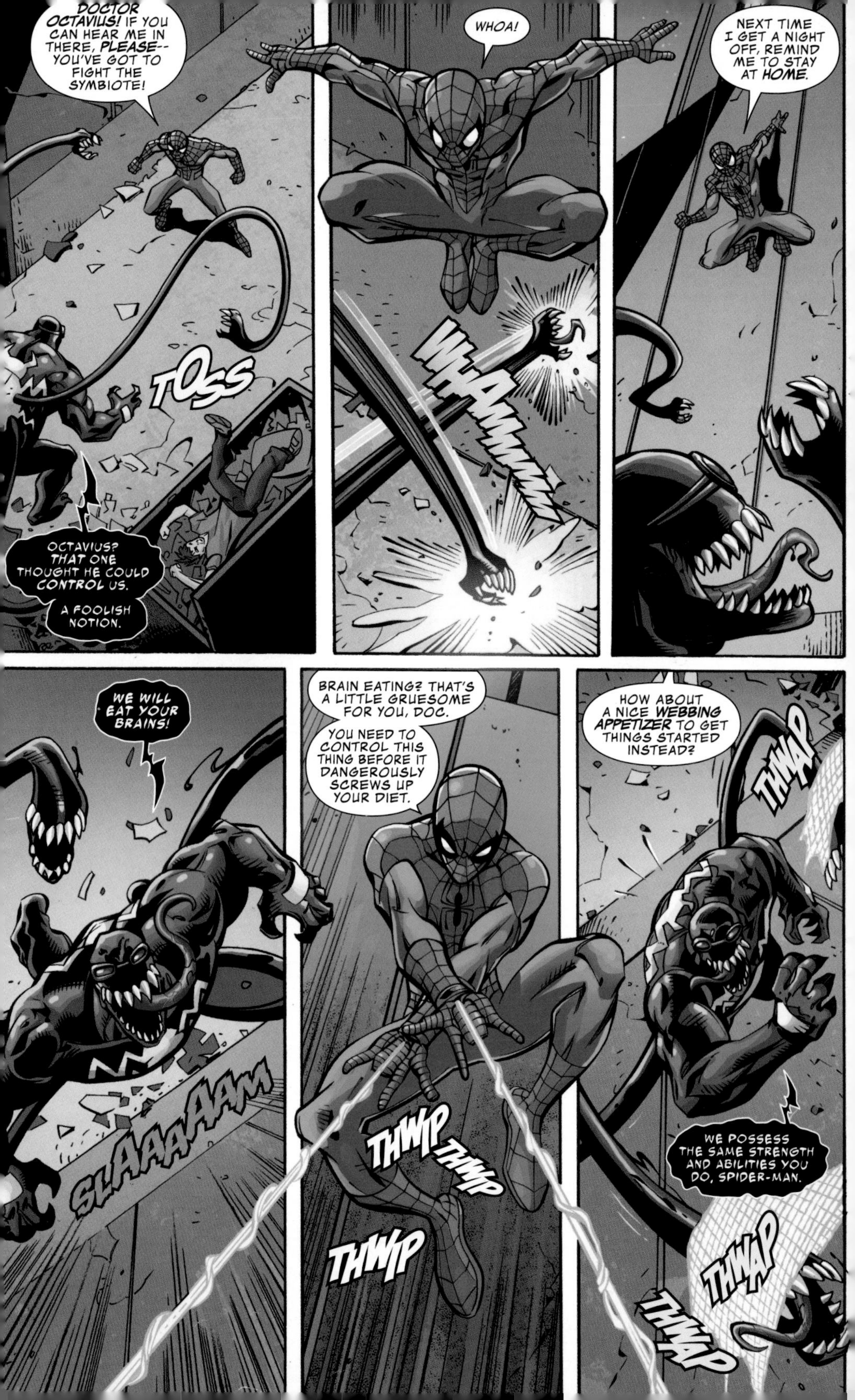
DOCTOR OCTAVIUS! IF YOU CAN HEAR ME IN THERE, PLEASE-- YOU'VE GOT TO FIGHT THE SYMBIOTE!
TOSS
OCTAVIUS? THAT ONE THOUGHT HE COULD CONTROL US.
A FOOLISH NOTION.
WHOA!
WHAMMMMM
NEXT TIME I GET A NIGHT OFF, REMIND ME TO STAY AT HOME.
WE WILL EAT YOUR BRAINS!
SLAAAAAM
BRAIN EATING? THAT'S A LITTLE GRUESOME FOR YOU, DOC.
YOU NEED TO CONTROL THIS THING BEFORE IT DANGEROUSLY SCREWS UP YOUR DIET.
THWIP
THWIP
THWIP
HOW ABOUT A NICE WEBBING APPETIZER TO GET THINGS STARTED INSTEAD?
THWAP
WE POSSESS THE SAME STRENGTH AND ABILITIES YOU DO, SPIDER-MAN.
THWAP
THWAP

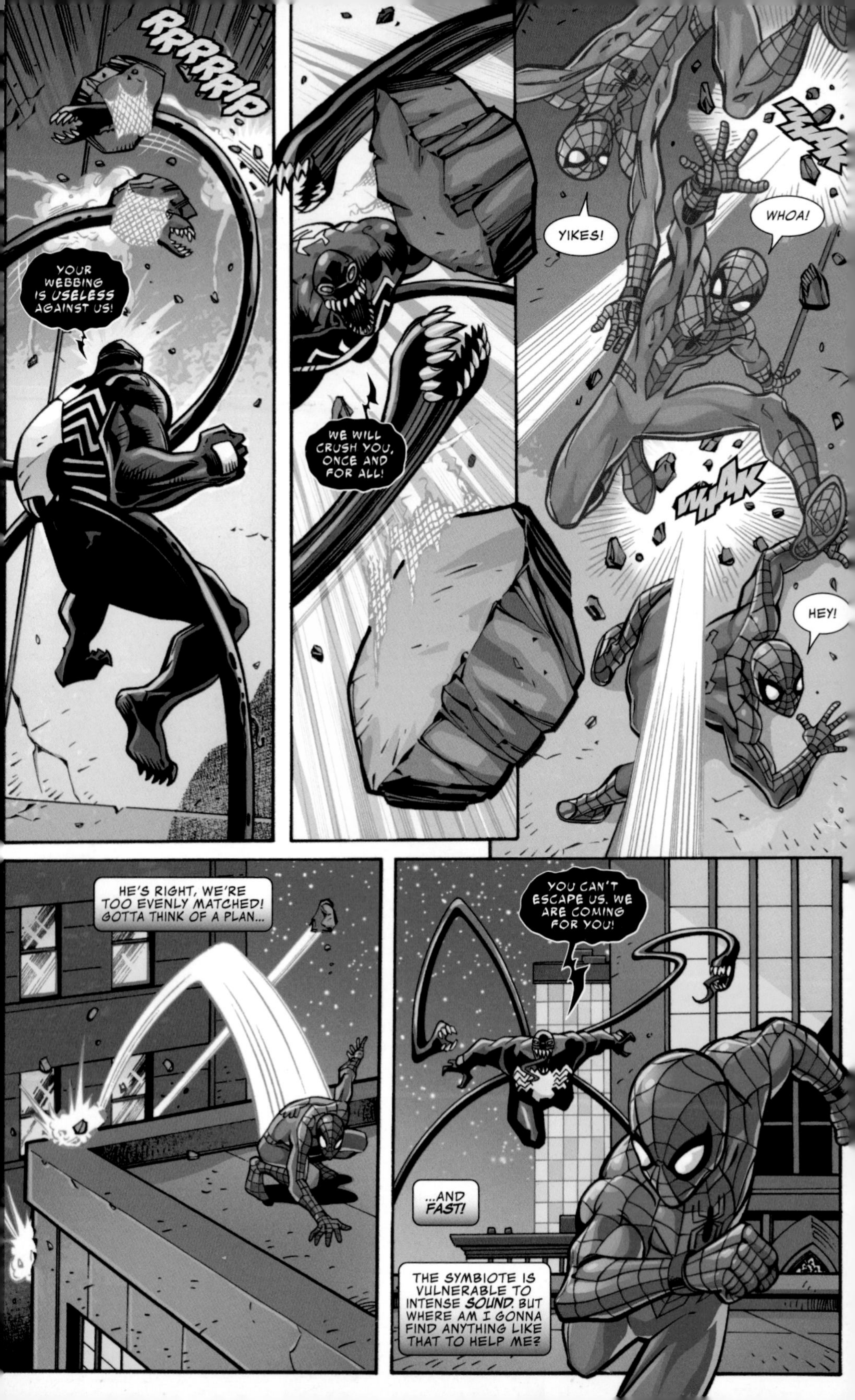
RRRRRIP
YOUR WEBBING IS USELESS AGAINST US!
WE WILL CRUSH YOU, ONCE AND FOR ALL!
WHAK
YIKES!
WHOA!
WHAK
HEY!
HE'S RIGHT, WE'RE TOO EVENLY MATCHED! GOTTA THINK OF A PLAN...
YOU CAN'T ESCAPE US. WE ARE COMING FOR YOU!
...AND FAST!
THE SYMBIOTE IS VULNERABLE TO INTENSE SOUND. BUT WHERE AM I GONNA FIND ANYTHING LIKE THAT TO HELP ME?

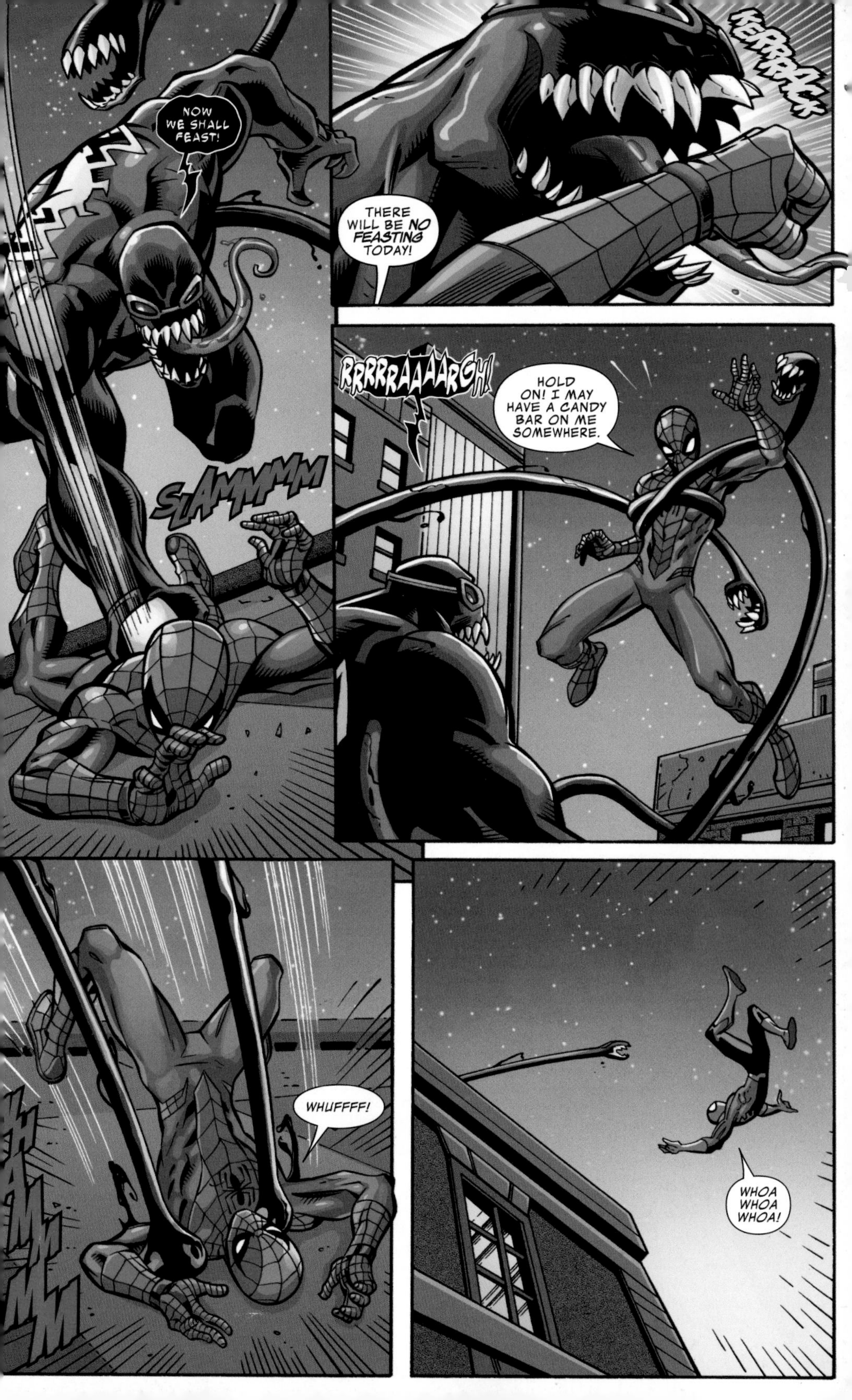
NOW WE SHALL FEAST!
KERRACK
THERE WILL BE NO FEASTING TODAY!
SLAMMMMM
RRRRRAAAAARGH!
HOLD ON! I MAY HAVE A CANDY BAR ON ME SOMEWHERE.
WHAMMM
WHUFFFF!
WHOA WHOA WHOA!

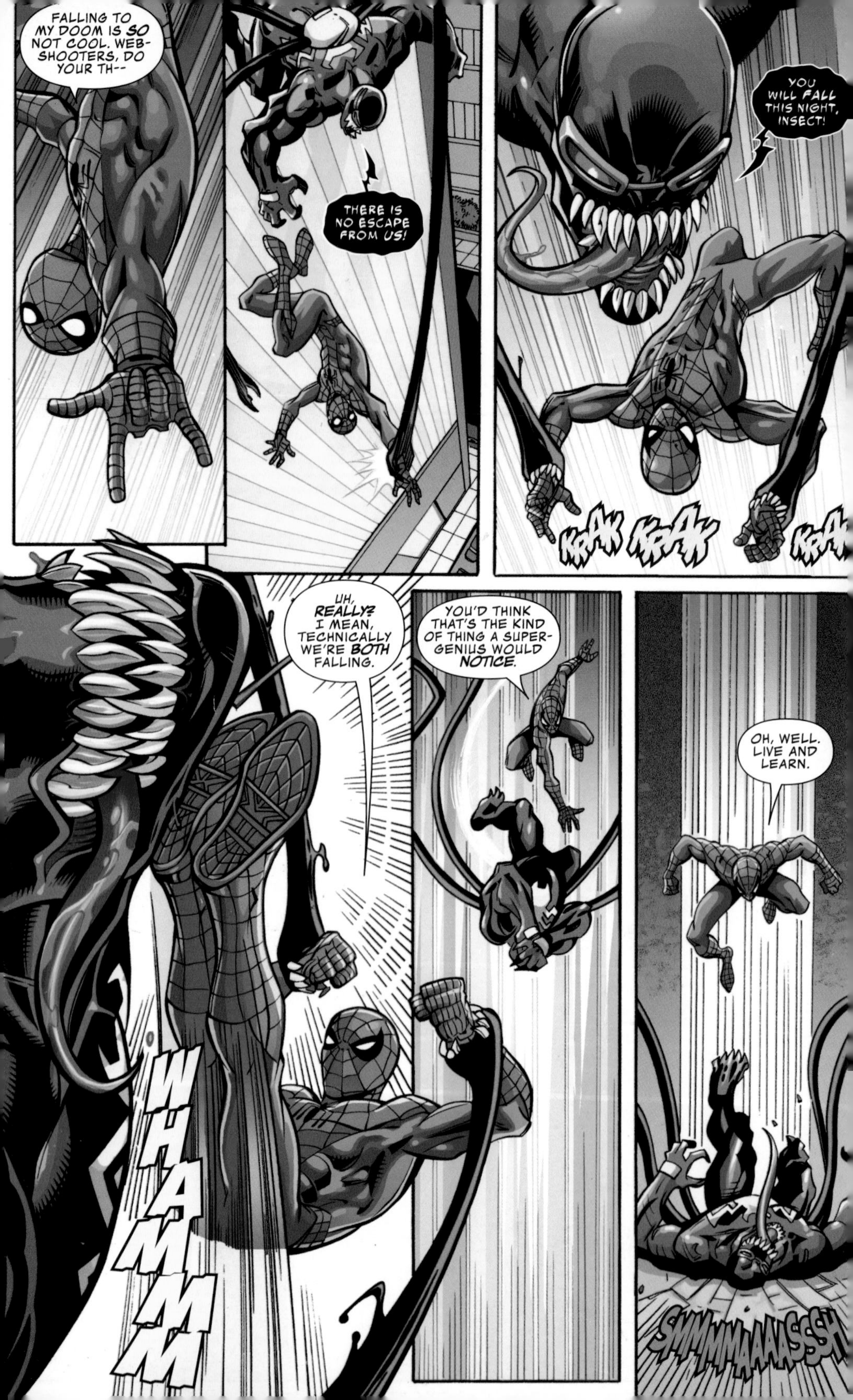
FALLING TO MY DOOM IS SO NOT COOL. WEB-SHOOTERS, DO YOUR TH--
THERE IS NO ESCAPE FROM US!
YOU WILL FALL THIS NIGHT, INSECT!
KRAK KRAK KRAK
UH, REALLY? I MEAN, TECHNICALLY WE'RE BOTH FALLING.
WHAMM
YOU'D THINK THAT'S THE KIND OF THING A SUPER-GENIUS WOULD NOTICE.
OH, WELL. LIVE AND LEARN.
SMMMMAAAASSSH

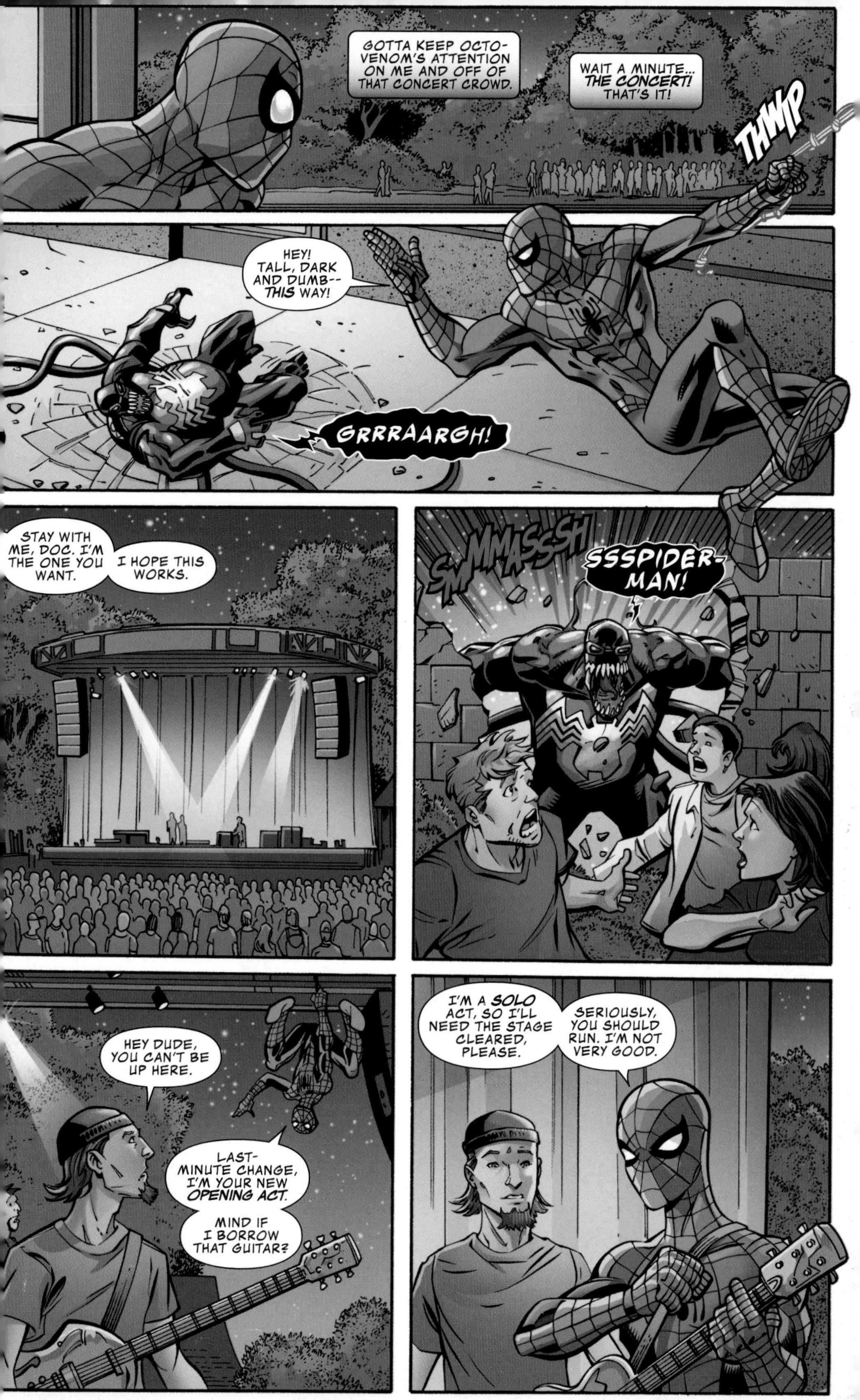
GOTTA KEEP OCTO-VENOM'S ATTENTION ON ME AND OFF OF THAT CONCERT CROWD.
WAIT A MINUTE... THE CONCERT! THAT'S IT!
THWIP
HEY! TALL, DARK AND DUMB-- THIS WAY!
GRRRAARGH!
STAY WITH ME, DOC. I'M THE ONE YOU WANT.
I HOPE THIS WORKS.
SMMMASSSH
SSSPIDER-MAN!
HEY DUDE, YOU CAN'T BE UP HERE.
LAST-MINUTE CHANGE, I'M YOUR NEW OPENING ACT.
MIND IF I BORROW THAT GUITAR?
I'M A SOLO ACT, SO I'LL NEED THE STAGE CLEARED, PLEASE.
SERIOUSLY, YOU SHOULD RUN. I'M NOT VERY GOOD.

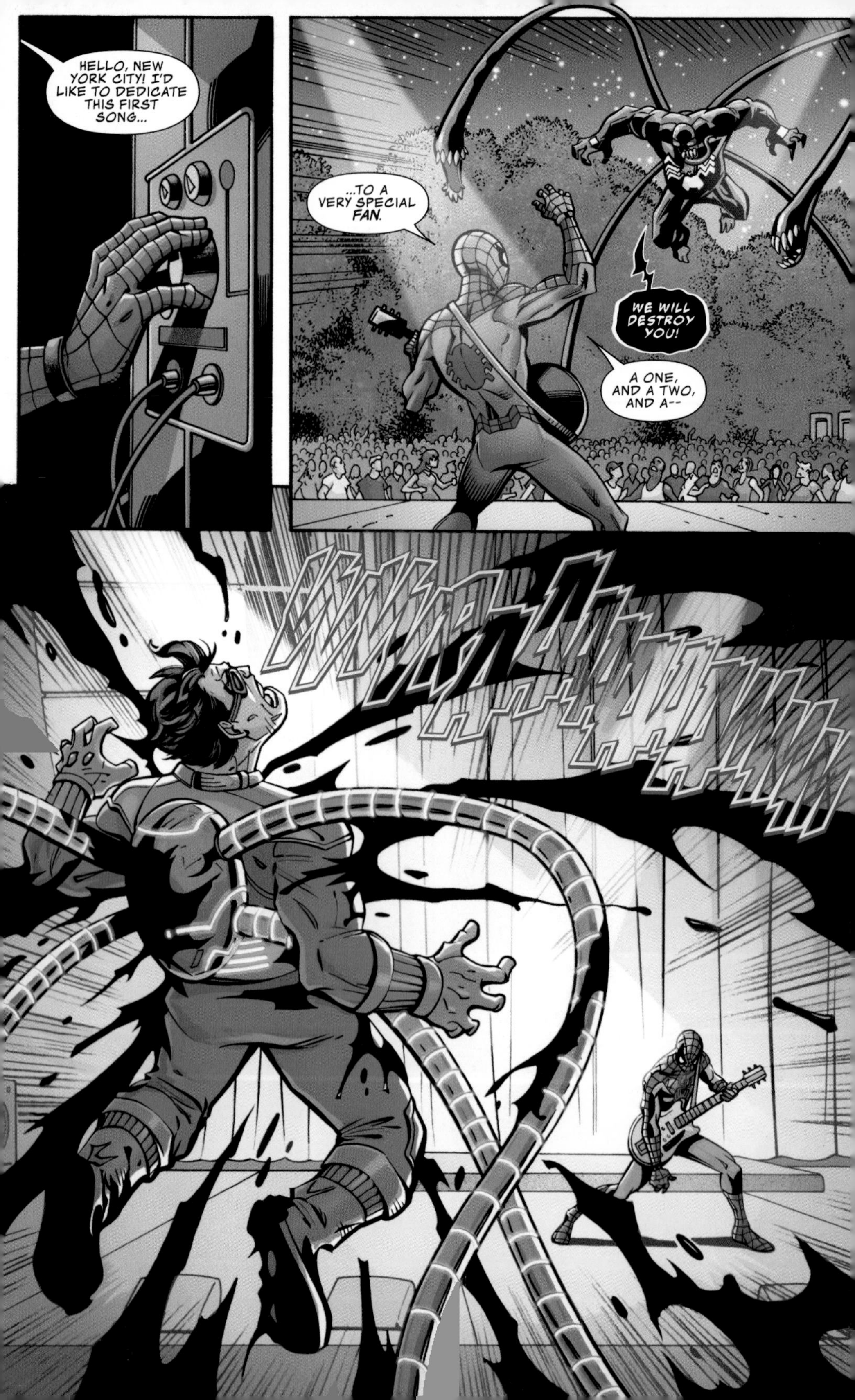
HELLO, NEW YORK CITY! I'D LIKE TO DEDICATE THIS FIRST SONG...
...TO A VERY SPECIAL FAN.
WE WILL DESTROY YOU!
A ONE, AND A TWO, AND A--

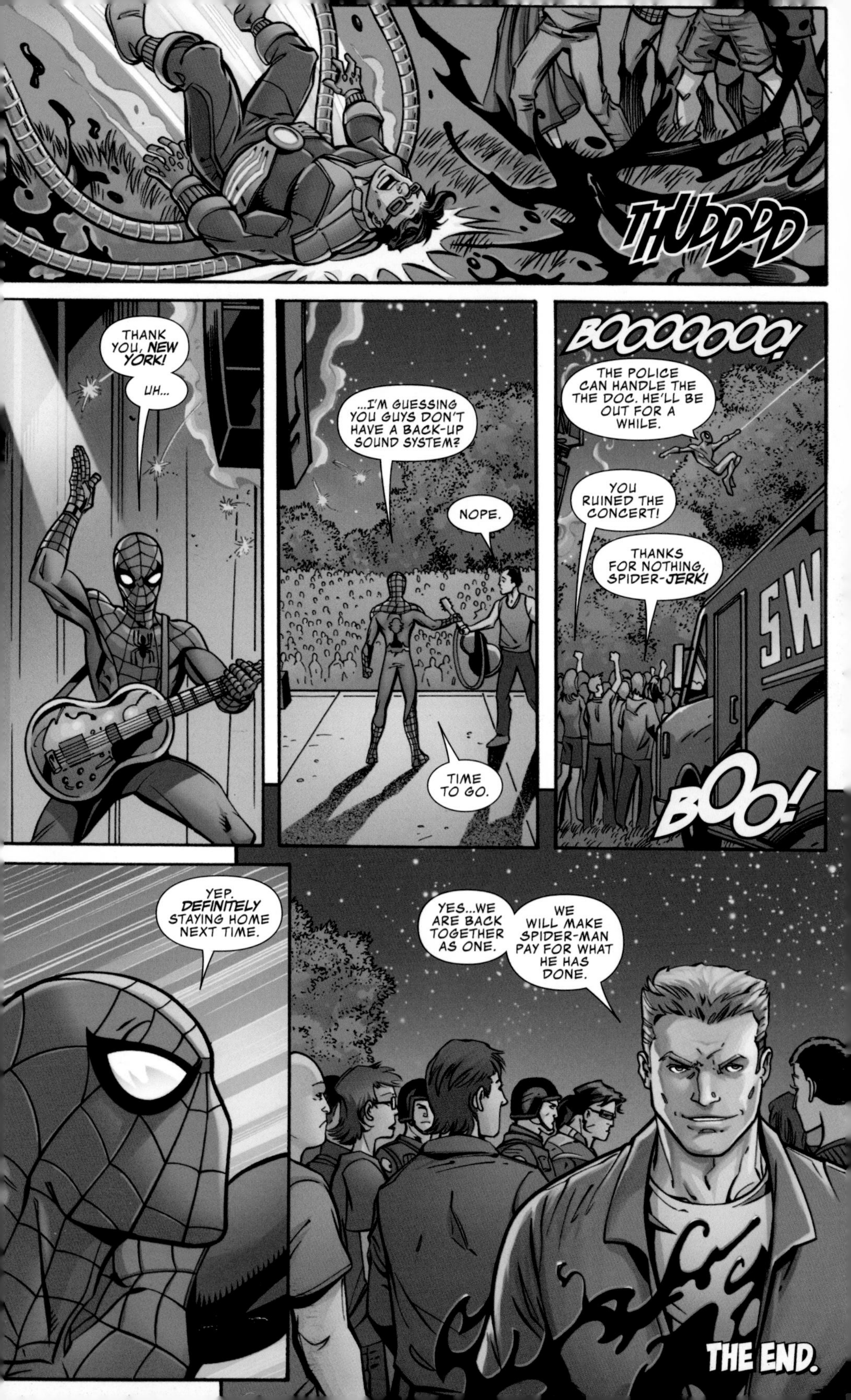
THUDDDD
THANK YOU, NEW YORK!
UH...
...I'M GUESSING YOU GUYS DON'T HAVE A BACK-UP SOUND SYSTEM?
NOPE.
TIME TO GO.
BOOOOOOO!
THE POLICE CAN HANDLE THE THE DOC. HE'LL BE OUT FOR A WHILE.
YOU RUINED THE CONCERT!
THANKS FOR NOTHING, SPIDER-JERK!
BOO!
YEP. DEFINITELY STAYING HOME NEXT TIME.
YES...WE ARE BACK TOGETHER AS ONE.
WE WILL MAKE SPIDER-MAN PAY FOR WHAT HE HAS DONE.
THE END.

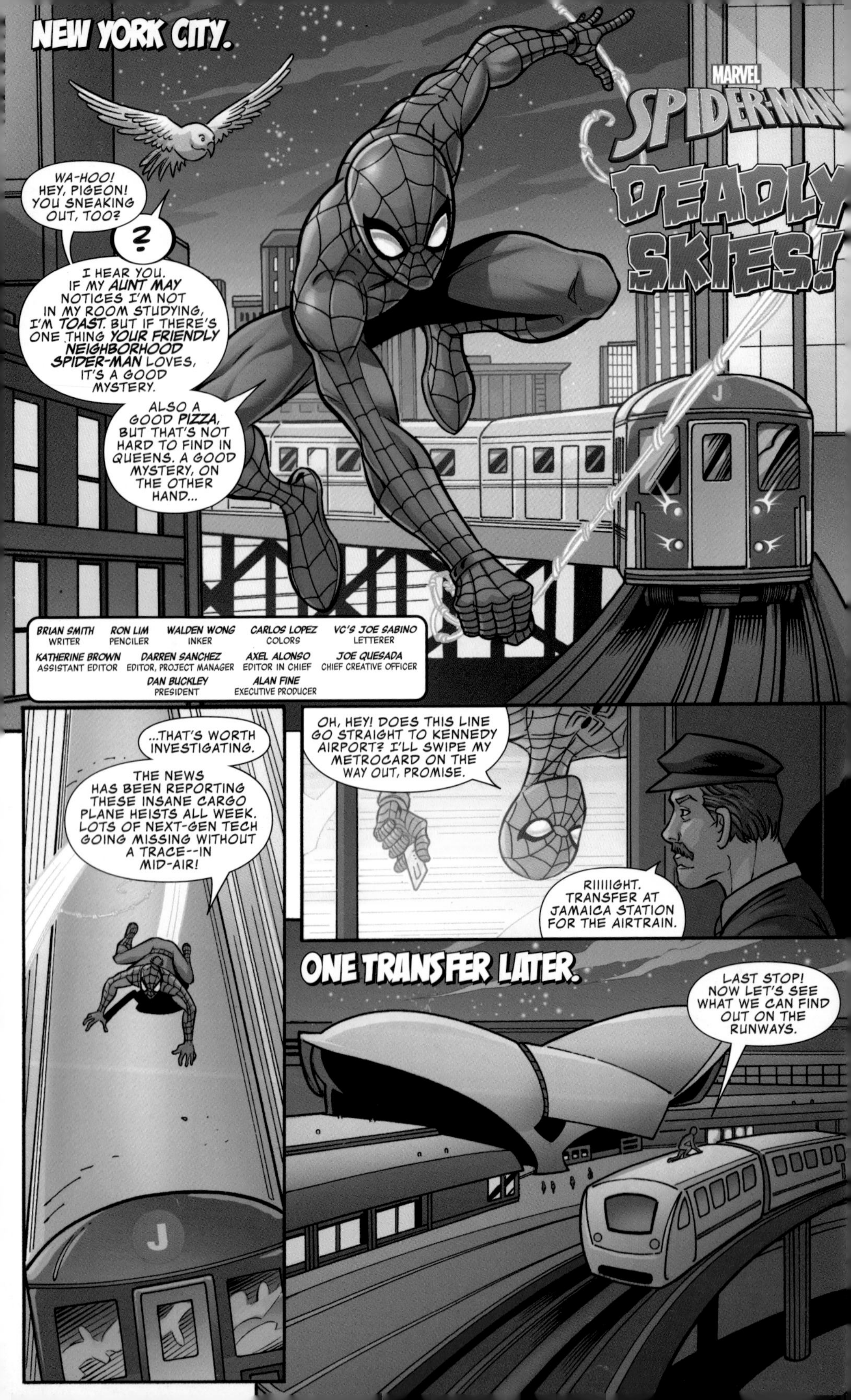
NEW YORK CITY.
MARVEL
SPIDER-MAN
DEADLY SKIES!
WA-HOO! HEY, PIGEON! YOU SNEAKING OUT, TOO?
?
I HEAR YOU. IF MY AUNT MAY NOTICES I'M NOT IN MY ROOM STUDYING, I'M TOAST. BUT IF THERE'S ONE THING YOUR FRIENDLY NEIGHBORHOOD SPIDER-MAN LOVES, IT'S A GOOD MYSTERY.
ALSO A GOOD PIZZA, BUT THAT'S NOT HARD TO FIND IN QUEENS. A GOOD MYSTERY, ON THE OTHER HAND...
BRIAN SMITH WRITER RON LIM PENCILER WALDEN WONG INKER CARLOS LOPEZ COLORS VC'S JOE SABINO LETTERER
KATHERINE BROWN ASSISTANT EDITOR DARREN SANCHEZ EDITOR, PROJECT MANAGER AXEL ALONSO EDITOR IN CHIEF JOE QUESADA CHIEF CREATIVE OFFICER
DAN BUCKLEY PRESIDENT ALAN FINE EXECUTIVE PRODUCER
...THAT'S WORTH INVESTIGATING.
THE NEWS HAS BEEN REPORTING THESE INSANE CARGO PLANE HEISTS ALL WEEK. LOTS OF NEXT-GEN TECH GOING MISSING WITHOUT A TRACE--IN MID-AIR!
OH, HEY! DOES THIS LINE GO STRAIGHT TO KENNEDY AIRPORT? I'LL SWIPE MY METROCARD ON THE WAY OUT, PROMISE.
RIIIIIGHT. TRANSFER AT JAMAICA STATION FOR THE AIRTRAIN.
ONE TRANSFER LATER.
LAST STOP! NOW LET'S SEE WHAT WE CAN FIND OUT ON THE RUNWAYS.

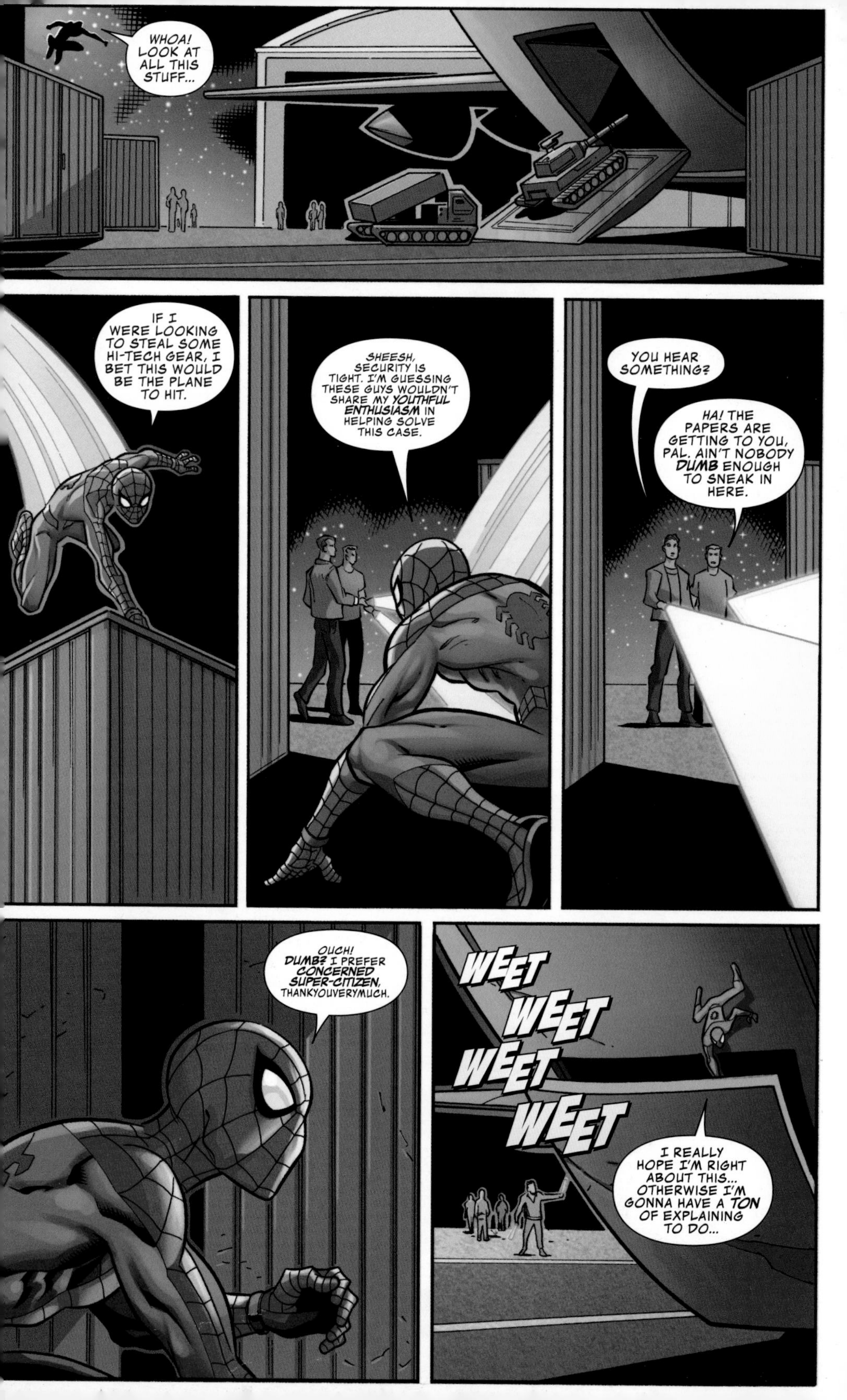
WHOA! LOOK AT ALL THIS STUFF...
IF I WERE LOOKING TO STEAL SOME HI-TECH GEAR, I BET THIS WOULD BE THE PLANE TO HIT.
SHEESH, SECURITY IS TIGHT. I'M GUESSING THESE GUYS WOULDN'T SHARE MY YOUTHFUL ENTHUSIASM IN HELPING SOLVE THIS CASE.
YOU HEAR SOMETHING?
HA! THE PAPERS ARE GETTING TO YOU, PAL. AIN'T NOBODY DUMB ENOUGH TO SNEAK IN HERE.
OUCH! DUMB? I PREFER CONCERNED SUPER-CITIZEN, THANKYOUVERYMUCH.
WEET
WEET
WEET
WEET
I REALLY HOPE I'M RIGHT ABOUT THIS... OTHERWISE I'M GONNA HAVE A TON OF EXPLAINING TO DO...

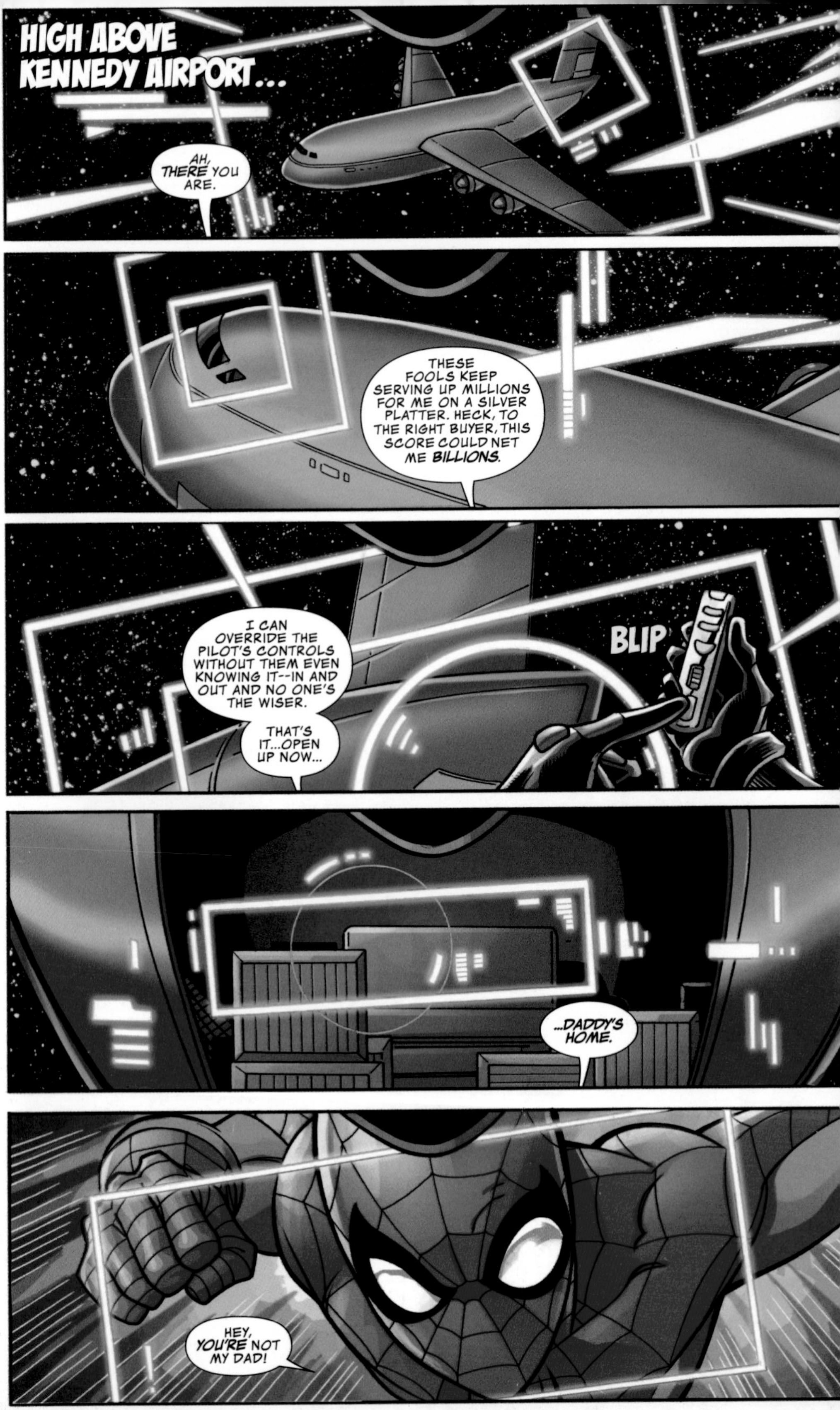
HIGH ABOVE KENNEDY AIRPORT...
AH, THERE YOU ARE.
THESE FOOLS KEEP SERVING UP MILLIONS FOR ME ON A SILVER PLATTER. HECK, TO THE RIGHT BUYER, THIS SCORE COULD NET ME BILLIONS.
I CAN OVERRIDE THE PILOT'S CONTROLS WITHOUT THEM EVEN KNOWING IT--IN AND OUT AND NO ONE'S THE WISER.
THAT'S IT...OPEN UP NOW...
BLIP
...DADDY'S HOME.
HEY, YOU'RE NOT MY DAD!

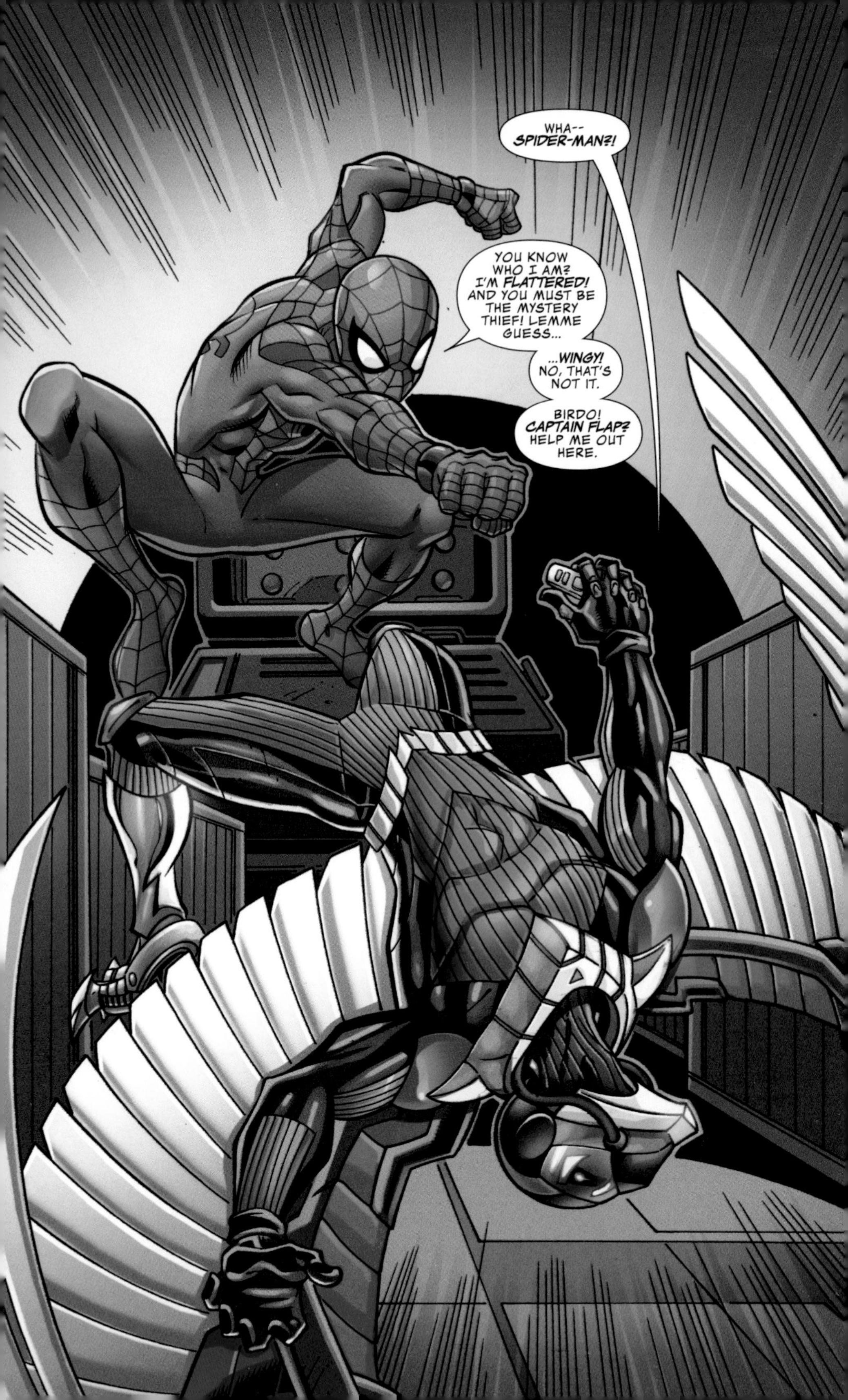
WHA-- SPIDER-MAN?!
YOU KNOW WHO I AM? I'M FLATTERED! AND YOU MUST BE THE MYSTERY THIEF! LEMME GUESS...
...WINGY! NO, THAT'S NOT IT.
BIRDO! CAPTAIN FLAP? HELP ME OUT HERE.

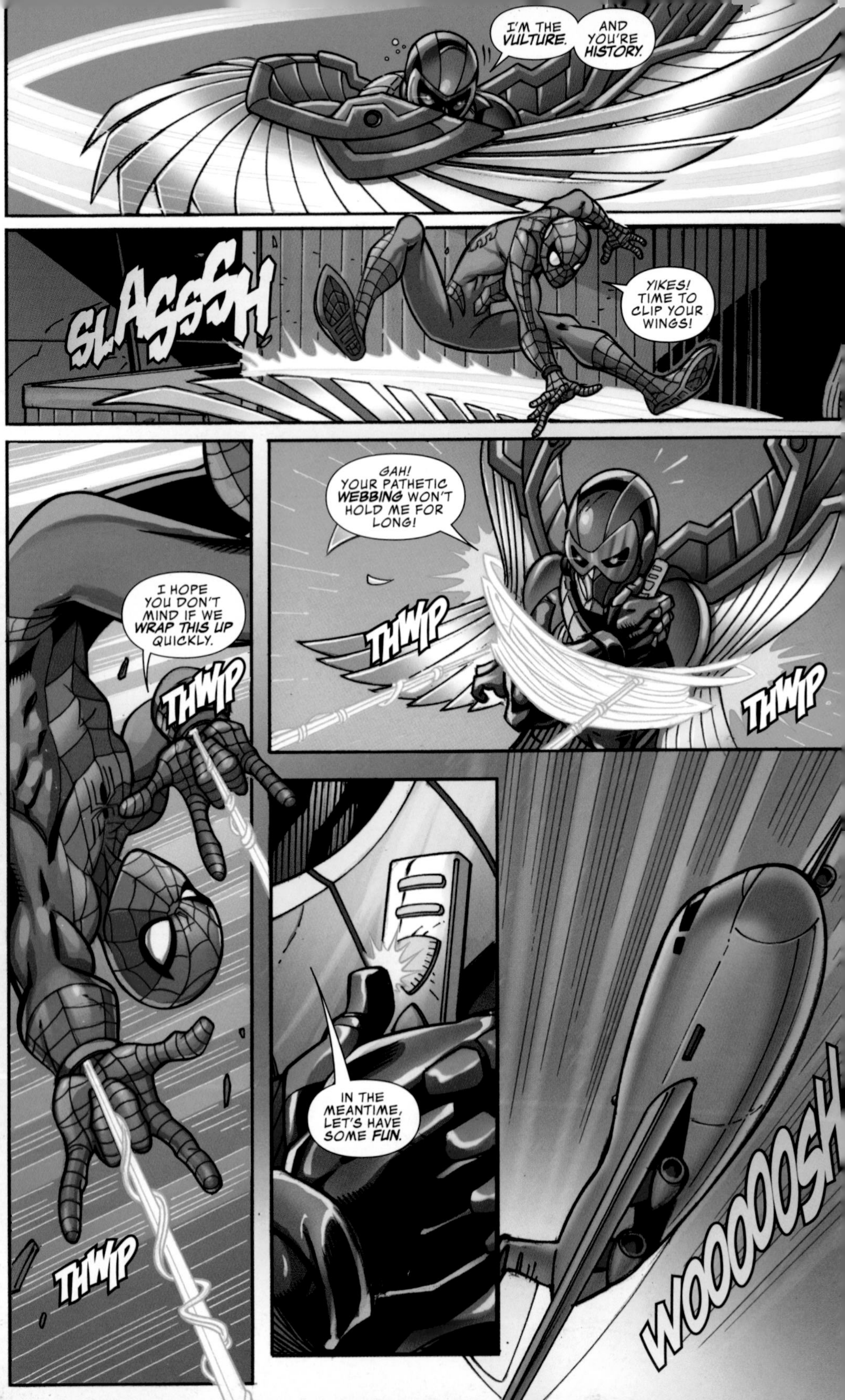

I'M THE VULTURE.
AND YOU'RE HISTORY.
SLASSSH
YIKES! TIME TO CLIP YOUR WINGS!
I HOPE YOU DON'T MIND IF WE WRAP THIS UP QUICKLY.
THWIP
THWIP
GAH! YOUR PATHETIC WEBBING WON'T HOLD ME FOR LONG!
THWIP
THWIP
IN THE MEANTIME, LET'S HAVE SOME FUN.
WOOOOOSH

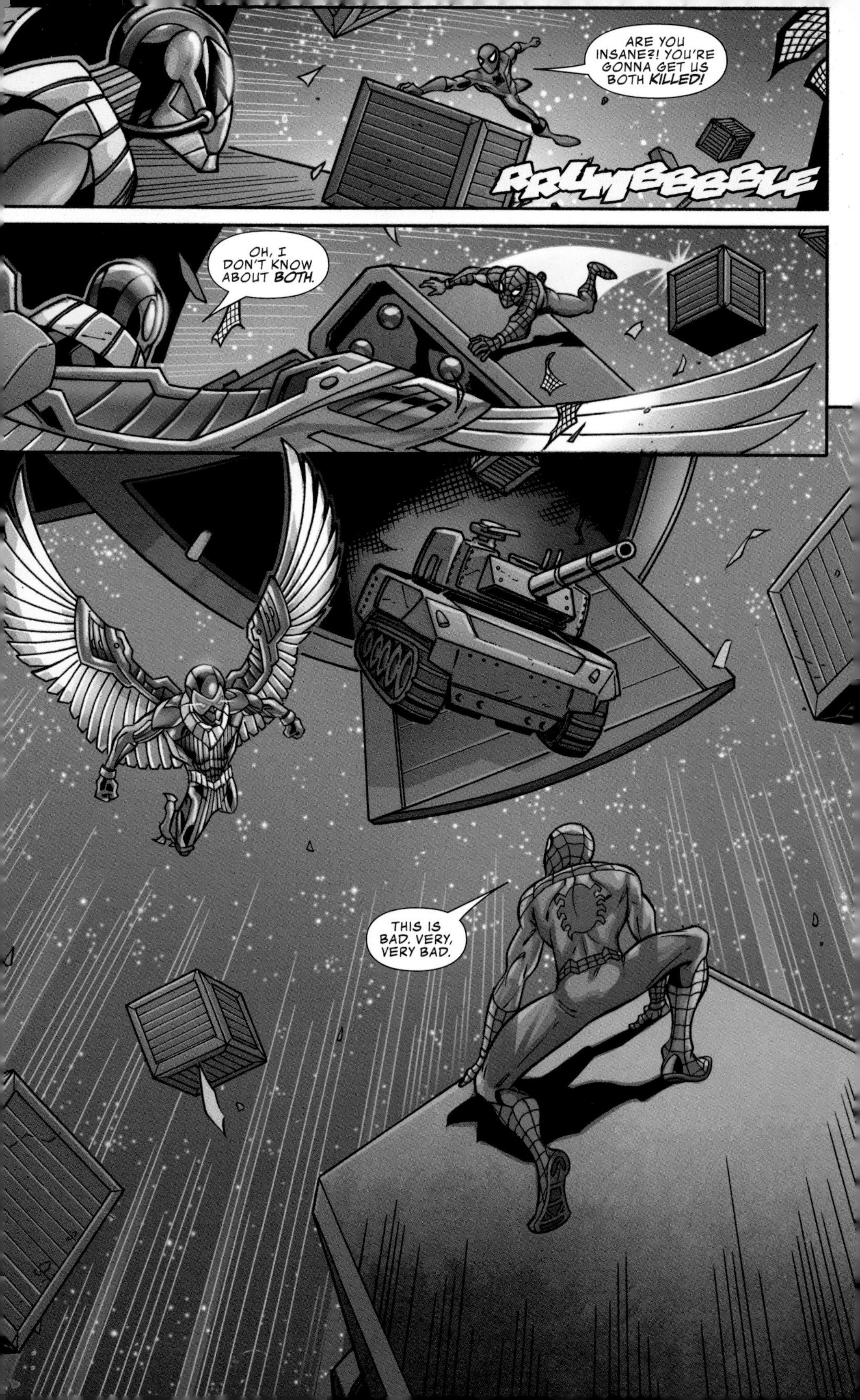
ARE YOU INSANE?! YOU'RE GONNA GET US BOTH KILLED!
RRUMBBBBLE
OH, I DON'T KNOW ABOUT BOTH.
THIS IS BAD. VERY, VERY BAD.

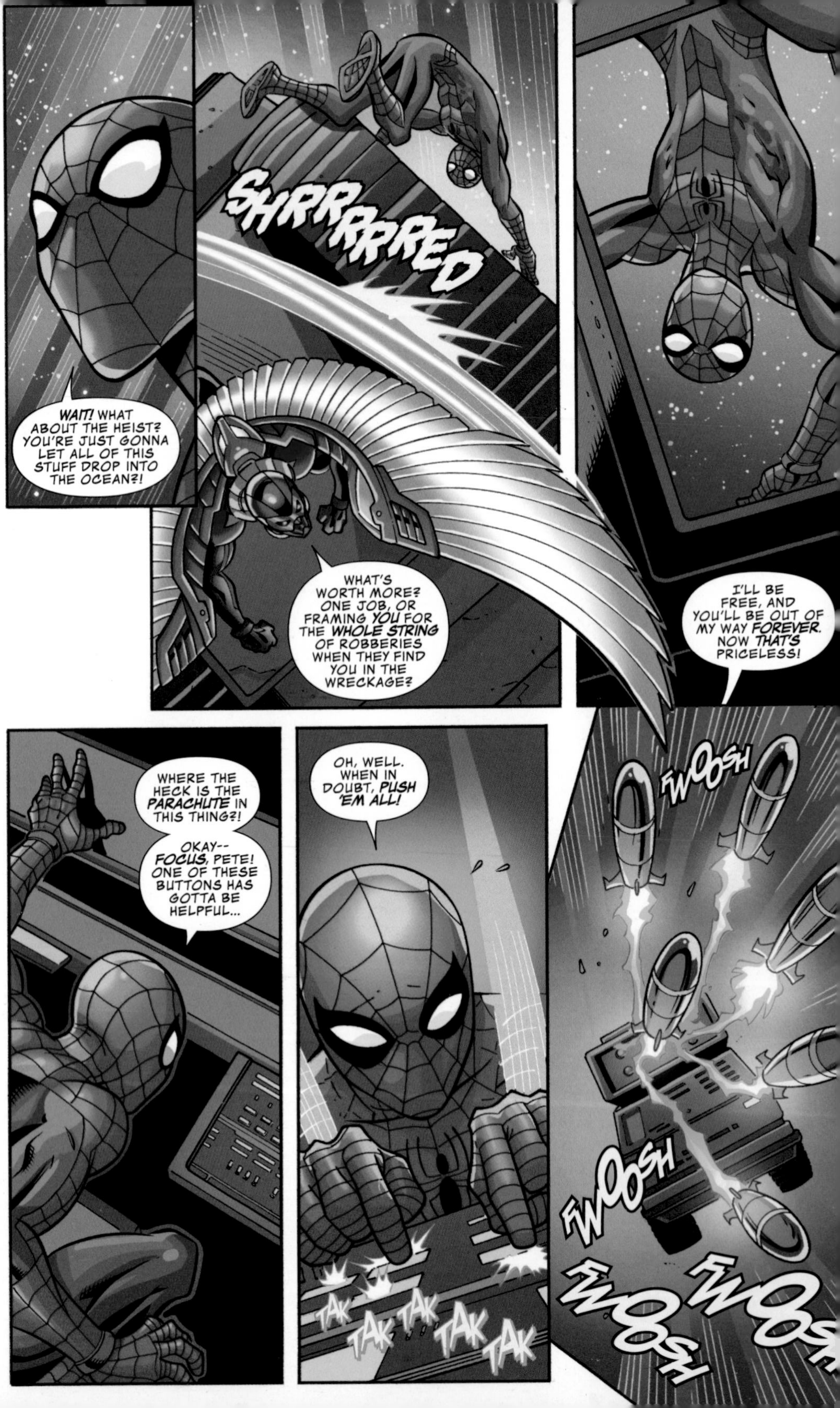
WAIT! WHAT ABOUT THE HEIST? YOU'RE JUST GONNA LET ALL OF THIS STUFF DROP INTO THE OCEAN?!
SHRRRRRED
WHAT'S WORTH MORE? ONE JOB, OR FRAMING YOU FOR THE WHOLE STRING OF ROBBERIES WHEN THEY FIND YOU IN THE WRECKAGE?
I'LL BE FREE, AND YOU'LL BE OUT OF MY WAY FOREVER. NOW THAT'S PRICELESS!
WHERE THE HECK IS THE PARACHUTE IN THIS THING?!
OKAY-- FOCUS, PETE! ONE OF THESE BUTTONS HAS GOTTA BE HELPFUL...
OH, WELL. WHEN IN DOUBT, PUSH 'EM ALL!
TAK TAK TAK TAK TAK TAK
FWOOSH
FWOOSH
FWOOSH
FWOOSH

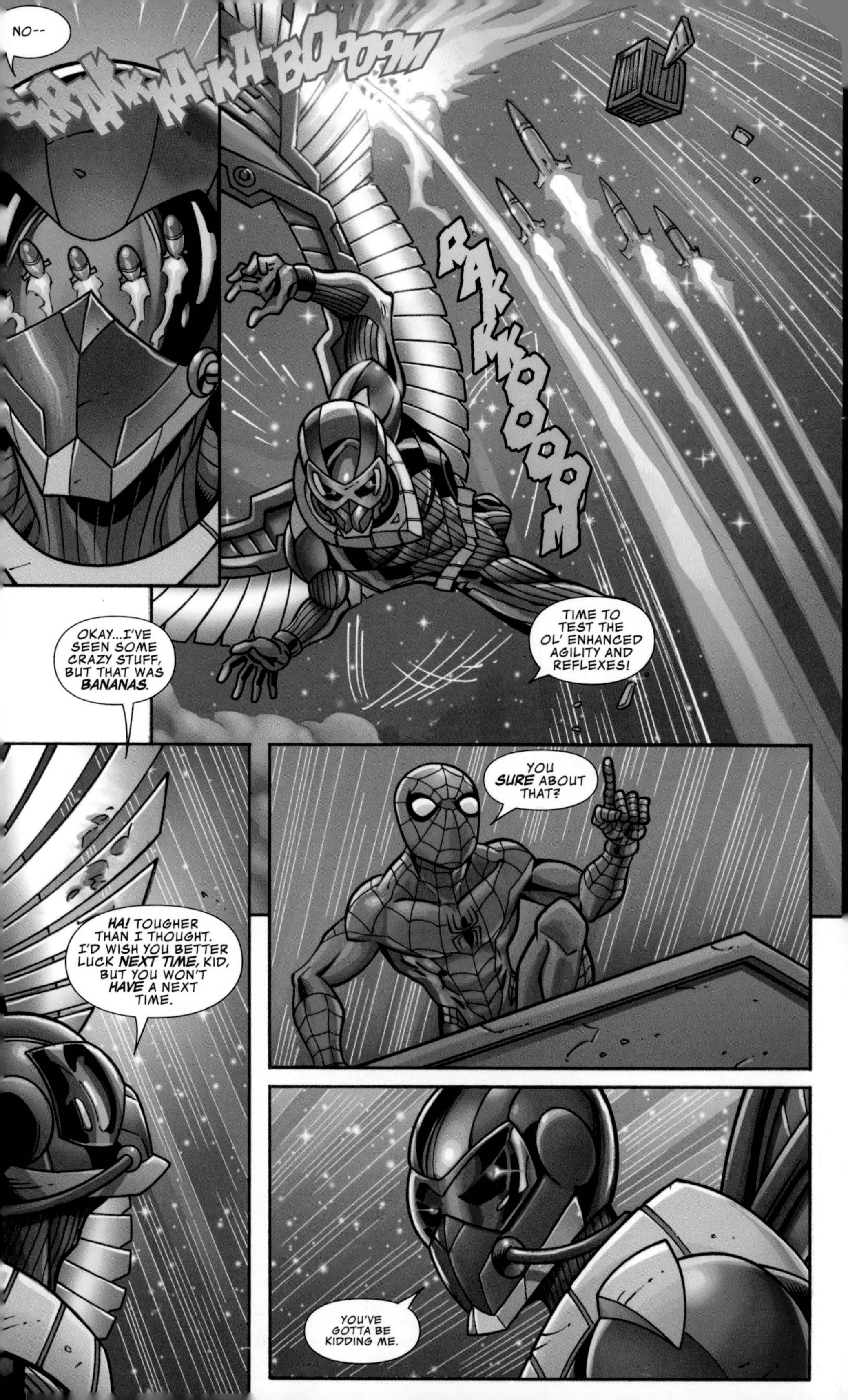
NO--
SKRAKKA-KA-BOOOOM
RAKKOOOOOM
TIME TO TEST THE OL' ENHANCED AGILITY AND REFLEXES!
OKAY...I'VE SEEN SOME CRAZY STUFF, BUT THAT WAS BANANAS.
HA! TOUGHER THAN I THOUGHT. I'D WISH YOU BETTER LUCK NEXT TIME, KID, BUT YOU WON'T HAVE A NEXT TIME.
YOU SURE ABOUT THAT?
YOU'VE GOTTA BE KIDDING ME.

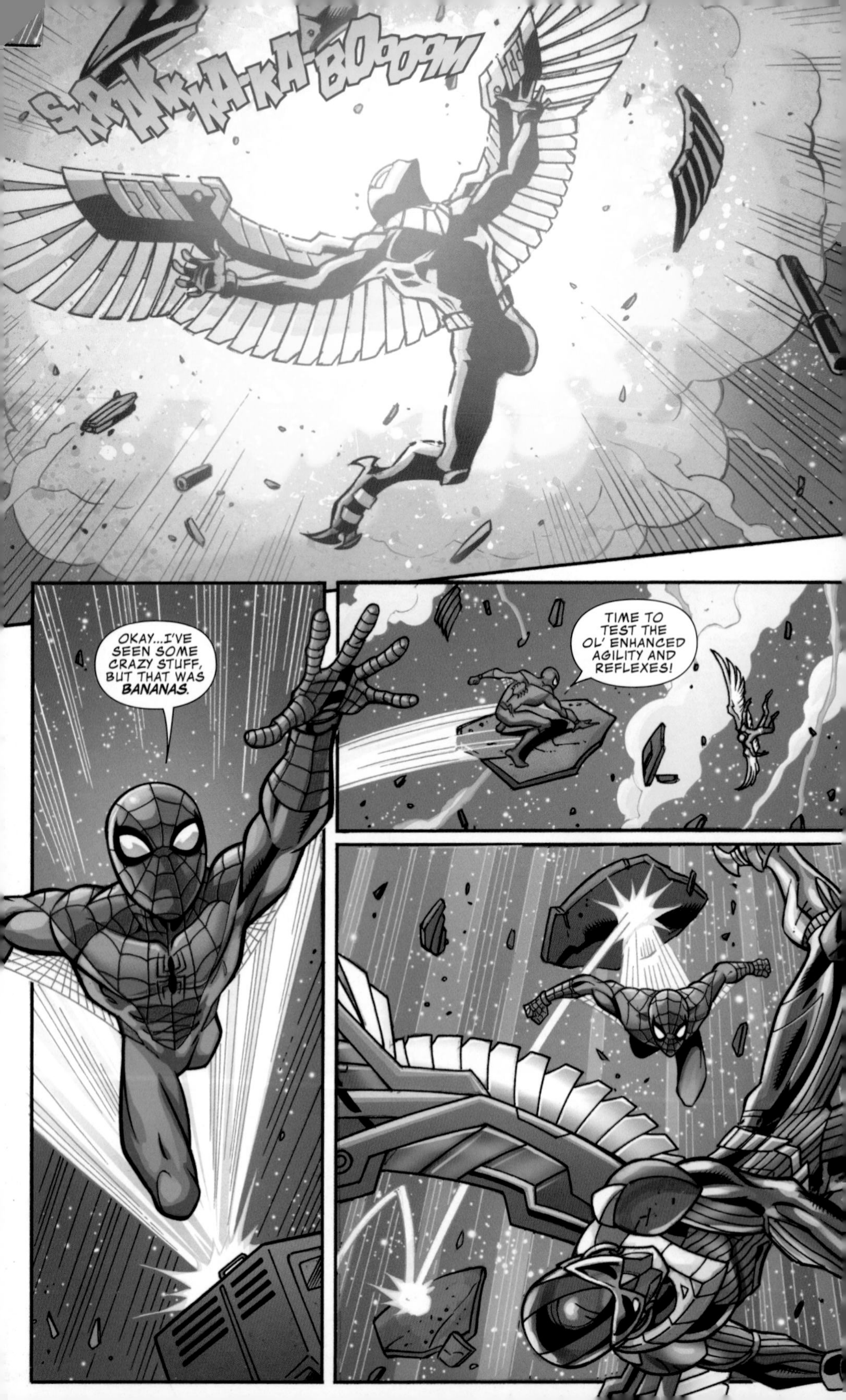
SKRAK-KA-KA-BOOOOM
OKAY...I'VE SEEN SOME CRAZY STUFF, BUT THAT WAS BANANAS.
TIME TO TEST THE OL' ENHANCED AGILITY AND REFLEXES!

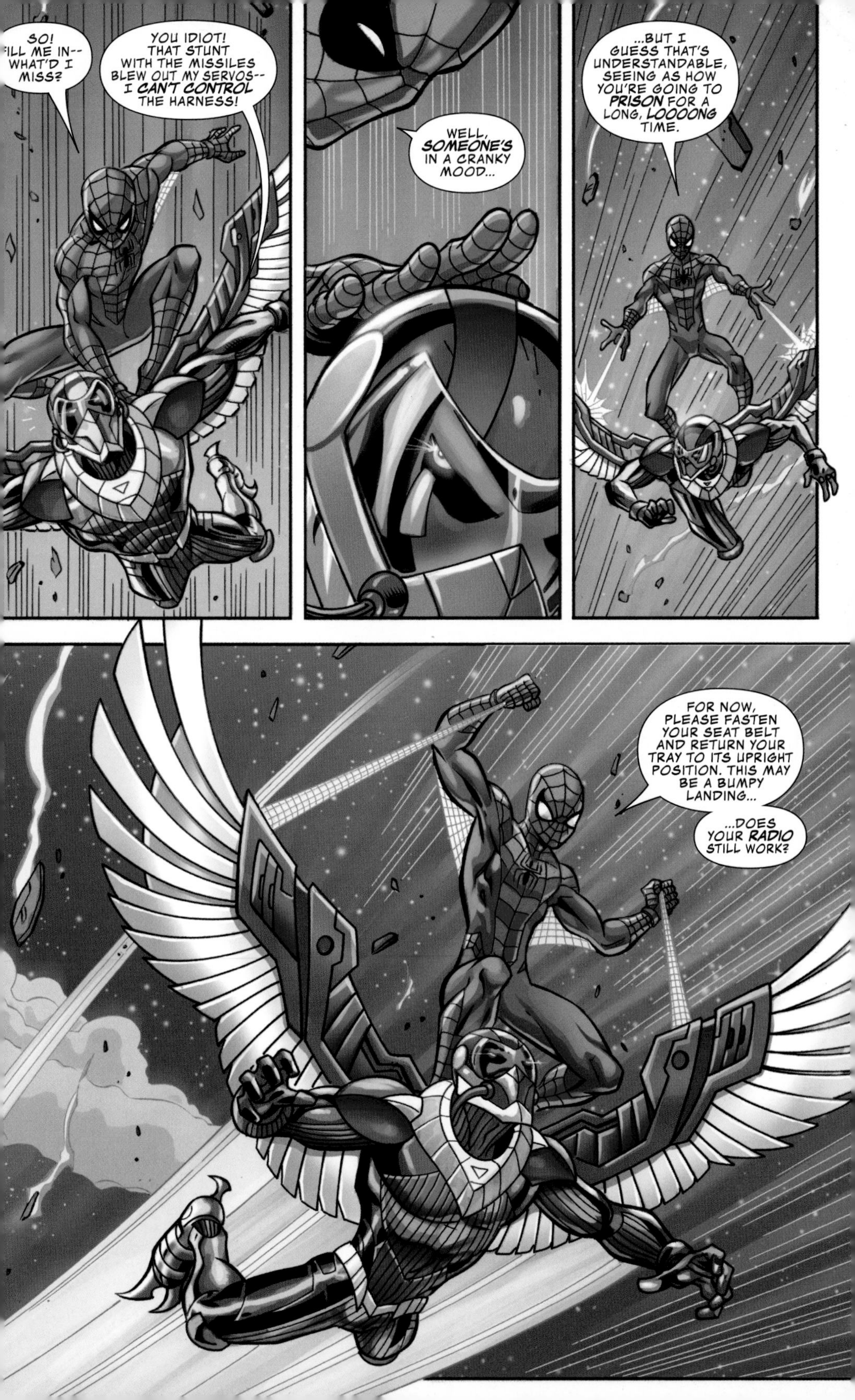
SO! FILL ME IN-- WHAT'D I MISS?
YOU IDIOT! THAT STUNT WITH THE MISSILES BLEW OUT MY SERVOS-- I CAN'T CONTROL THE HARNESS!
WELL, SOMEONE'S IN A CRANKY MOOD...
...BUT I GUESS THAT'S UNDERSTANDABLE, SEEING AS HOW YOU'RE GOING TO PRISON FOR A LONG, LOOOONG TIME.
FOR NOW, PLEASE FASTEN YOUR SEAT BELT AND RETURN YOUR TRAY TO ITS UPRIGHT POSITION. THIS MAY BE A BUMPY LANDING...
...DOES YOUR RADIO STILL WORK?

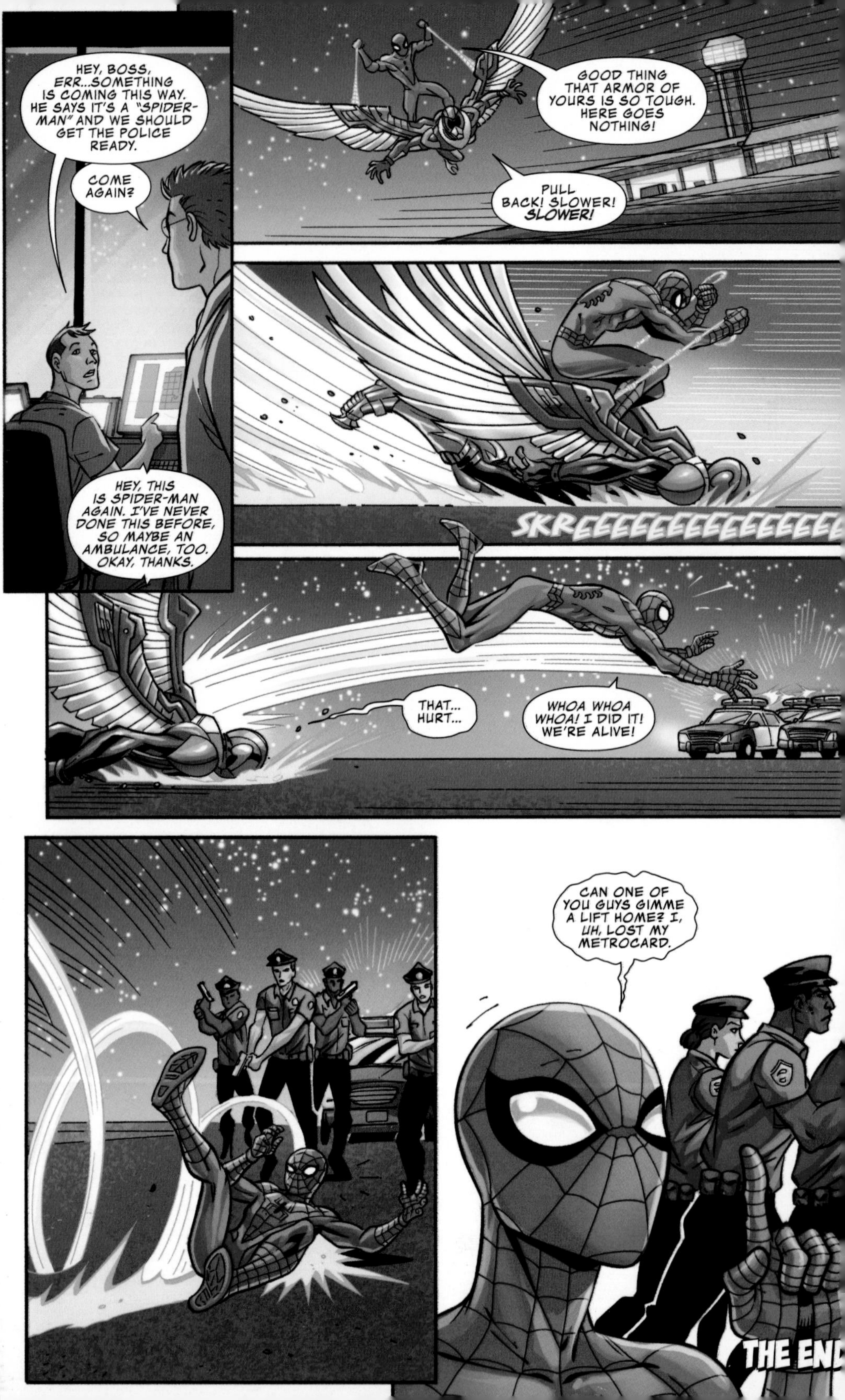
HEY, BOSS, ERR...SOMETHING IS COMING THIS WAY. HE SAYS IT'S A "SPIDER-MAN" AND WE SHOULD GET THE POLICE READY.
COME AGAIN?
HEY, THIS IS SPIDER-MAN AGAIN. I'VE NEVER DONE THIS BEFORE, SO MAYBE AN AMBULANCE, TOO. OKAY, THANKS.
GOOD THING THAT ARMOR OF YOURS IS SO TOUGH. HERE GOES NOTHING!
PULL BACK! SLOWER! SLOWER!
SKREEEEEEEEEEEEEEEE
THAT... HURT...
WHOA WHOA WHOA! I DID IT! WE'RE ALIVE!
CAN ONE OF YOU GUYS GIMME A LIFT HOME? I, UH, LOST MY METROCARD.
THE END

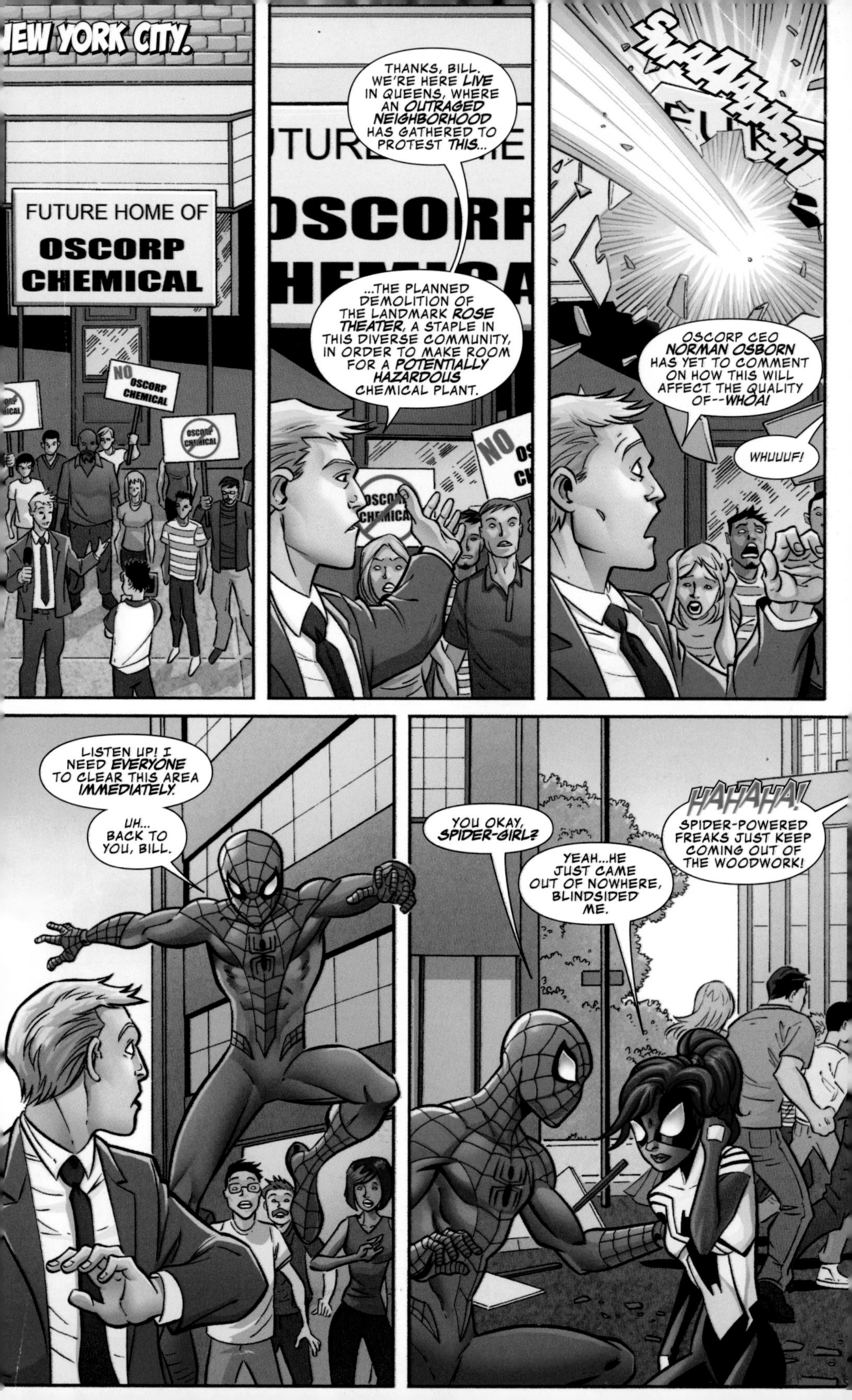
NEW YORK CITY.
FUTURE HOME OF OSCORP CHEMICAL
NO OSCORP CHEMICAL
THANKS, BILL. WE'RE HERE LIVE IN QUEENS, WHERE AN OUTRAGED NEIGHBORHOOD HAS GATHERED TO PROTEST THIS...
...THE PLANNED DEMOLITION OF THE LANDMARK ROSE THEATER, A STAPLE IN THIS DIVERSE COMMUNITY, IN ORDER TO MAKE ROOM FOR A POTENTIALLY HAZARDOUS CHEMICAL PLANT.
SWADAAASH
OSCORP CEO NORMAN OSBORN HAS YET TO COMMENT ON HOW THIS WILL AFFECT THE QUALITY OF--WHOA!
WHUUUF!
LISTEN UP! I NEED EVERYONE TO CLEAR THIS AREA IMMEDIATELY.
UH... BACK TO YOU, BILL.
YOU OKAY, SPIDER-GIRL?
YEAH...HE JUST CAME OUT OF NOWHERE, BLINDSIDED ME.
HAHAHA!
SPIDER-POWERED FREAKS JUST KEEP COMING OUT OF THE WOODWORK!

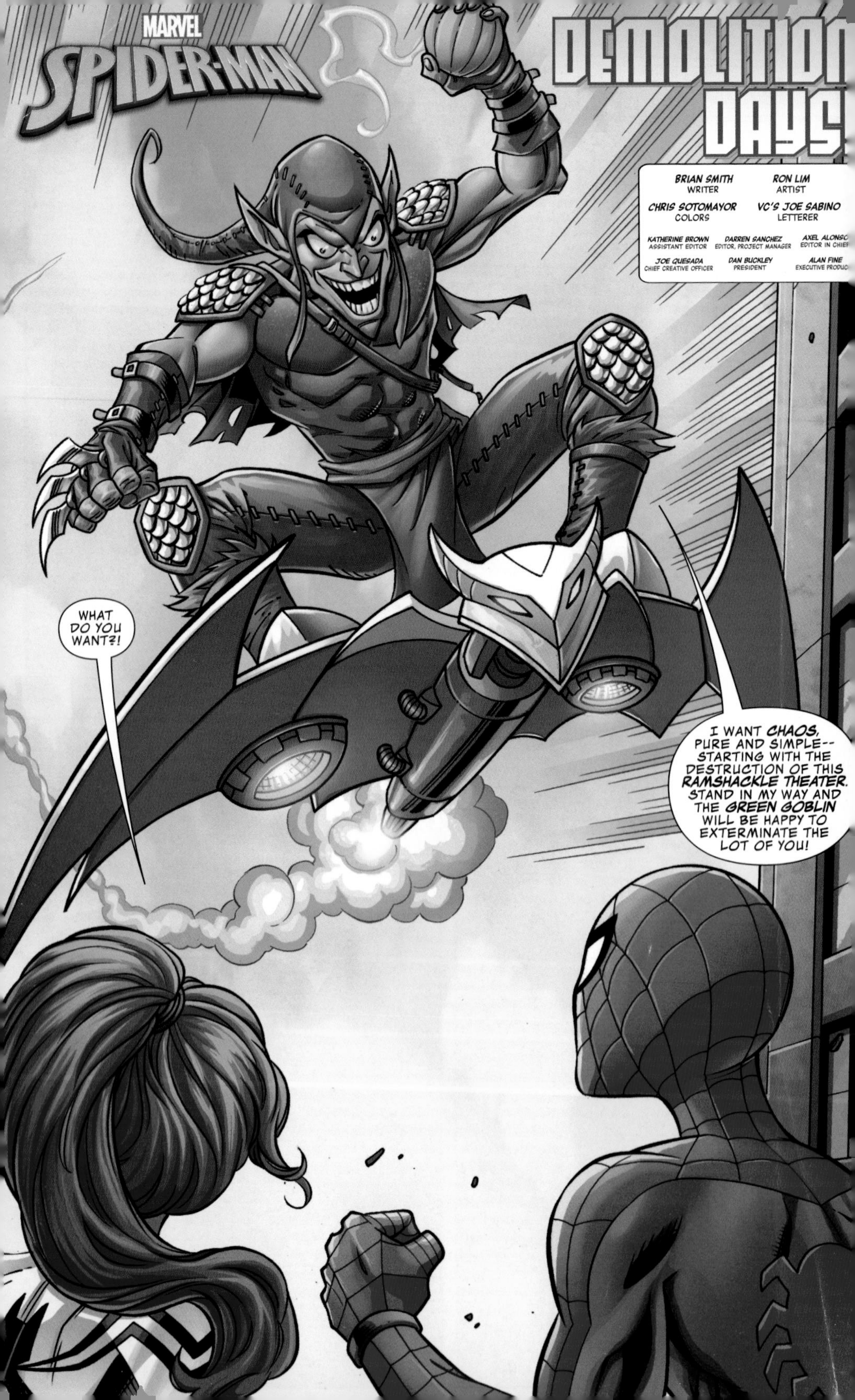
MARVEL
SPIDER-MAN
DEMOLITION DAYS
BRIAN SMITH WRITER
RON LIM ARTIST
CHRIS SOTOMAYOR COLORS
VC'S JOE SABINO LETTERER
KATHERINE BROWN ASSISTANT EDITOR
DARREN SANCHEZ EDITOR, PROJECT MANAGER
AXEL ALONSO EDITOR IN CHIEF
JOE QUESADA CHIEF CREATIVE OFFICER
DAN BUCKLEY PRESIDENT
ALAN FINE EXECUTIVE PRODUC
WHAT DO YOU WANT?!
I WANT CHAOS, PURE AND SIMPLE--STARTING WITH THE DESTRUCTION OF THIS RAMSHACKLE THEATER. STAND IN MY WAY AND THE GREEN GOBLIN WILL BE HAPPY TO EXTERMINATE THE LOT OF YOU!

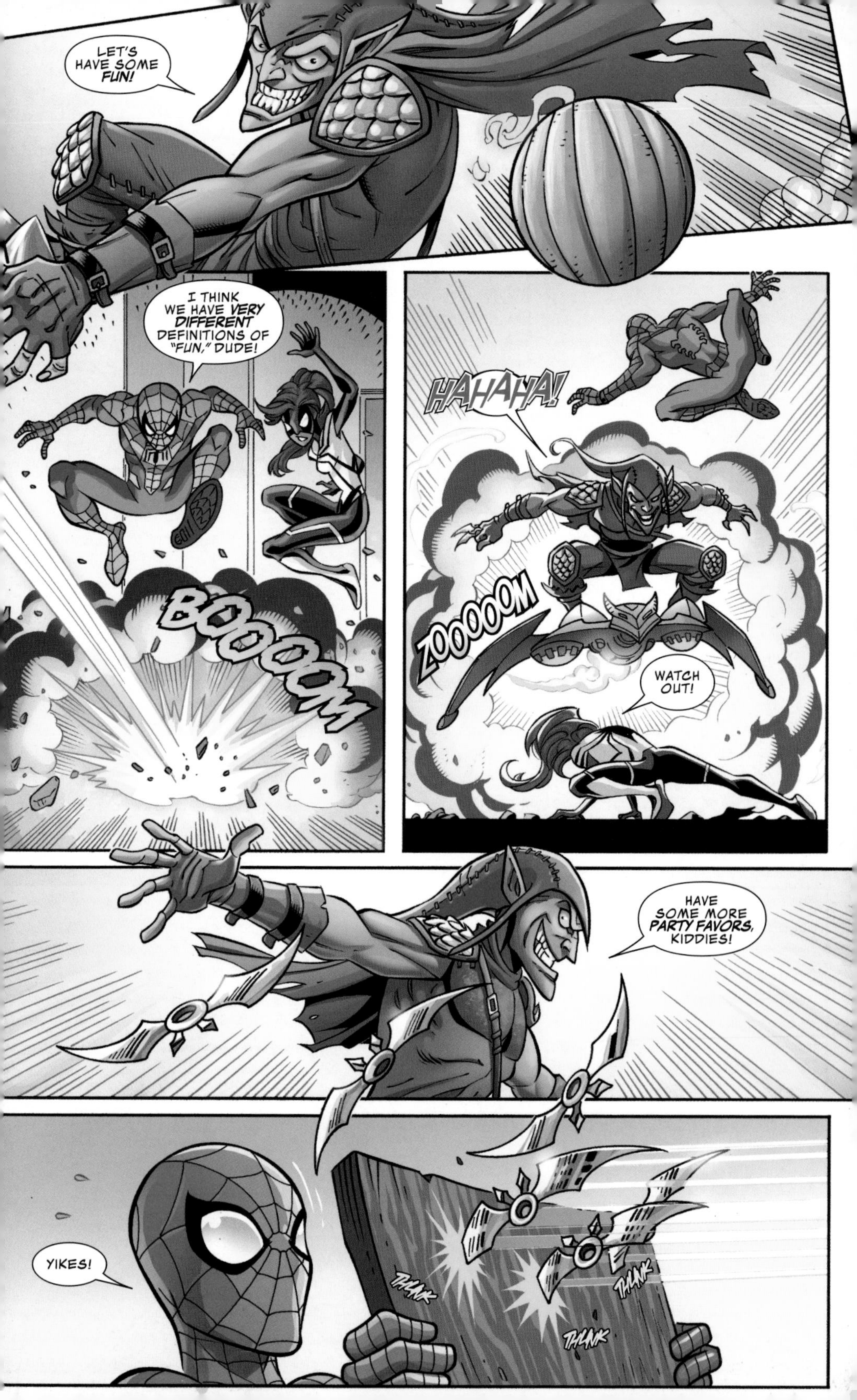
LET'S HAVE SOME FUN!
I THINK WE HAVE VERY DIFFERENT DEFINITIONS OF "FUN," DUDE!
BOOOOM
HAHAHA!
ZOOOOOM
WATCH OUT!
HAVE SOME MORE PARTY FAVORS, KIDDIES!
YIKES!
THUNK
THUNK
THUNK

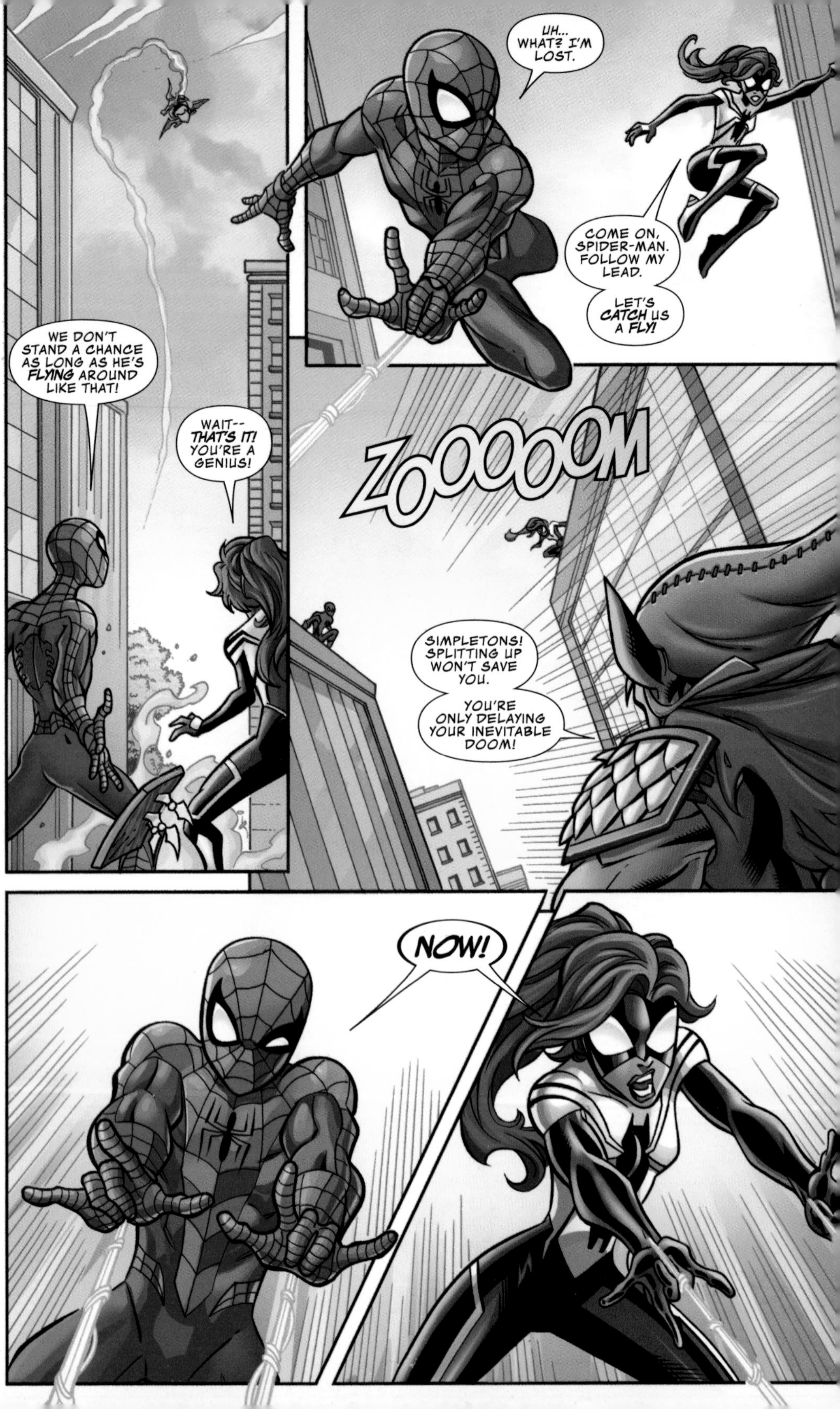
WE DON'T STAND A CHANCE AS LONG AS HE'S FLYING AROUND LIKE THAT!
WAIT-- THAT'S IT! YOU'RE A GENIUS!
UH... WHAT? I'M LOST.
COME ON, SPIDER-MAN. FOLLOW MY LEAD.
LET'S CATCH US A FLY!
ZOOOOOOM
SIMPLETONS! SPLITTING UP WON'T SAVE YOU.
YOU'RE ONLY DELAYING YOUR INEVITABLE DOOM!
NOW!

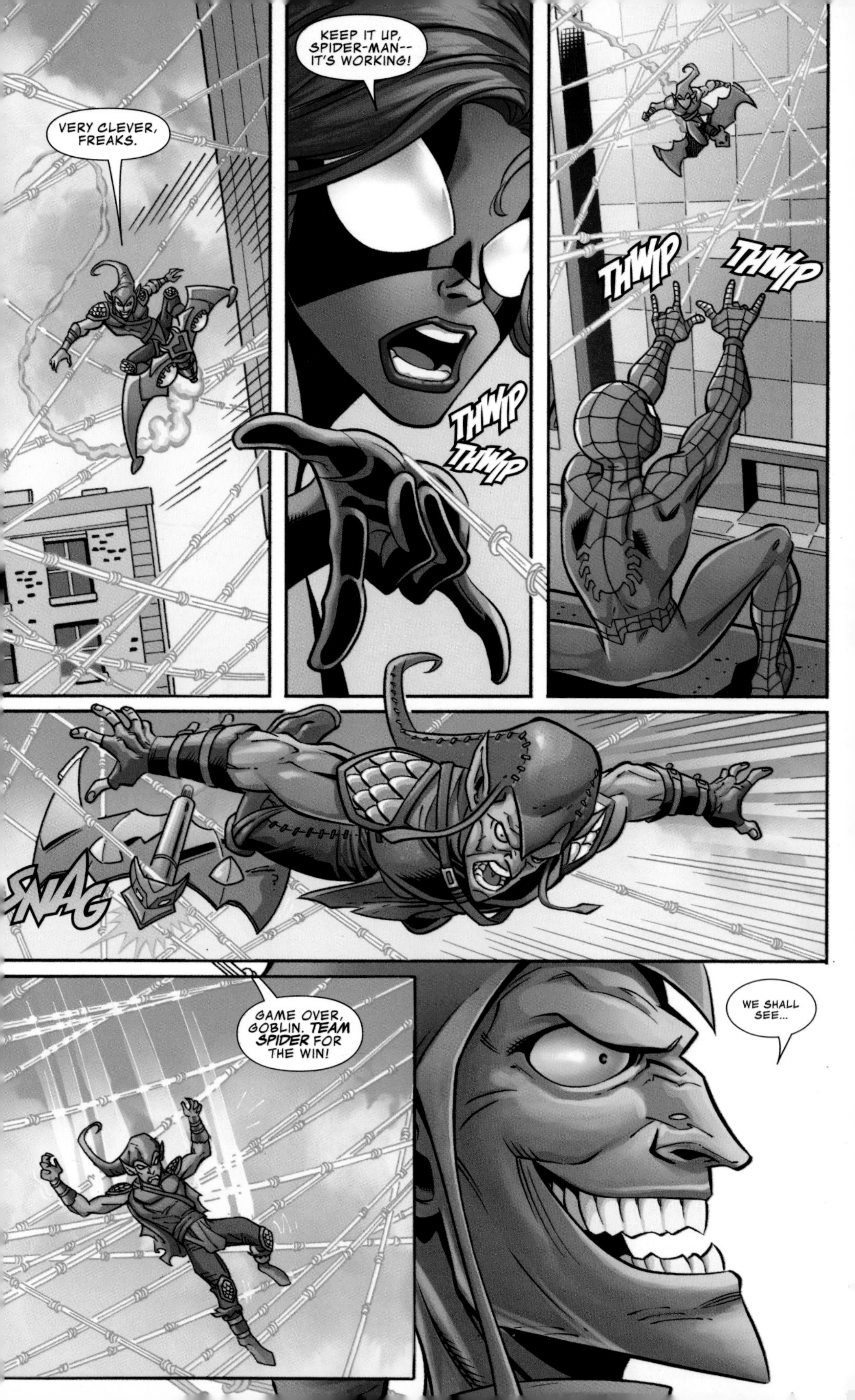
VERY CLEVER, FREAKS.
KEEP IT UP, SPIDER-MAN-- IT'S WORKING!
THWIP
THWIP
THWIP
THWIP
SNAG
GAME OVER, GOBLIN. TEAM SPIDER FOR THE WIN!
WE SHALL SEE...

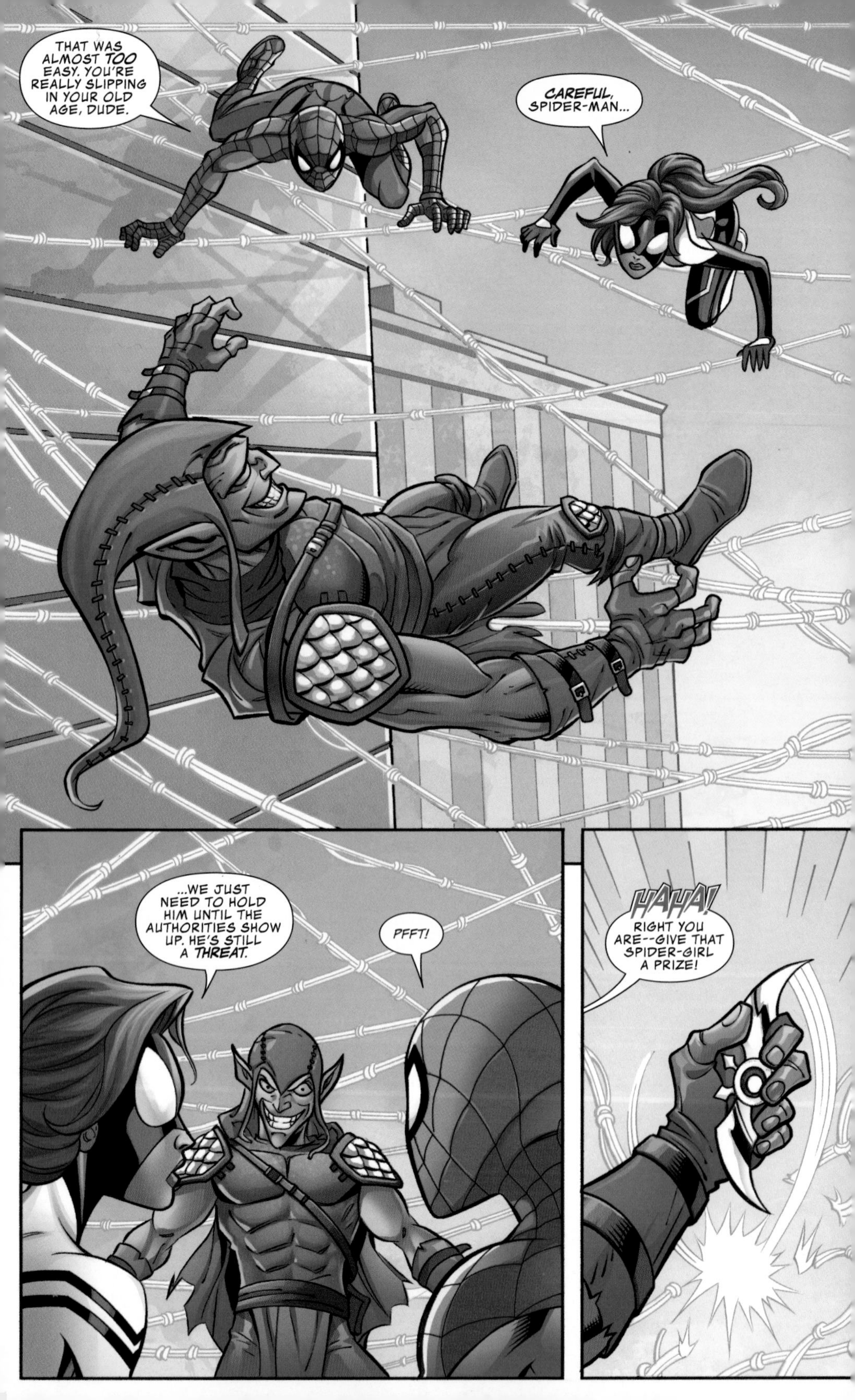
THAT WAS ALMOST TOO EASY. YOU'RE REALLY SLIPPING IN YOUR OLD AGE, DUDE.
CAREFUL, SPIDER-MAN...
...WE JUST NEED TO HOLD HIM UNTIL THE AUTHORITIES SHOW UP. HE'S STILL A THREAT.
PFFT!
HAHA!
RIGHT YOU ARE--GIVE THAT SPIDER-GIRL A PRIZE!

≷HURK≷

YOU SHOULD'VE LISTENED TO YOUR FRIEND, SPIDER-WHELP-- YOUR ARROGANCE IS ABSOLUTELY **SHOCKING!**

BZZZZZTTT

POINT TAKEN...BUT WORK ON YOUR JOKES...

AS FOR **YOU**, I'M A MAN OF MY WORD...

NO! SPIDER-MAN!

...ENJOY YOUR **PRIZE!** HAHAHA!

MY **SPIDER-SENSE** IS GOING BANANAS...

WHOA! THAT WAS CLOSE!

NOW TO **EXPEDITE** THIS DEMOLITION!

ZZZZZOOOOOOMM

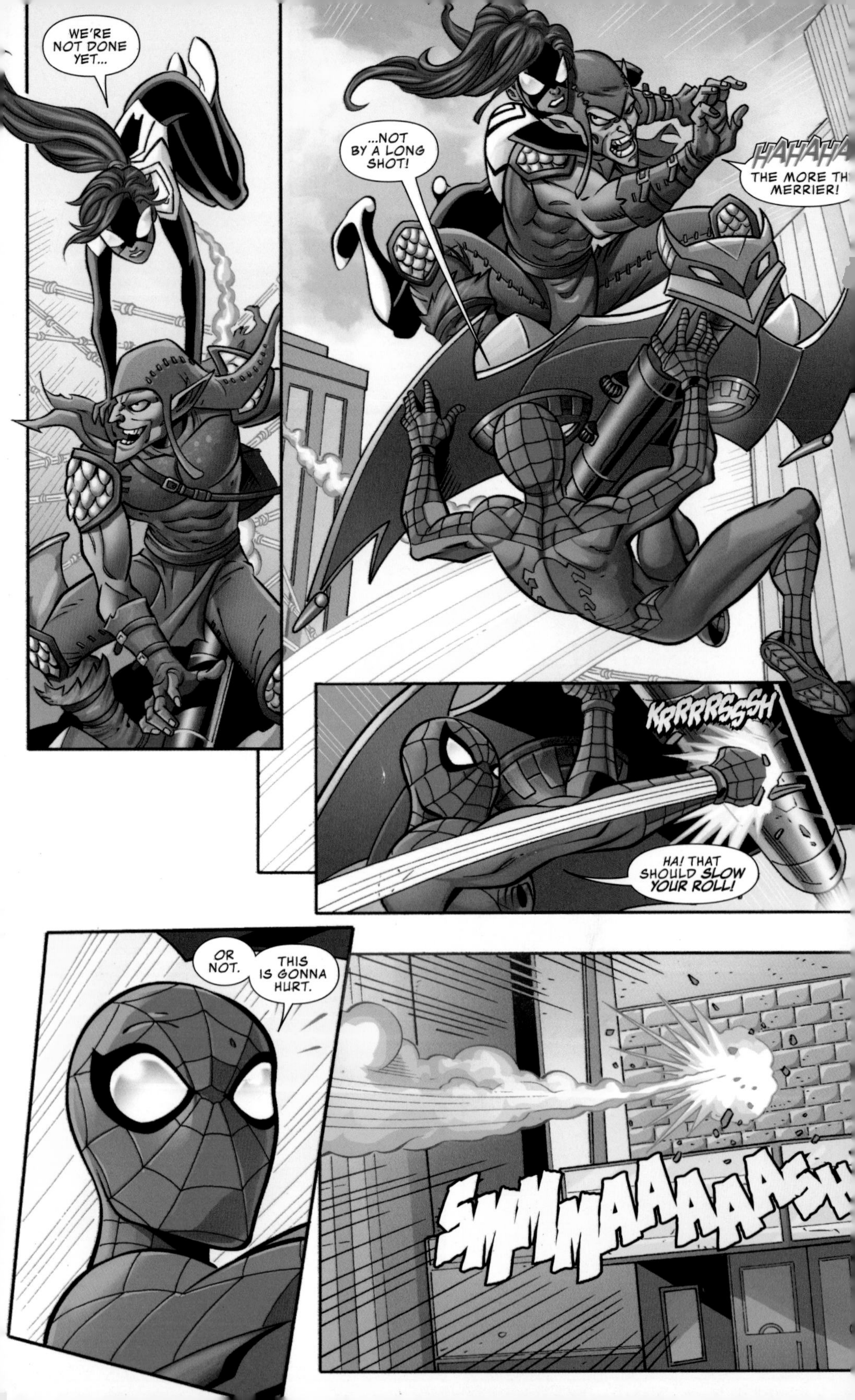

WE'RE NOT DONE YET...
...NOT BY A LONG SHOT!
HAHAHA! THE MORE THE MERRIER!
KRRRRSSSH
HA! THAT SHOULD SLOW YOUR ROLL!
OR NOT.
THIS IS GONNA HURT.
SHMMAAAAAASH

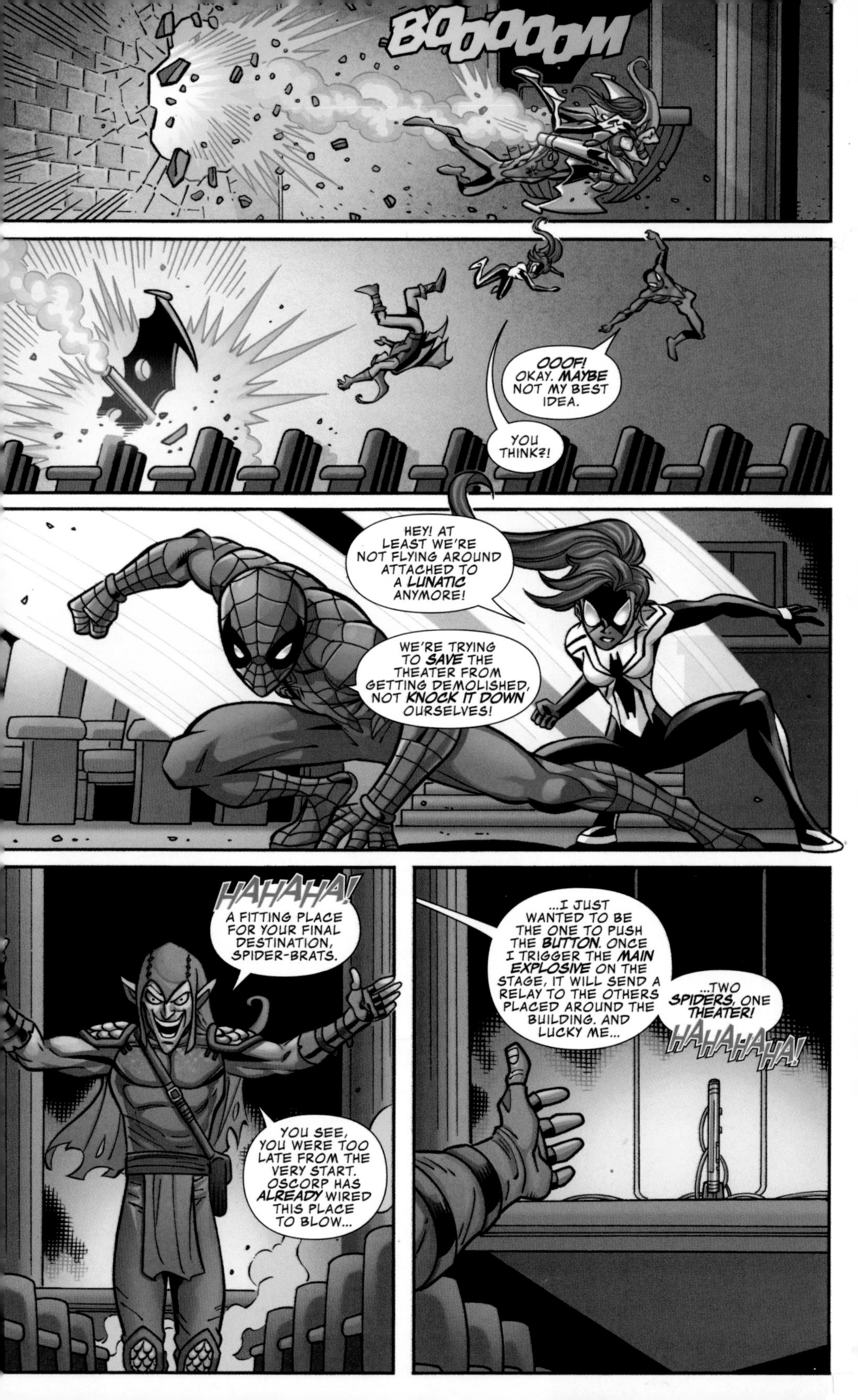
BOOOOOOM
OOOF! OKAY. MAYBE NOT MY BEST IDEA.
YOU THINK?!
HEY! AT LEAST WE'RE NOT FLYING AROUND ATTACHED TO A LUNATIC ANYMORE!
WE'RE TRYING TO SAVE THE THEATER FROM GETTING DEMOLISHED, NOT KNOCK IT DOWN OURSELVES!
HAHAHA!
A FITTING PLACE FOR YOUR FINAL DESTINATION, SPIDER-BRATS.
YOU SEE, YOU WERE TOO LATE FROM THE VERY START. OSCORP HAS ALREADY WIRED THIS PLACE TO BLOW...
...I JUST WANTED TO BE THE ONE TO PUSH THE BUTTON. ONCE I TRIGGER THE MAIN EXPLOSIVE ON THE STAGE, IT WILL SEND A RELAY TO THE OTHERS PLACED AROUND THE BUILDING. AND LUCKY ME...
...TWO SPIDERS, ONE THEATER!
HAHAHAHA!

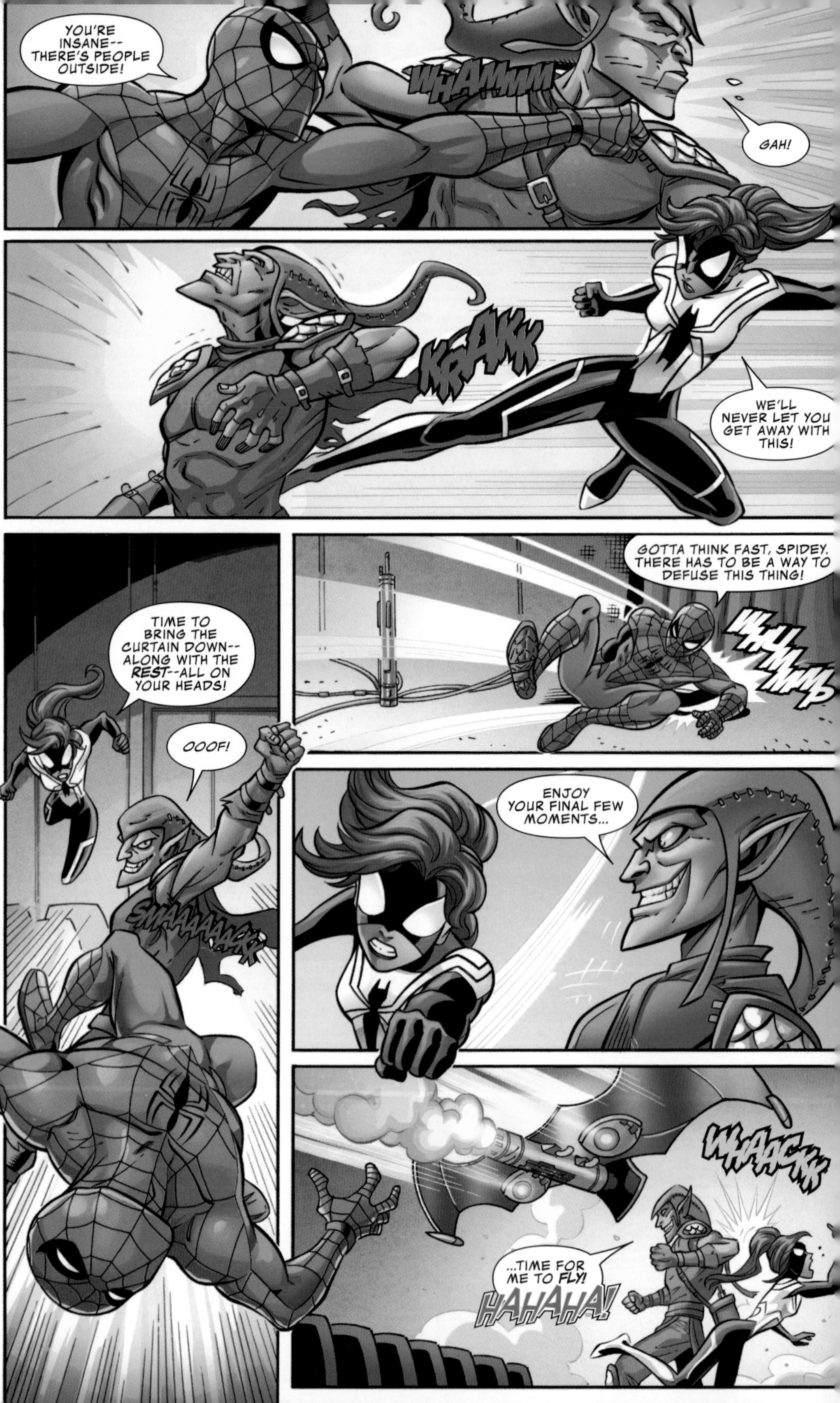
YOU'RE INSANE--THERE'S PEOPLE OUTSIDE!
WHAMMM
GAH!
KRAKK
WE'LL NEVER LET YOU GET AWAY WITH THIS!
TIME TO BRING THE CURTAIN DOWN--ALONG WITH THE REST--ALL ON YOUR HEADS!
OOOF!
SMAAAAAACK
GOTTA THINK FAST, SPIDEY. THERE HAS TO BE A WAY TO DEFUSE THIS THING!
WHUMMP
ENJOY YOUR FINAL FEW MOMENTS...
WHACK
...TIME FOR ME TO FLY!
HAHAHA!

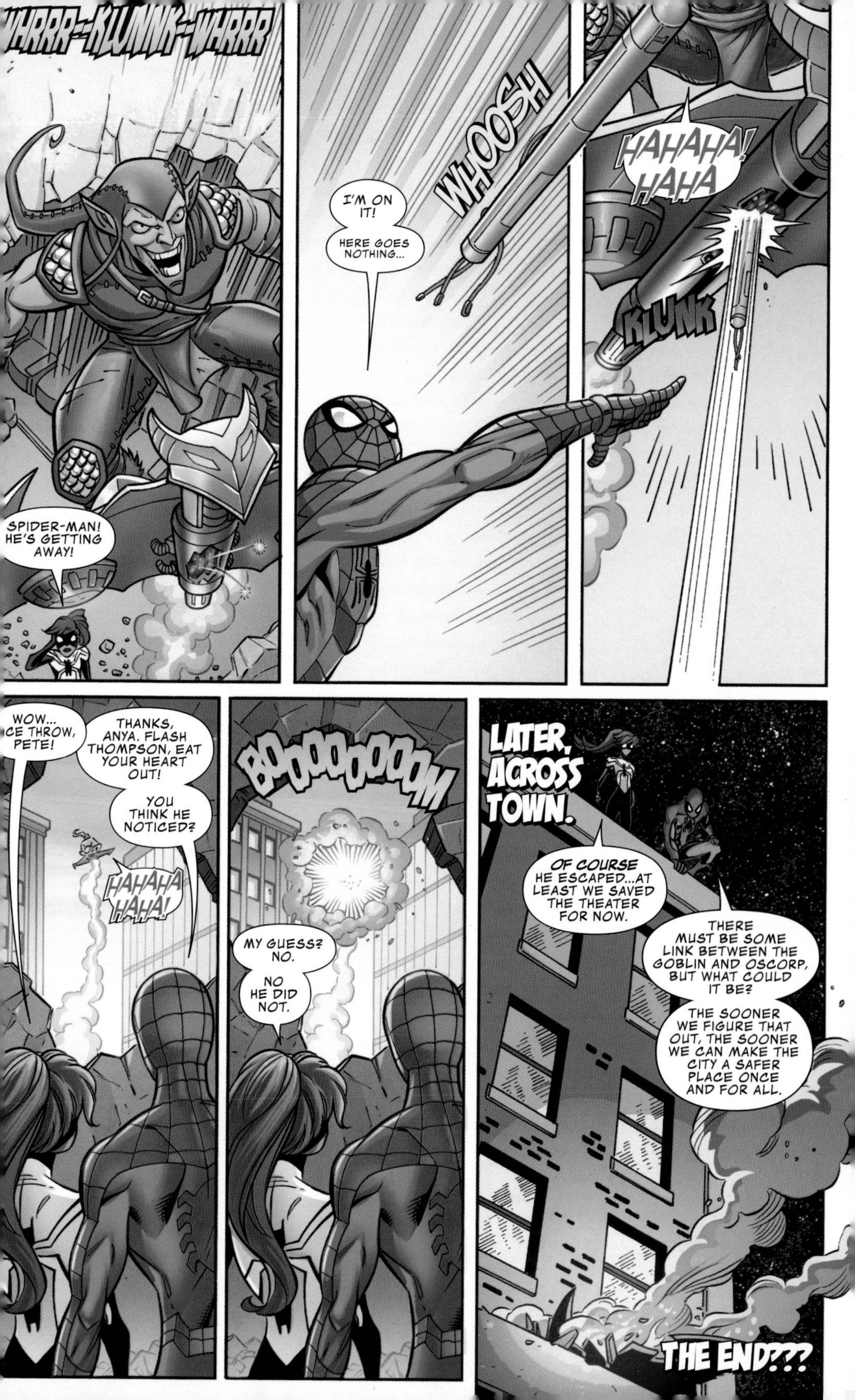
WHRRR-KLUNNK-WHRRR
SPIDER-MAN! HE'S GETTING AWAY!
I'M ON IT!
HERE GOES NOTHING...
WHOOSH
HAHAHA! HAHA
KLUNK
WOW... CE THROW, PETE!
THANKS, ANYA. FLASH THOMPSON, EAT YOUR HEART OUT!
YOU THINK HE NOTICED?
HAHAHA HAHA!
BOOOOOOOOM
MY GUESS? NO.
NO HE DID NOT.
LATER, ACROSS TOWN.
OF COURSE HE ESCAPED...AT LEAST WE SAVED THE THEATER FOR NOW.
THERE MUST BE SOME LINK BETWEEN THE GOBLIN AND OSCORP, BUT WHAT COULD IT BE?
THE SOONER WE FIGURE THAT OUT, THE SOONER WE CAN MAKE THE CITY A SAFER PLACE ONCE AND FOR ALL.
THE END???

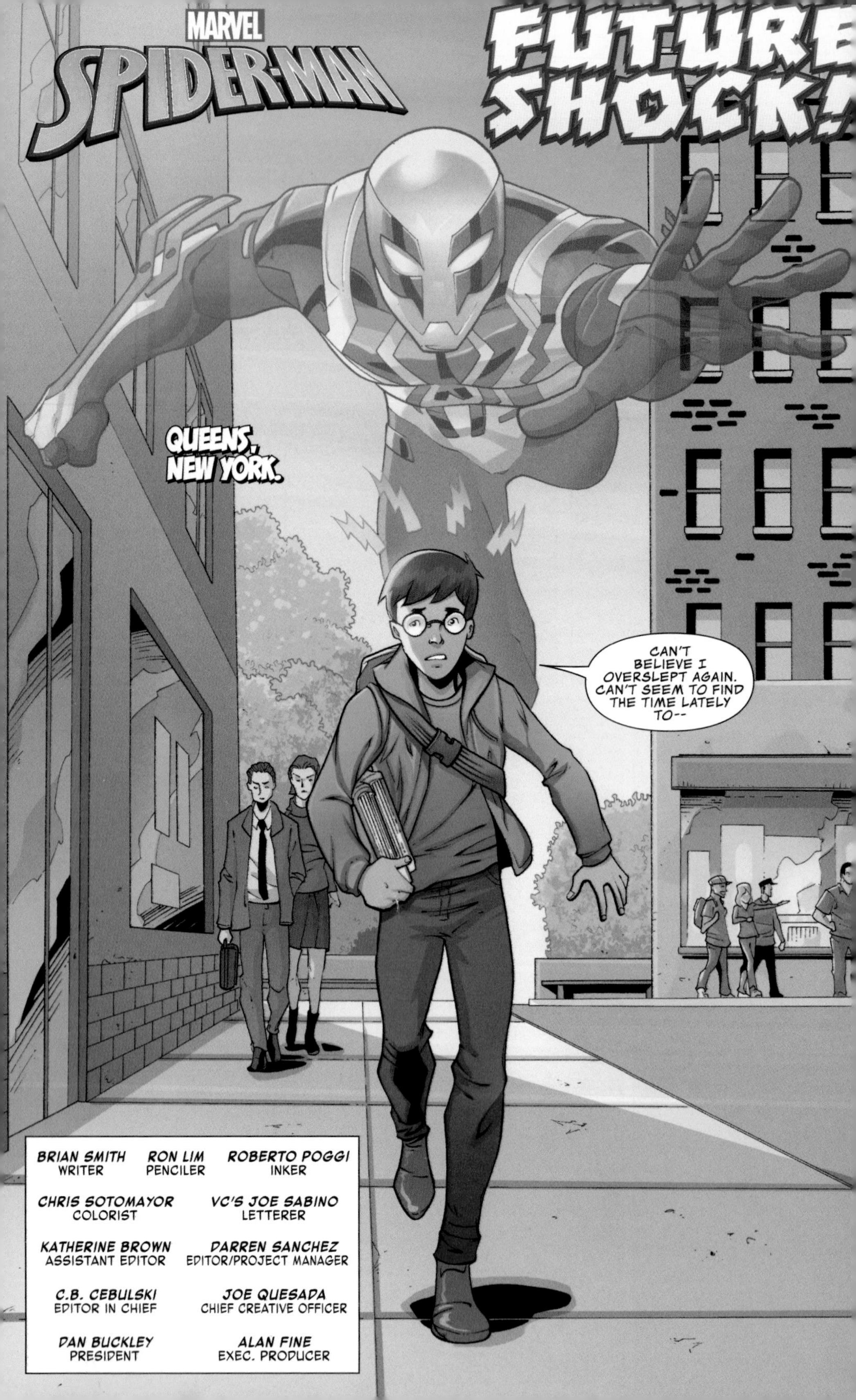
MARVEL
SPIDER-MAN
FUTURE SHOCK!
QUEENS, NEW YORK.
CAN'T BELIEVE I OVERSLEPT AGAIN. CAN'T SEEM TO FIND THE TIME LATELY TO--
BRIAN SMITH WRITER
RON LIM PENCILER
ROBERTO POGGI INKER
CHRIS SOTOMAYOR COLORIST
VC'S JOE SABINO LETTERER
KATHERINE BROWN ASSISTANT EDITOR
DARREN SANCHEZ EDITOR/PROJECT MANAGER
C.B. CEBULSKI EDITOR IN CHIEF
JOE QUESADA CHIEF CREATIVE OFFICER
DAN BUCKLEY PRESIDENT
ALAN FINE EXEC. PRODUCER

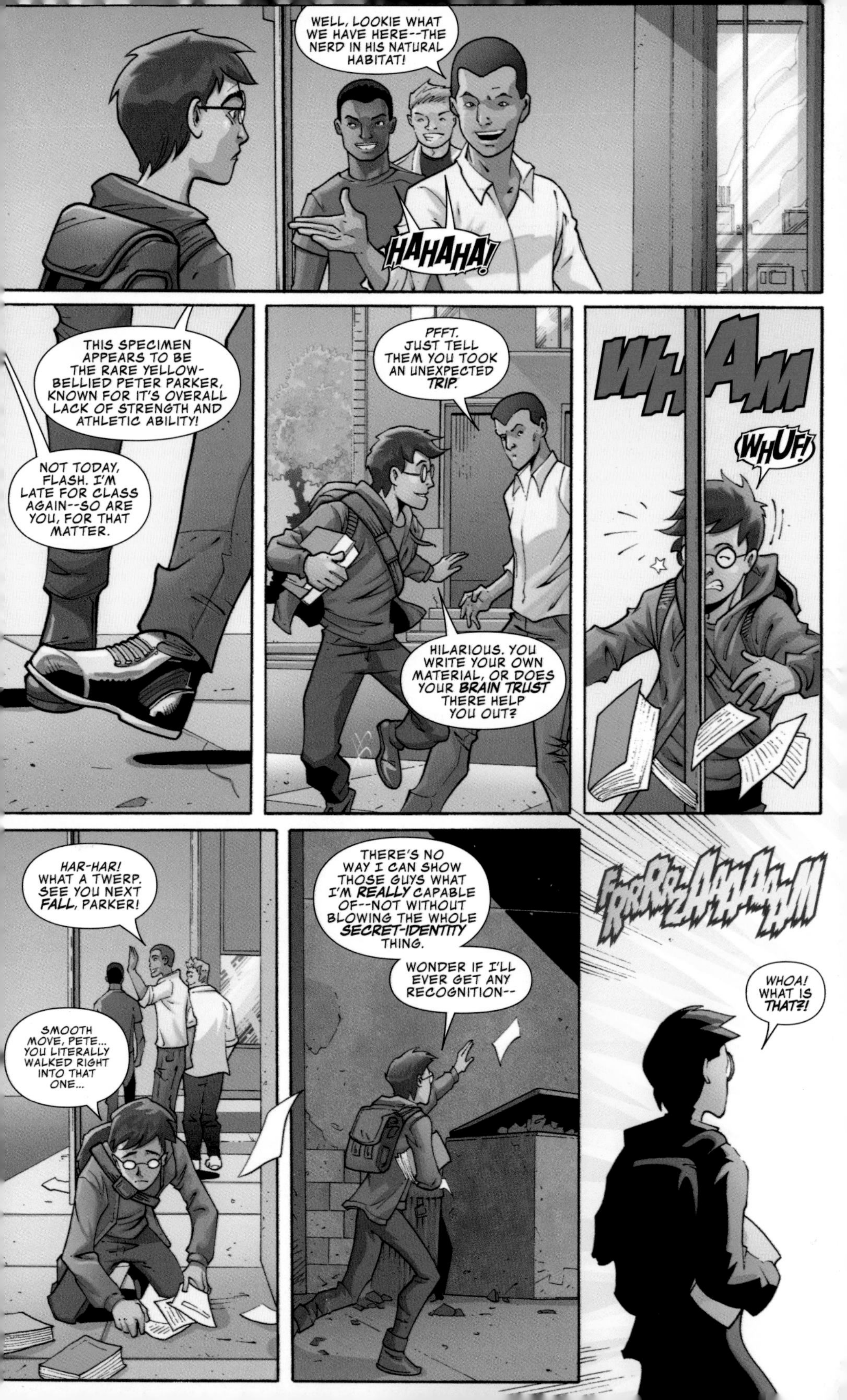
WELL, LOOKIE WHAT WE HAVE HERE--THE NERD IN HIS NATURAL HABITAT!
HAHAHA!
THIS SPECIMEN APPEARS TO BE THE RARE YELLOW-BELLIED PETER PARKER, KNOWN FOR IT'S OVERALL LACK OF STRENGTH AND ATHLETIC ABILITY!
NOT TODAY, FLASH. I'M LATE FOR CLASS AGAIN--SO ARE YOU, FOR THAT MATTER.
PFFT. JUST TELL THEM YOU TOOK AN UNEXPECTED TRIP.
HILARIOUS. YOU WRITE YOUR OWN MATERIAL, OR DOES YOUR BRAIN TRUST THERE HELP YOU OUT?
WHAM
WHUF!
HAR-HAR! WHAT A TWERP. SEE YOU NEXT FALL, PARKER!
SMOOTH MOVE, PETE... YOU LITERALLY WALKED RIGHT INTO THAT ONE...
THERE'S NO WAY I CAN SHOW THOSE GUYS WHAT I'M REALLY CAPABLE OF--NOT WITHOUT BLOWING THE WHOLE SECRET-IDENTITY THING.
WONDER IF I'LL EVER GET ANY RECOGNITION--
FRRRRZAAAAAM
WHOA! WHAT IS THAT?!

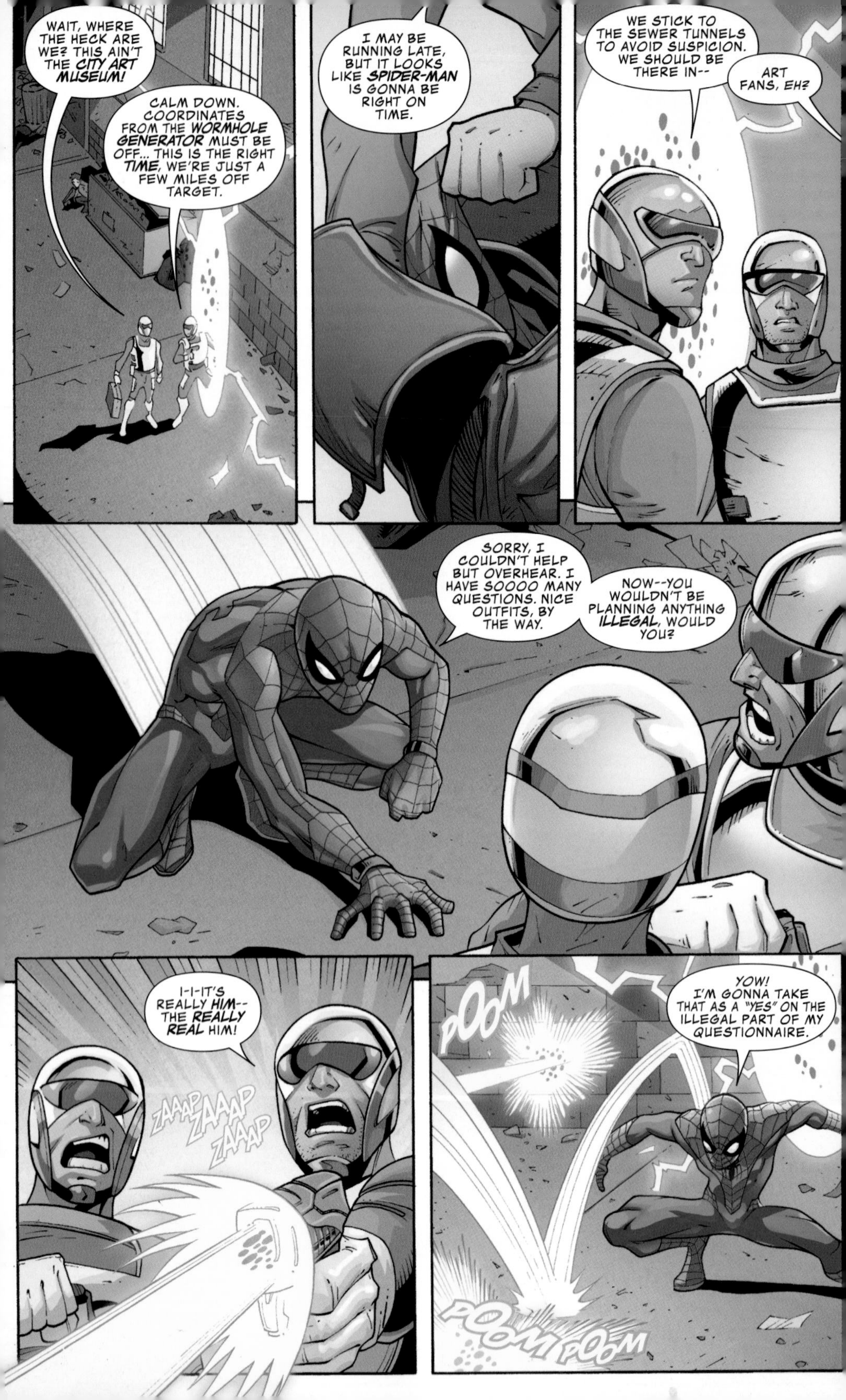
WAIT, WHERE THE HECK ARE WE? THIS AIN'T THE CITY ART MUSEUM!
CALM DOWN. COORDINATES FROM THE WORMHOLE GENERATOR MUST BE OFF... THIS IS THE RIGHT TIME, WE'RE JUST A FEW MILES OFF TARGET.
I MAY BE RUNNING LATE, BUT IT LOOKS LIKE SPIDER-MAN IS GONNA BE RIGHT ON TIME.
WE STICK TO THE SEWER TUNNELS TO AVOID SUSPICION. WE SHOULD BE THERE IN--
ART FANS, EH?
SORRY, I COULDN'T HELP BUT OVERHEAR. I HAVE SOOOO MANY QUESTIONS. NICE OUTFITS, BY THE WAY.
NOW--YOU WOULDN'T BE PLANNING ANYTHING ILLEGAL, WOULD YOU?
I-I-IT'S REALLY HIM-- THE REALLY REAL HIM!
ZAAAP ZAAAP ZAAAP
POOM
YOW! I'M GONNA TAKE THAT AS A "YES" ON THE ILLEGAL PART OF MY QUESTIONNAIRE.
POOM POOM

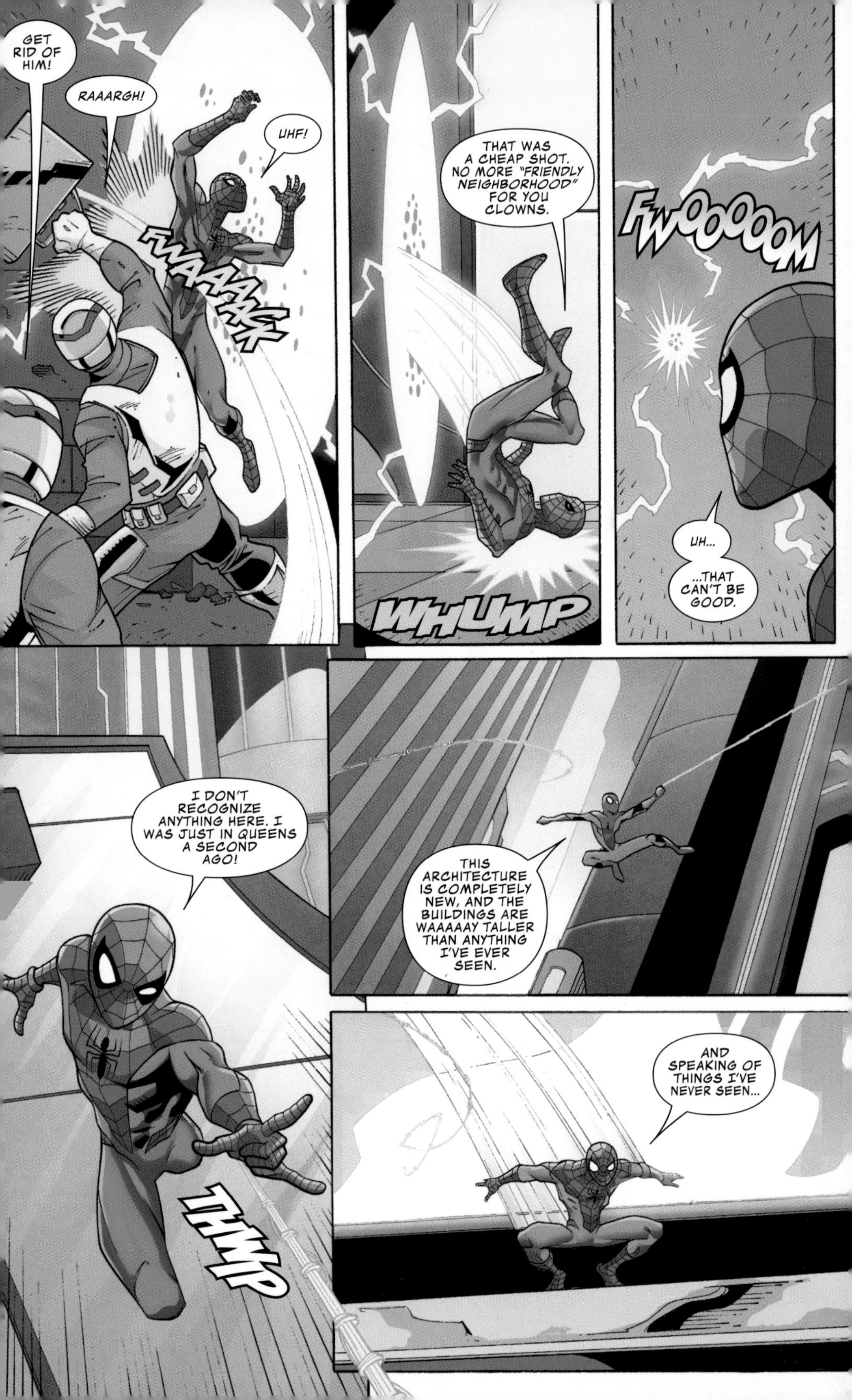
GET RID OF HIM!
RAAARGH!
UHF!
FWAAAK
THAT WAS A CHEAP SHOT. NO MORE "FRIENDLY NEIGHBORHOOD" FOR YOU CLOWNS.
WHUMP
FWOOOOOM
UH...
...THAT CAN'T BE GOOD.
I DON'T RECOGNIZE ANYTHING HERE. I WAS JUST IN QUEENS A SECOND AGO!
THWIP
THIS ARCHITECTURE IS COMPLETELY NEW, AND THE BUILDINGS ARE WAAAAAY TALLER THAN ANYTHING I'VE EVER SEEN.
AND SPEAKING OF THINGS I'VE NEVER SEEN...

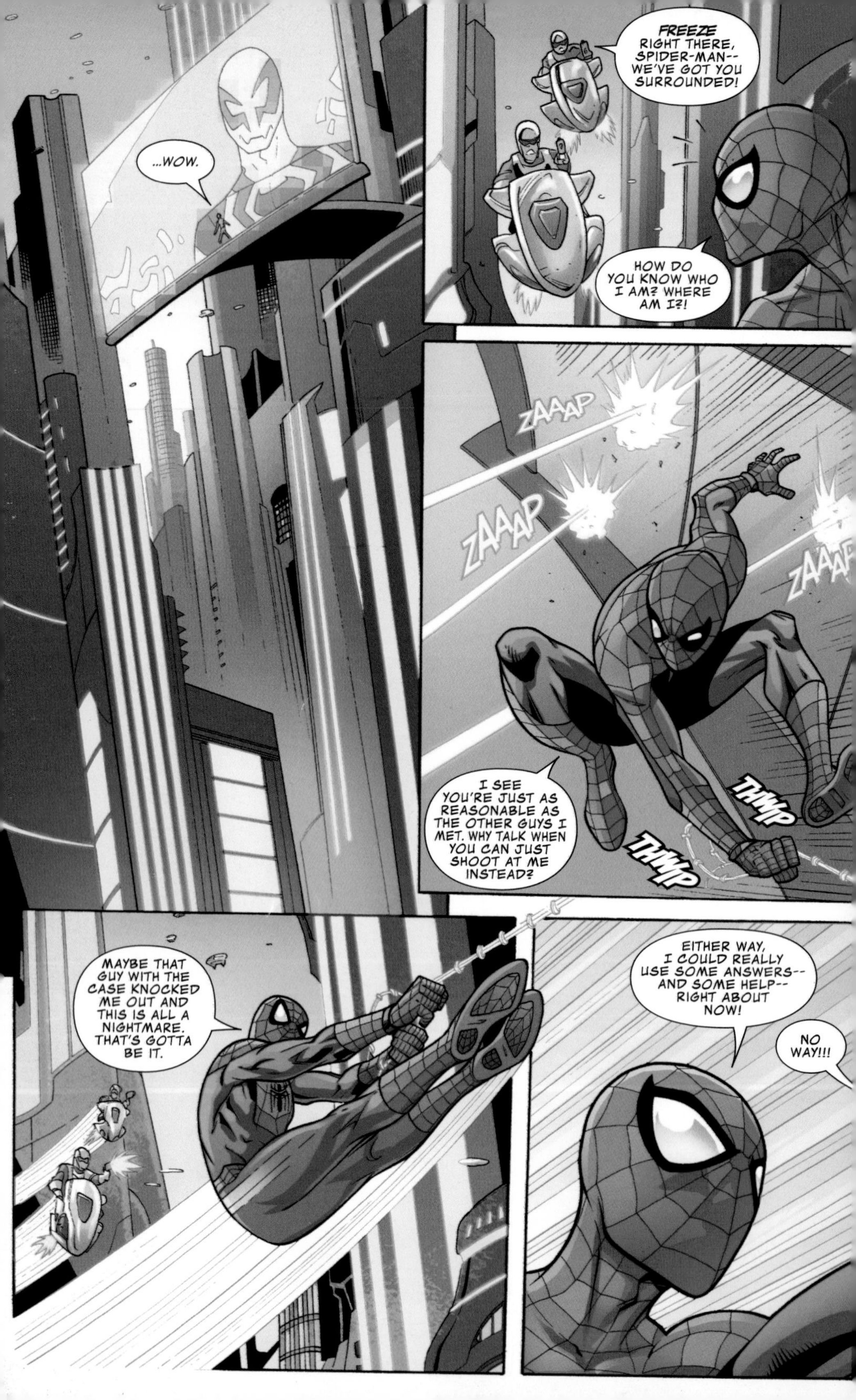
...WOW.
FREEZE RIGHT THERE, SPIDER-MAN-- WE'VE GOT YOU SURROUNDED!
HOW DO YOU KNOW WHO I AM? WHERE AM I?!
ZAAAP
ZAAAP
ZAAAP
I SEE YOU'RE JUST AS REASONABLE AS THE OTHER GUYS I MET. WHY TALK WHEN YOU CAN JUST SHOOT AT ME INSTEAD?
THMP
THMP
MAYBE THAT GUY WITH THE CASE KNOCKED ME OUT AND THIS IS ALL A NIGHTMARE. THAT'S GOTTA BE IT.
EITHER WAY, I COULD REALLY USE SOME ANSWERS-- AND SOME HELP-- RIGHT ABOUT NOW!
NO WAY!!!

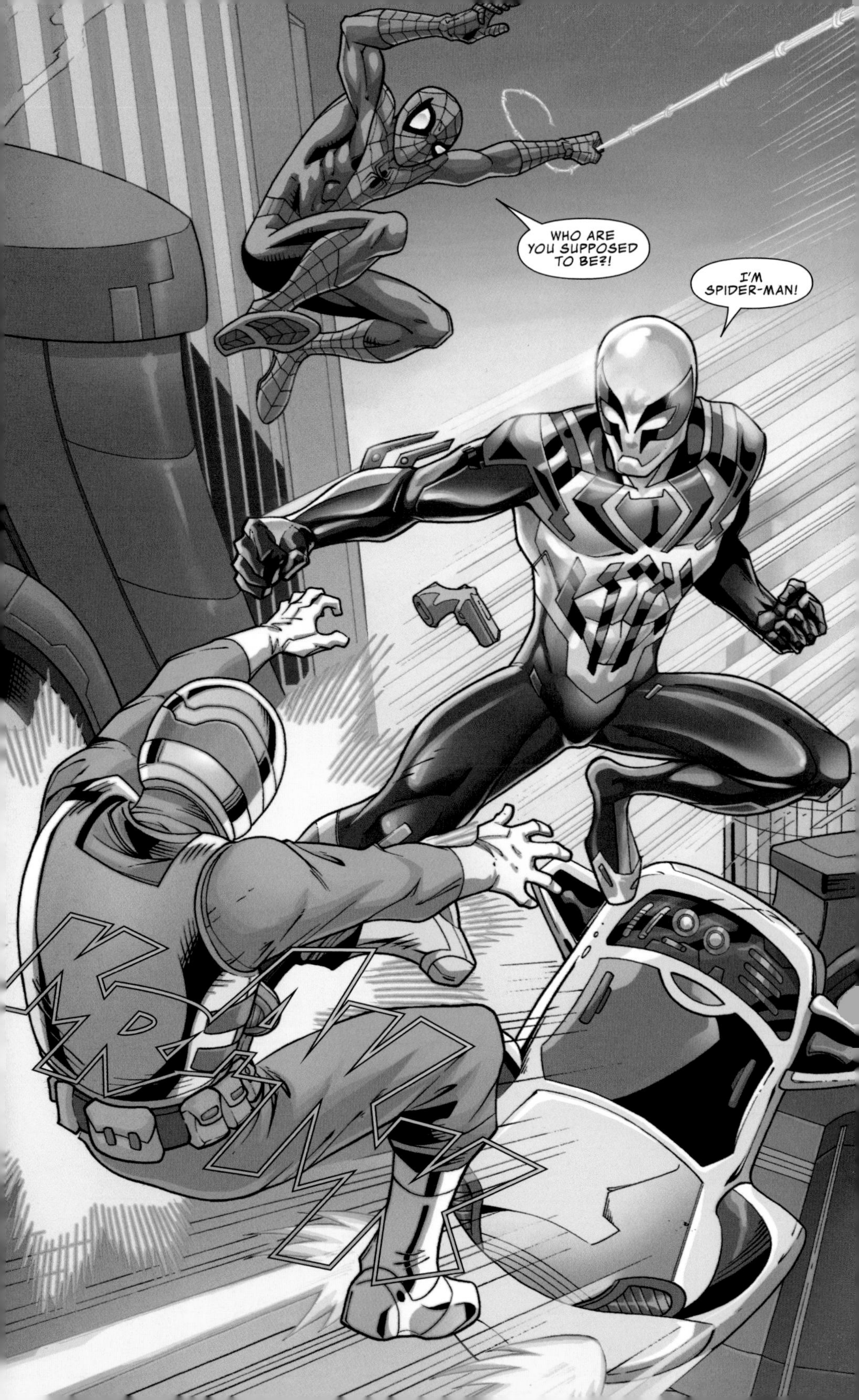

WHO ARE YOU SUPPOSED TO BE?!
I'M SPIDER-MAN!

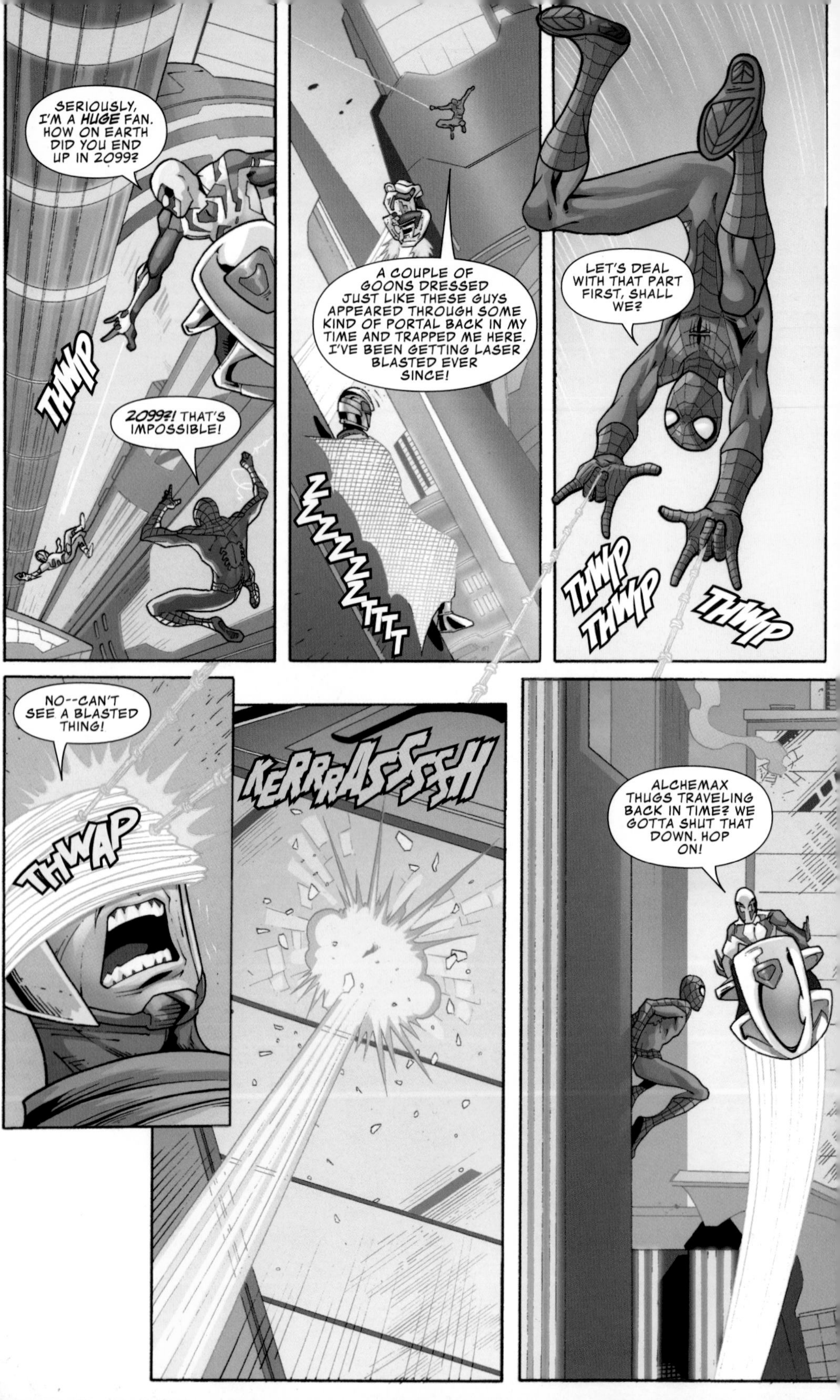
SERIOUSLY, I'M A HUGE FAN. HOW ON EARTH DID YOU END UP IN 2099?
THWIP
2099?! THAT'S IMPOSSIBLE!
A COUPLE OF GOONS DRESSED JUST LIKE THESE GUYS APPEARED THROUGH SOME KIND OF PORTAL BACK IN MY TIME AND TRAPPED ME HERE. I'VE BEEN GETTING LASER BLASTED EVER SINCE!
ZZZZZTTTT
LET'S DEAL WITH THAT PART FIRST, SHALL WE?
THWIP THWIP
THWIP
NO--CAN'T SEE A BLASTED THING!
THWAP
KERRRASSSSH
ALCHEMAX THUGS TRAVELING BACK IN TIME? WE GOTTA SHUT THAT DOWN. HOP ON!

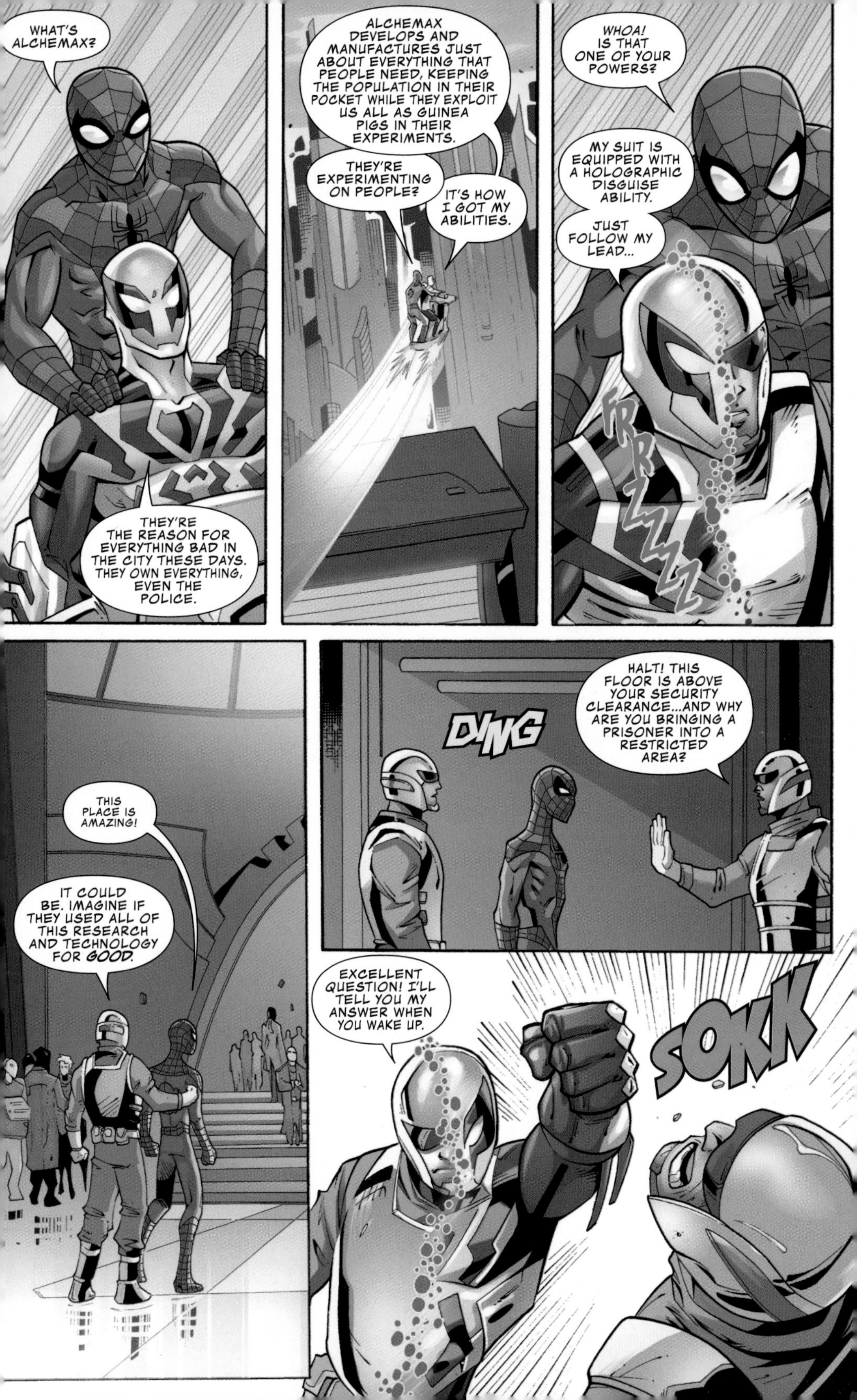
WHAT'S ALCHEMAX?
THEY'RE THE REASON FOR EVERYTHING BAD IN THE CITY THESE DAYS. THEY OWN EVERYTHING, EVEN THE POLICE.
ALCHEMAX DEVELOPS AND MANUFACTURES JUST ABOUT EVERYTHING THAT PEOPLE NEED, KEEPING THE POPULATION IN THEIR POCKET WHILE THEY EXPLOIT US ALL AS GUINEA PIGS IN THEIR EXPERIMENTS.
THEY'RE EXPERIMENTING ON PEOPLE?
IT'S HOW I GOT MY ABILITIES.
WHOA! IS THAT ONE OF YOUR POWERS?
MY SUIT IS EQUIPPED WITH A HOLOGRAPHIC DISGUISE ABILITY.
JUST FOLLOW MY LEAD...
FRRZZZZZ
THIS PLACE IS AMAZING!
IT COULD BE. IMAGINE IF THEY USED ALL OF THIS RESEARCH AND TECHNOLOGY FOR GOOD.
DING
HALT! THIS FLOOR IS ABOVE YOUR SECURITY CLEARANCE...AND WHY ARE YOU BRINGING A PRISONER INTO A RESTRICTED AREA?
EXCELLENT QUESTION! I'LL TELL YOU MY ANSWER WHEN YOU WAKE UP.
SOKK

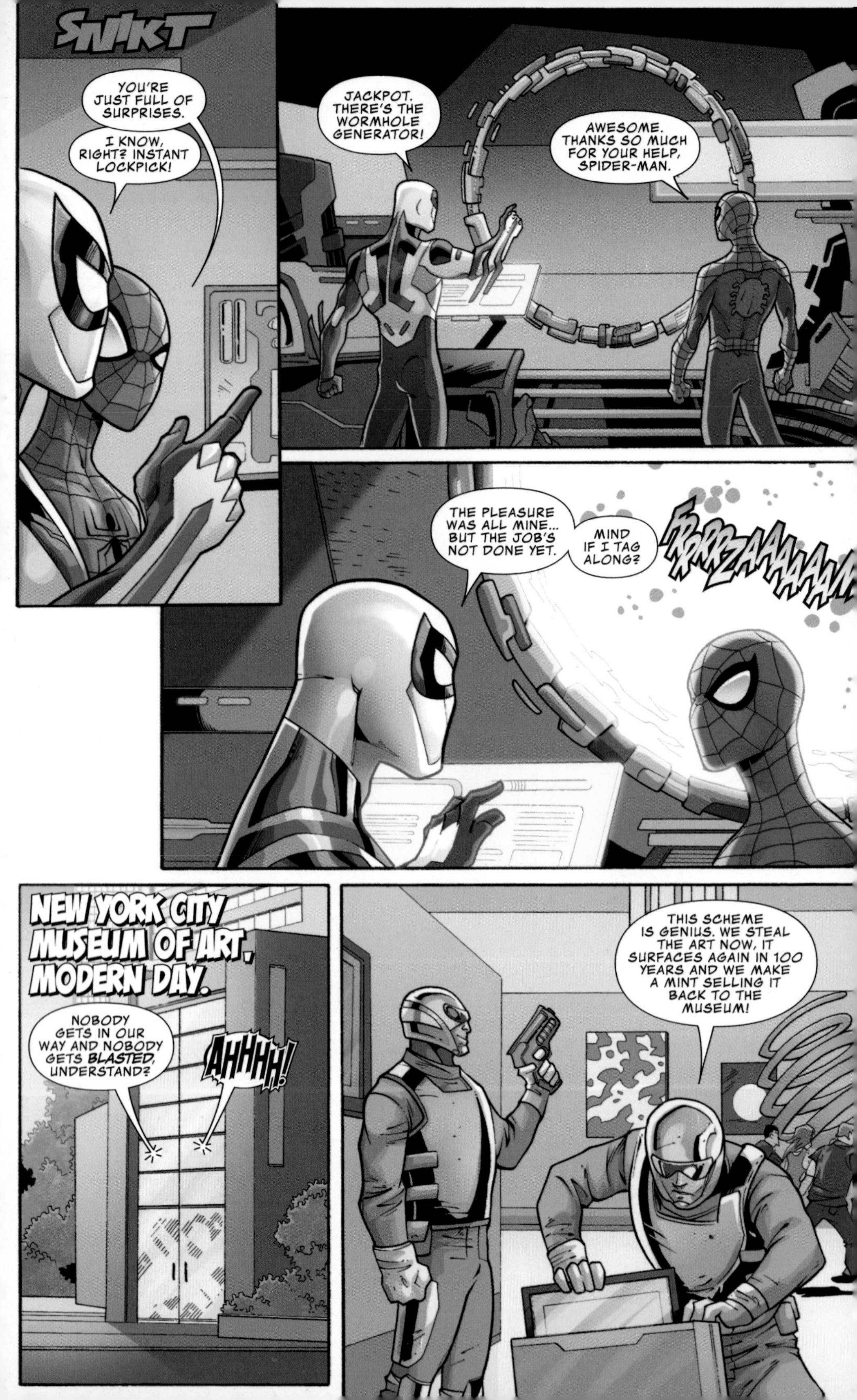

SNIKT
YOU'RE JUST FULL OF SURPRISES.
I KNOW, RIGHT? INSTANT LOCKPICK!
JACKPOT. THERE'S THE WORMHOLE GENERATOR!
AWESOME. THANKS SO MUCH FOR YOUR HELP, SPIDER-MAN.
THE PLEASURE WAS ALL MINE... BUT THE JOB'S NOT DONE YET.
MIND IF I TAG ALONG?
FRRRZAAAAAAM
NEW YORK CITY MUSEUM OF ART, MODERN DAY.
NOBODY GETS IN OUR WAY AND NOBODY GETS BLASTED, UNDERSTAND?
AHHHH!
THIS SCHEME IS GENIUS. WE STEAL THE ART NOW, IT SURFACES AGAIN IN 100 YEARS AND WE MAKE A MINT SELLING IT BACK TO THE MUSEUM!

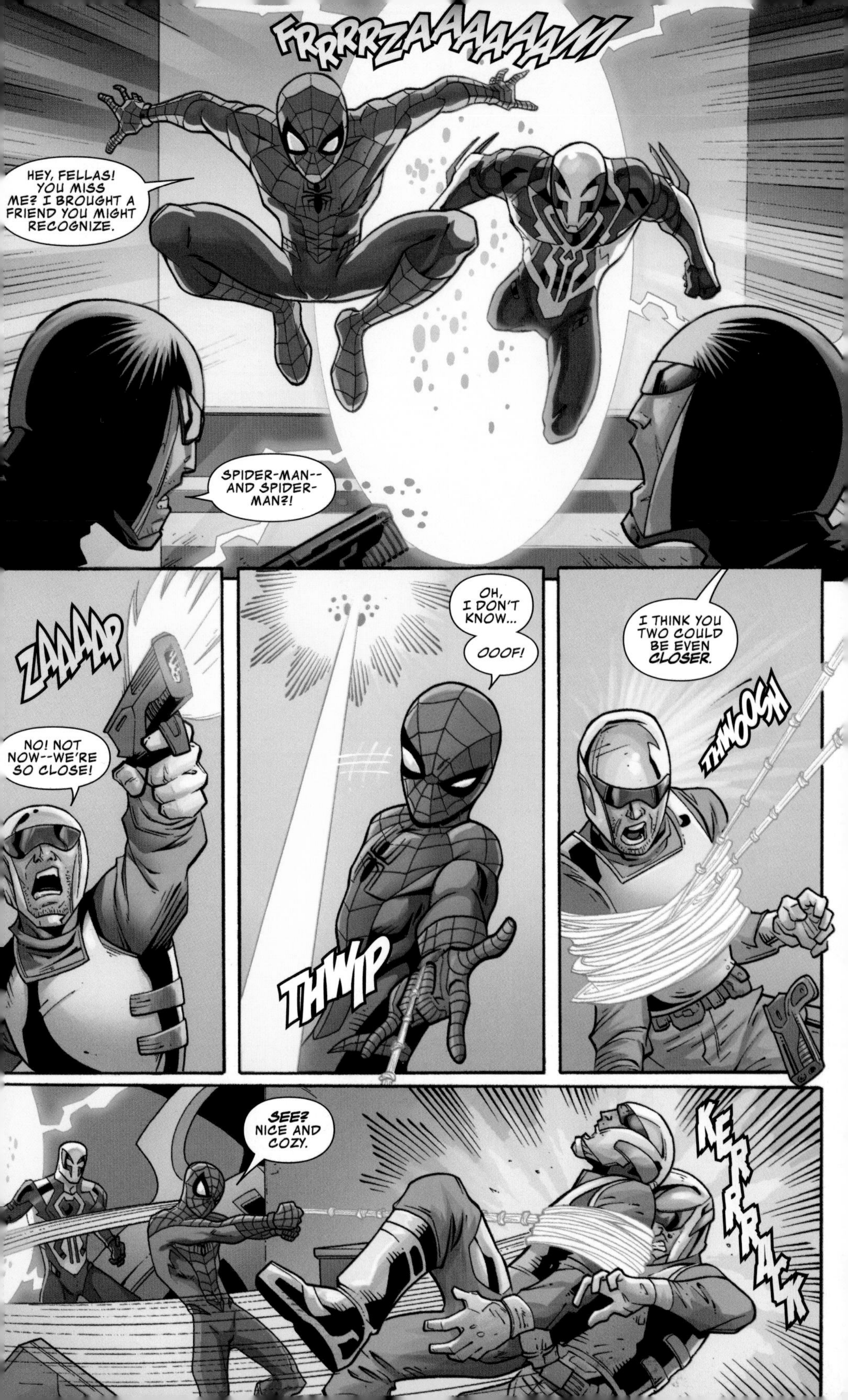
FRRRRZAAAAAAM
HEY, FELLAS! YOU MISS ME? I BROUGHT A FRIEND YOU MIGHT RECOGNIZE.
SPIDER-MAN-- AND SPIDER-MAN?!
ZAAAAP
NO! NOT NOW--WE'RE SO CLOSE!
OH, I DON'T KNOW...
OOOF!
THWIP
I THINK YOU TWO COULD BE EVEN CLOSER.
THWOOSH
SEE? NICE AND COZY.
KERRRACK

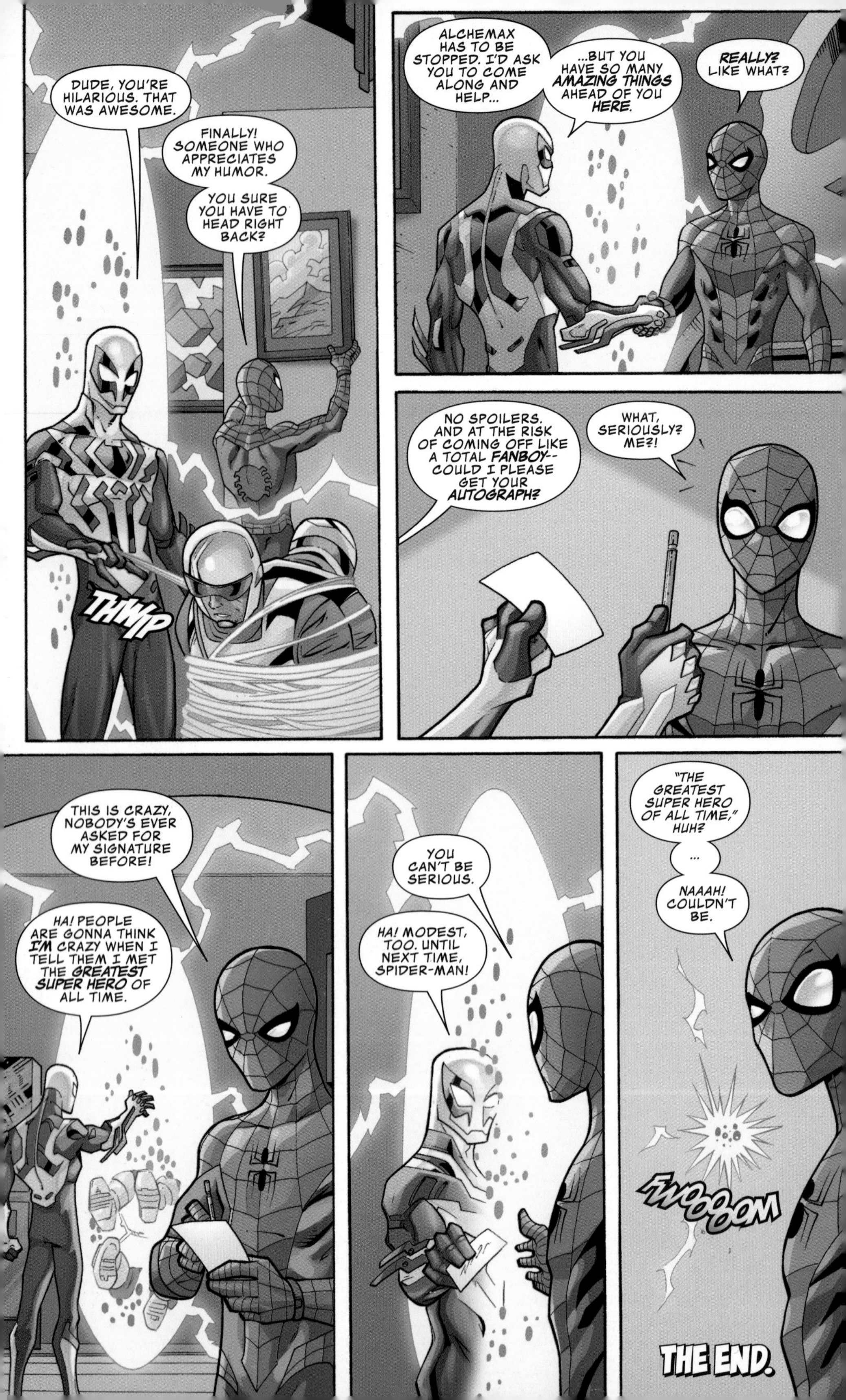
DUDE, YOU'RE HILARIOUS. THAT WAS AWESOME.
FINALLY! SOMEONE WHO APPRECIATES MY HUMOR.
YOU SURE YOU HAVE TO HEAD RIGHT BACK?
THWIP
ALCHEMAX HAS TO BE STOPPED. I'D ASK YOU TO COME ALONG AND HELP...
...BUT YOU HAVE SO MANY AMAZING THINGS AHEAD OF YOU HERE.
REALLY? LIKE WHAT?
NO SPOILERS. AND AT THE RISK OF COMING OFF LIKE A TOTAL FANBOY-- COULD I PLEASE GET YOUR AUTOGRAPH?
WHAT, SERIOUSLY? ME?!
THIS IS CRAZY, NOBODY'S EVER ASKED FOR MY SIGNATURE BEFORE!
HA! PEOPLE ARE GONNA THINK I'M CRAZY WHEN I TELL THEM I MET THE GREATEST SUPER HERO OF ALL TIME.
YOU CAN'T BE SERIOUS.
HA! MODEST, TOO. UNTIL NEXT TIME, SPIDER-MAN!
"THE GREATEST SUPER HERO OF ALL TIME," HUH?
...
NAAAH! COULDN'T BE.
FWOOOOOM
THE END.

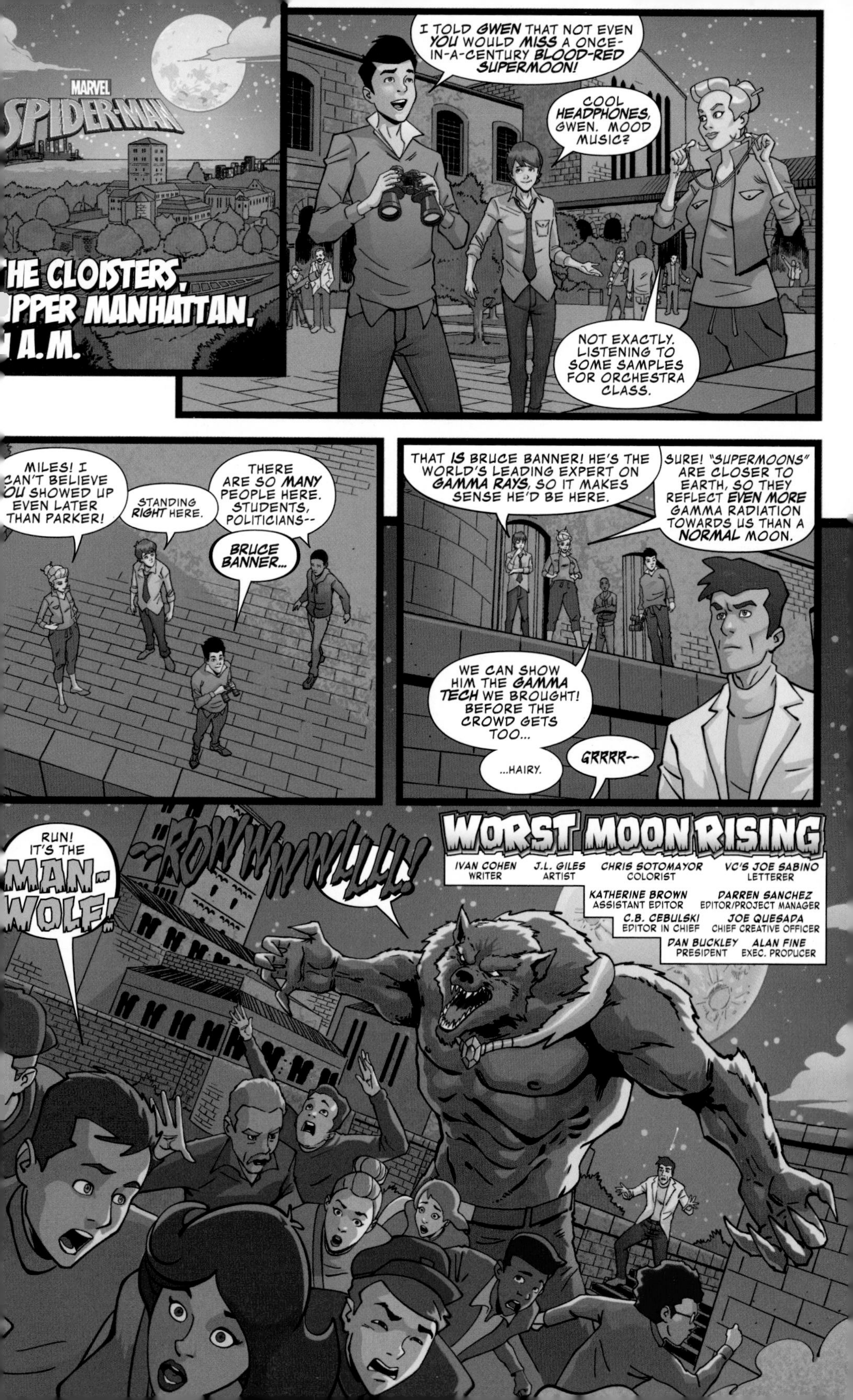
MARVEL
SPIDER-MAN
HE CLOISTERS,
PPER MANHATTAN,
A.M.
I TOLD GWEN THAT NOT EVEN YOU WOULD MISS A ONCE-IN-A-CENTURY BLOOD-RED SUPERMOON!
COOL HEADPHONES, GWEN. MOOD MUSIC?
NOT EXACTLY. LISTENING TO SOME SAMPLES FOR ORCHESTRA CLASS.
MILES! I CAN'T BELIEVE YOU SHOWED UP EVEN LATER THAN PARKER!
STANDING RIGHT HERE.
THERE ARE SO MANY PEOPLE HERE. STUDENTS, POLITICIANS--
BRUCE BANNER...
THAT IS BRUCE BANNER! HE'S THE WORLD'S LEADING EXPERT ON GAMMA RAYS, SO IT MAKES SENSE HE'D BE HERE.
SURE! "SUPERMOONS" ARE CLOSER TO EARTH, SO THEY REFLECT EVEN MORE GAMMA RADIATION TOWARDS US THAN A NORMAL MOON.
WE CAN SHOW HIM THE GAMMA TECH WE BROUGHT! BEFORE THE CROWD GETS TOO...
...HAIRY.
GRRRR--
RUN! IT'S THE MAN-WOLF!
--ROWWWWLLL!
WORST MOON RISING
IVAN COHEN WRITER
J.L. GILES ARTIST
CHRIS SOTOMAYOR COLORIST
VC'S JOE SABINO LETTERER
KATHERINE BROWN ASSISTANT EDITOR
DARREN SANCHEZ EDITOR/PROJECT MANAGER
C.B. CEBULSKI EDITOR IN CHIEF
JOE QUESADA CHIEF CREATIVE OFFICER
DAN BUCKLEY PRESIDENT
ALAN FINE EXEC. PRODUCER

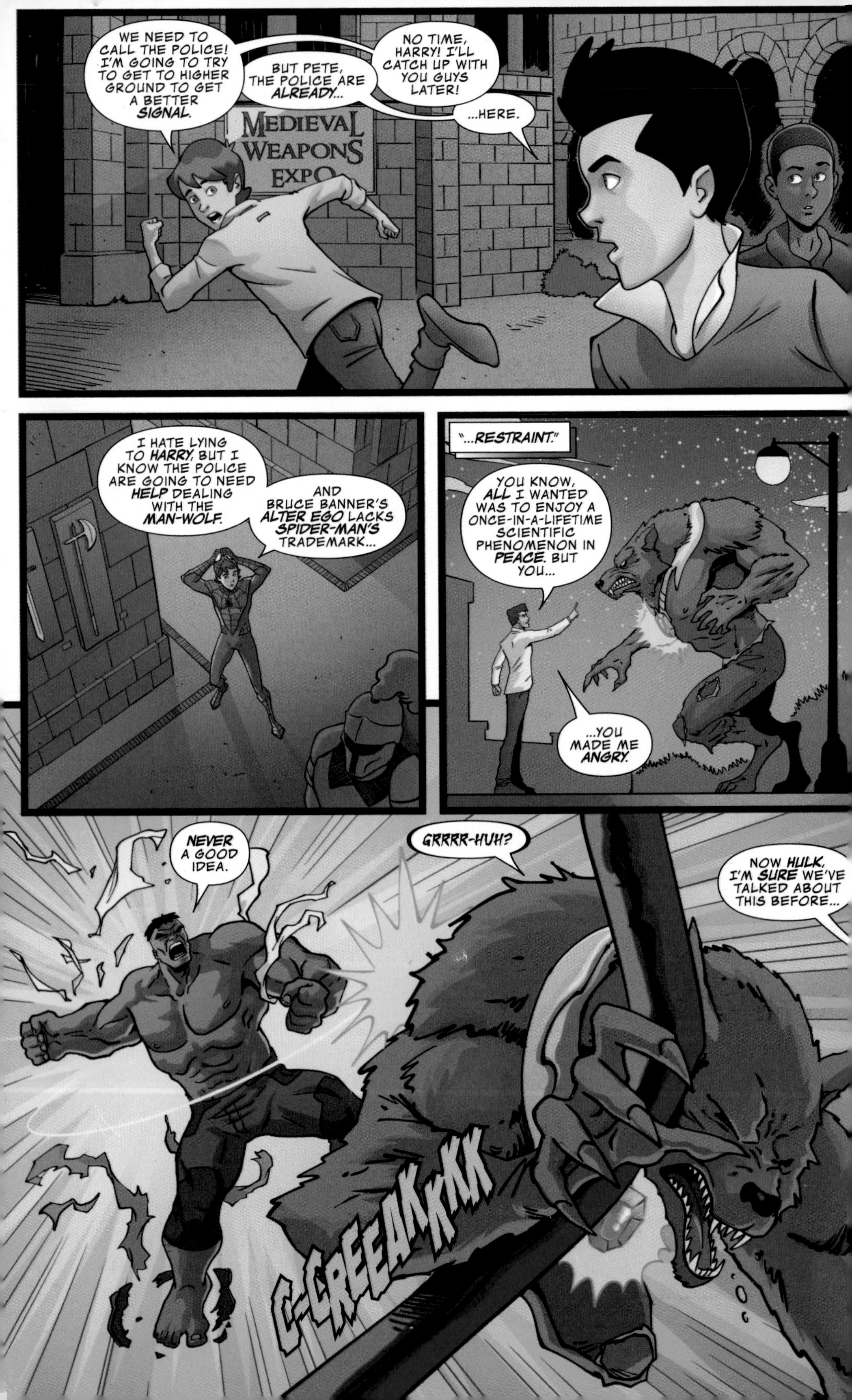
WE NEED TO CALL THE POLICE! I'M GOING TO TRY TO GET TO HIGHER GROUND TO GET A BETTER SIGNAL.
BUT PETE, THE POLICE ARE ALREADY...
NO TIME, HARRY! I'LL CATCH UP WITH YOU GUYS LATER!
...HERE.
MEDIEVAL WEAPONS EXPO
I HATE LYING TO HARRY, BUT I KNOW THE POLICE ARE GOING TO NEED HELP DEALING WITH THE MAN-WOLF.
AND BRUCE BANNER'S ALTER EGO LACKS SPIDER-MAN'S TRADEMARK...
"...RESTRAINT."
YOU KNOW, ALL I WANTED WAS TO ENJOY A ONCE-IN-A-LIFETIME SCIENTIFIC PHENOMENON IN PEACE. BUT YOU...
...YOU MADE ME ANGRY.
NEVER A GOOD IDEA.
GRRRR-HUH?
NOW HULK, I'M SURE WE'VE TALKED ABOUT THIS BEFORE...
C-CREEAKKKK

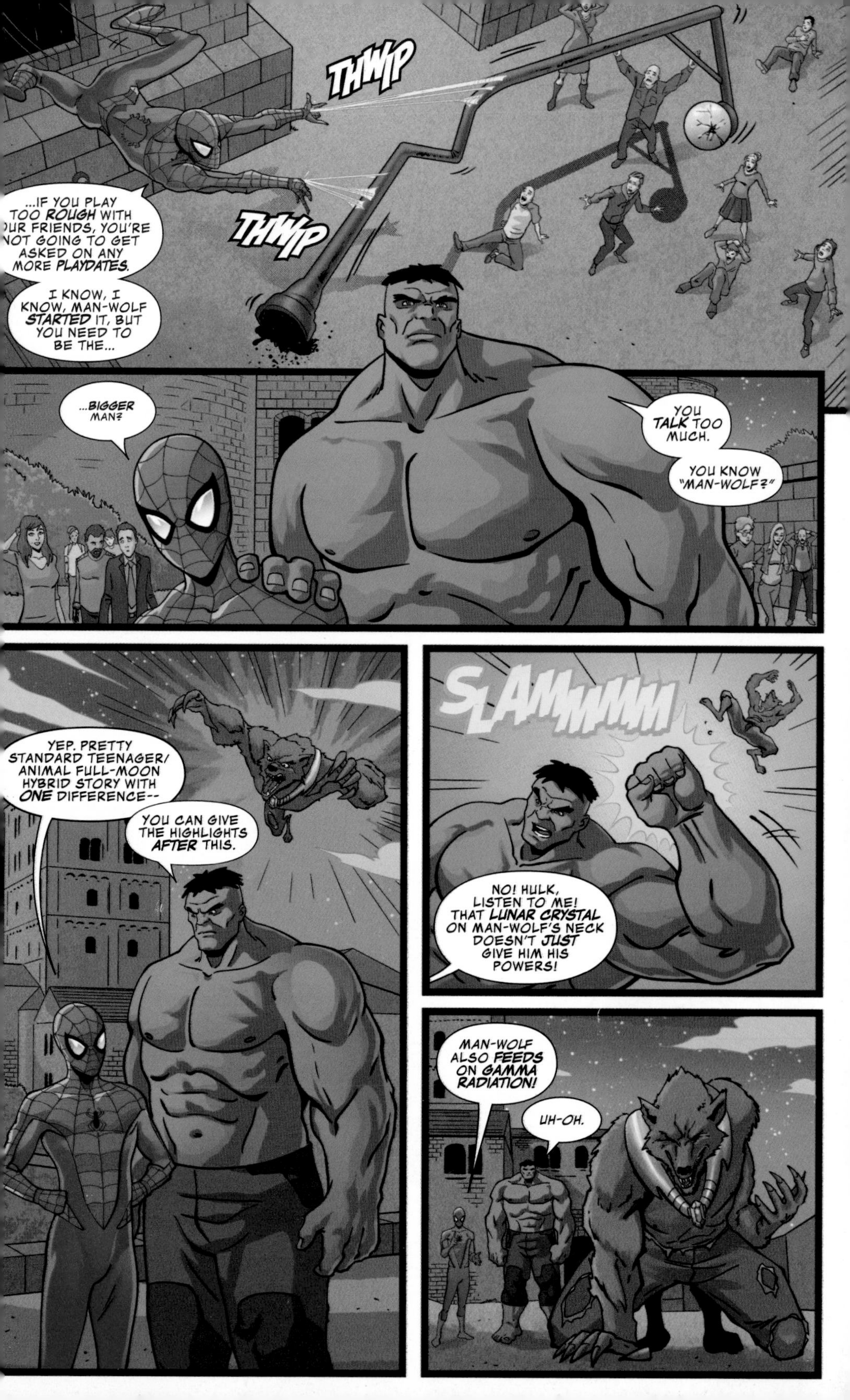
THWIP
THWIP
...IF YOU PLAY TOO ROUGH WITH OUR FRIENDS, YOU'RE NOT GOING TO GET ASKED ON ANY MORE PLAYDATES.
I KNOW, I KNOW, MAN-WOLF STARTED IT, BUT YOU NEED TO BE THE...
...BIGGER MAN?
YOU TALK TOO MUCH.
YOU KNOW "MAN-WOLF?"
YEP. PRETTY STANDARD TEENAGER/ ANIMAL FULL-MOON HYBRID STORY WITH ONE DIFFERENCE--
YOU CAN GIVE THE HIGHLIGHTS AFTER THIS.
SLAMMMMM
NO! HULK, LISTEN TO ME! THAT LUNAR CRYSTAL ON MAN-WOLF'S NECK DOESN'T JUST GIVE HIM HIS POWERS!
MAN-WOLF ALSO FEEDS ON GAMMA RADIATION!
UH-OH.

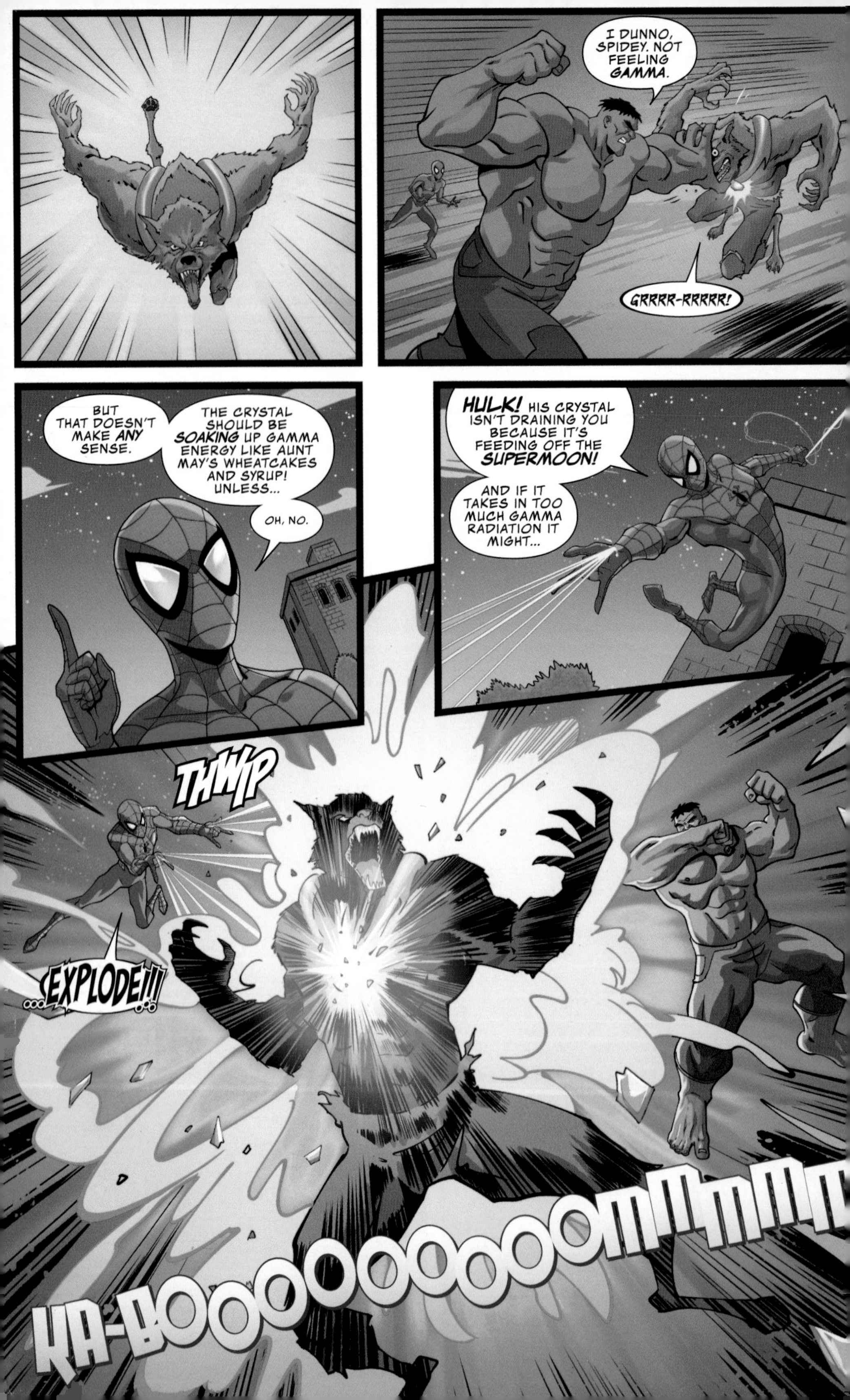
I DUNNO, SPIDEY. NOT FEELING GAMMA.
GRRRR-RRRRR!
BUT THAT DOESN'T MAKE ANY SENSE.
THE CRYSTAL SHOULD BE SOAKING UP GAMMA ENERGY LIKE AUNT MAY'S WHEATCAKES AND SYRUP! UNLESS...
OH, NO.
HULK! HIS CRYSTAL ISN'T DRAINING YOU BECAUSE IT'S FEEDING OFF THE SUPERMOON!
AND IF IT TAKES IN TOO MUCH GAMMA RADIATION IT MIGHT...
THWIP
...EXPLODE!!!
KA-BOOOOOOOOOOOMMMMMM

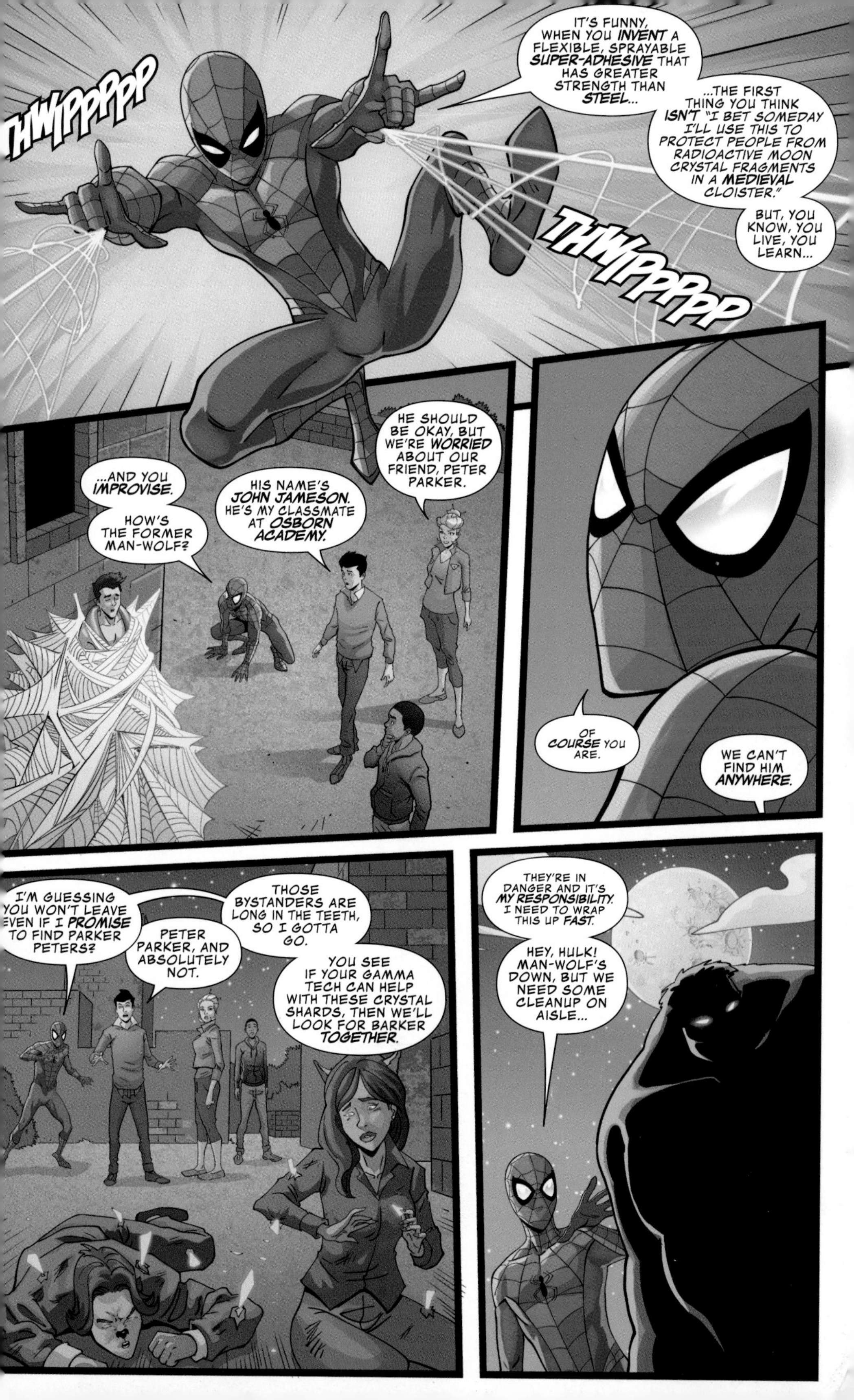
THWIPPPPP
IT'S FUNNY, WHEN YOU INVENT A FLEXIBLE, SPRAYABLE SUPER-ADHESIVE THAT HAS GREATER STRENGTH THAN STEEL...
...THE FIRST THING YOU THINK ISN'T "I BET SOMEDAY I'LL USE THIS TO PROTECT PEOPLE FROM RADIOACTIVE MOON CRYSTAL FRAGMENTS IN A MEDIEVAL CLOISTER."
BUT, YOU KNOW, YOU LIVE, YOU LEARN...
THWIPPPPPP
...AND YOU IMPROVISE.
HOW'S THE FORMER MAN-WOLF?
HIS NAME'S JOHN JAMESON. HE'S MY CLASSMATE AT OSBORN ACADEMY.
HE SHOULD BE OKAY, BUT WE'RE WORRIED ABOUT OUR FRIEND, PETER PARKER.
OF COURSE YOU ARE.
WE CAN'T FIND HIM ANYWHERE.
I'M GUESSING YOU WON'T LEAVE EVEN IF I PROMISE TO FIND PARKER PETERS?
PETER PARKER, AND ABSOLUTELY NOT.
THOSE BYSTANDERS ARE LONG IN THE TEETH, SO I GOTTA GO.
YOU SEE IF YOUR GAMMA TECH CAN HELP WITH THESE CRYSTAL SHARDS, THEN WE'LL LOOK FOR BARKER TOGETHER.
THEY'RE IN DANGER AND IT'S MY RESPONSIBILITY. I NEED TO WRAP THIS UP FAST.
HEY, HULK! MAN-WOLF'S DOWN, BUT WE NEED SOME CLEANUP ON AISLE...

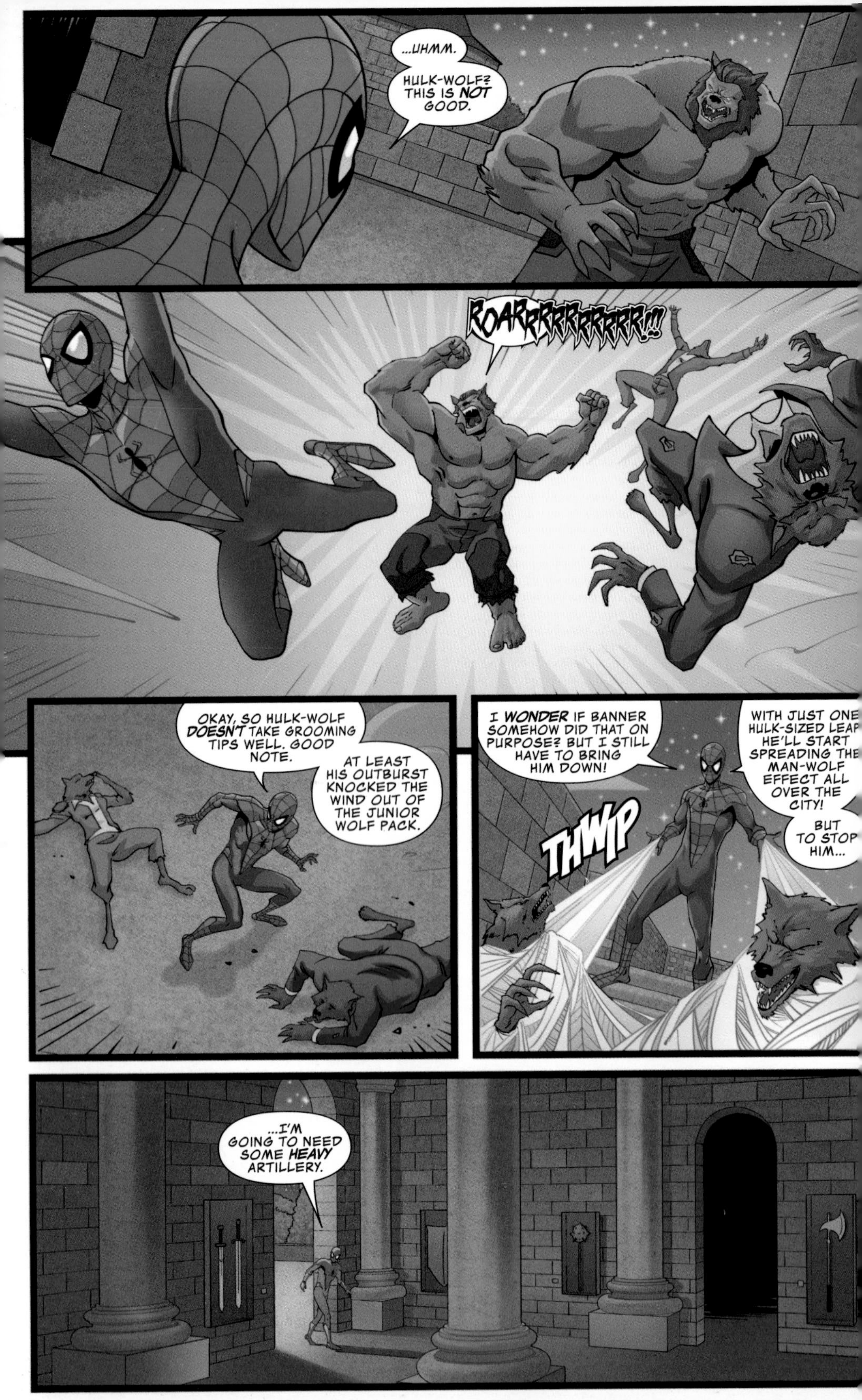
...UHMM.
HULK-WOLF? THIS IS NOT GOOD.
ROARRRRRRRRRR!!!
OKAY, SO HULK-WOLF DOESN'T TAKE GROOMING TIPS WELL. GOOD NOTE.
AT LEAST HIS OUTBURST KNOCKED THE WIND OUT OF THE JUNIOR WOLF PACK.
I WONDER IF BANNER SOMEHOW DID THAT ON PURPOSE? BUT I STILL HAVE TO BRING HIM DOWN!
THWIP
WITH JUST ONE HULK-SIZED LEAP HE'LL START SPREADING THE MAN-WOLF EFFECT ALL OVER THE CITY!
BUT TO STOP HIM...
...I'M GOING TO NEED SOME HEAVY ARTILLERY.

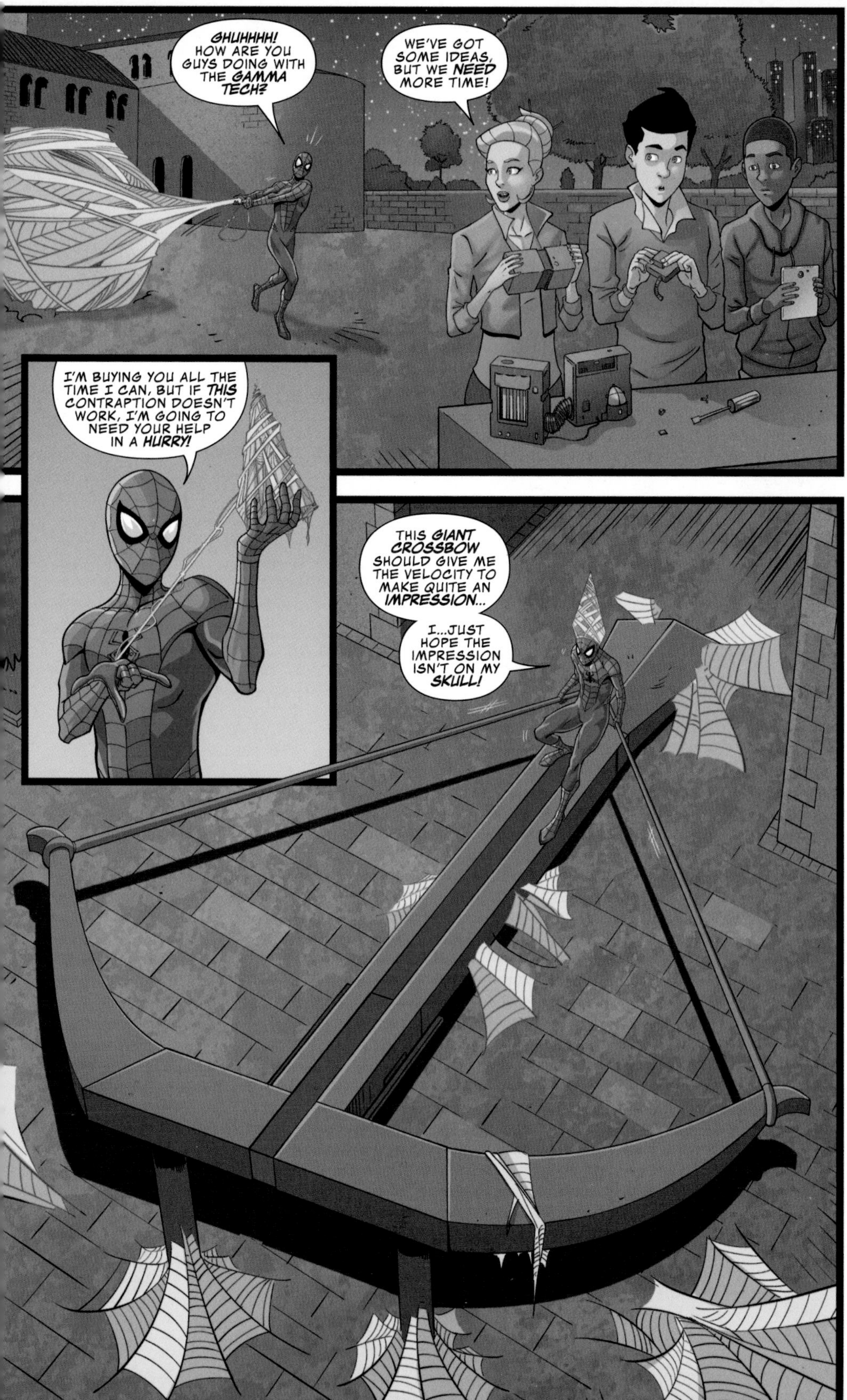
GHUHHHH! HOW ARE YOU GUYS DOING WITH THE GAMMA TECH?
WE'VE GOT SOME IDEAS, BUT WE NEED MORE TIME!
I'M BUYING YOU ALL THE TIME I CAN, BUT IF THIS CONTRAPTION DOESN'T WORK, I'M GOING TO NEED YOUR HELP IN A HURRY!
THIS GIANT CROSSBOW SHOULD GIVE ME THE VELOCITY TO MAKE QUITE AN IMPRESSION...
I...JUST HOPE THE IMPRESSION ISN'T ON MY SKULL!

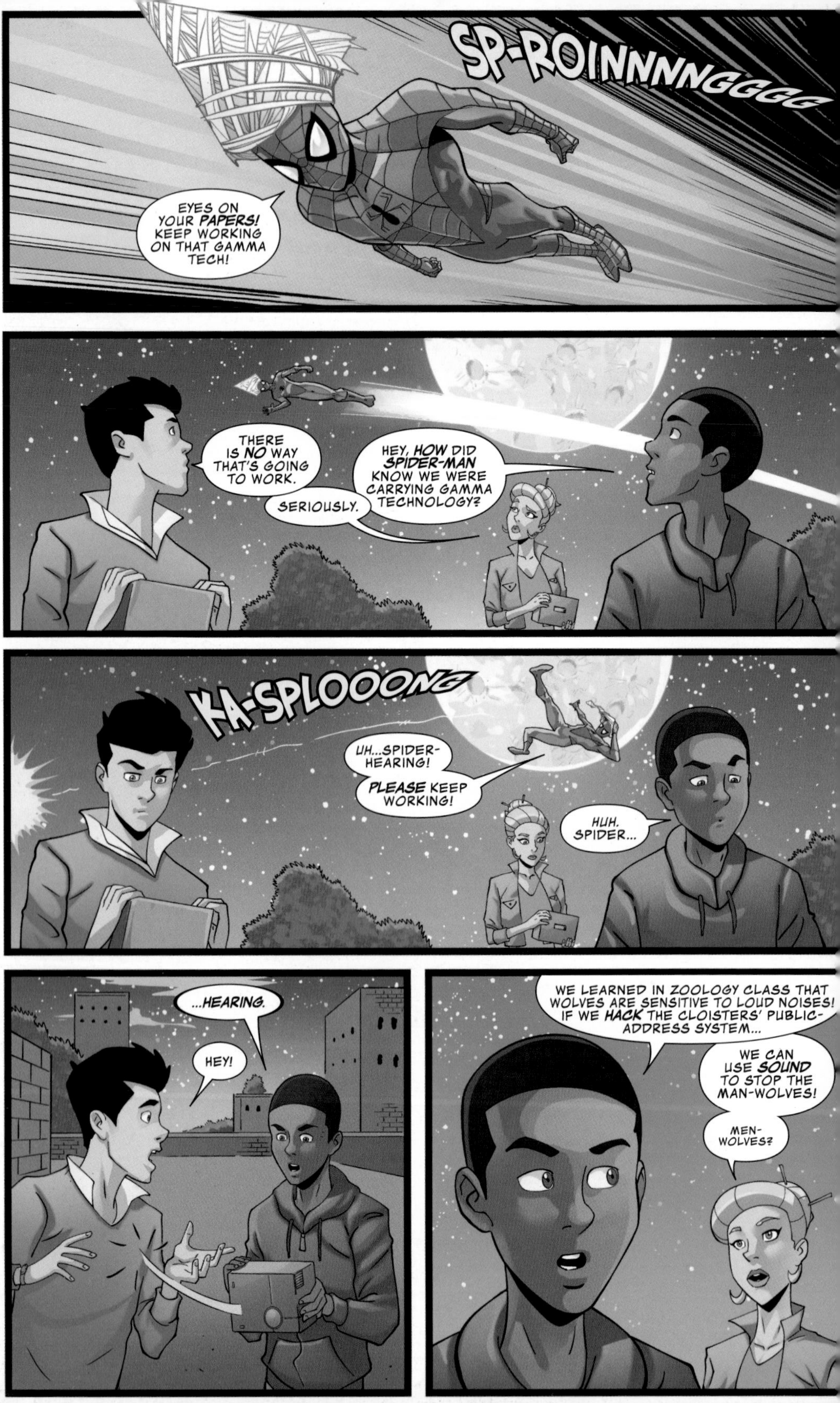
SP-ROINNNNGGGG
EYES ON YOUR PAPERS! KEEP WORKING ON THAT GAMMA TECH!
THERE IS NO WAY THAT'S GOING TO WORK.
SERIOUSLY.
HEY, HOW DID SPIDER-MAN KNOW WE WERE CARRYING GAMMA TECHNOLOGY?
KA-SPLOOOONG
UH...SPIDER-HEARING!
PLEASE KEEP WORKING!
HUH. SPIDER...
...HEARING.
HEY!
WE LEARNED IN ZOOLOGY CLASS THAT WOLVES ARE SENSITIVE TO LOUD NOISES! IF WE HACK THE CLOISTERS' PUBLIC-ADDRESS SYSTEM...
WE CAN USE SOUND TO STOP THE MAN-WOLVES!
MEN-WOLVES?

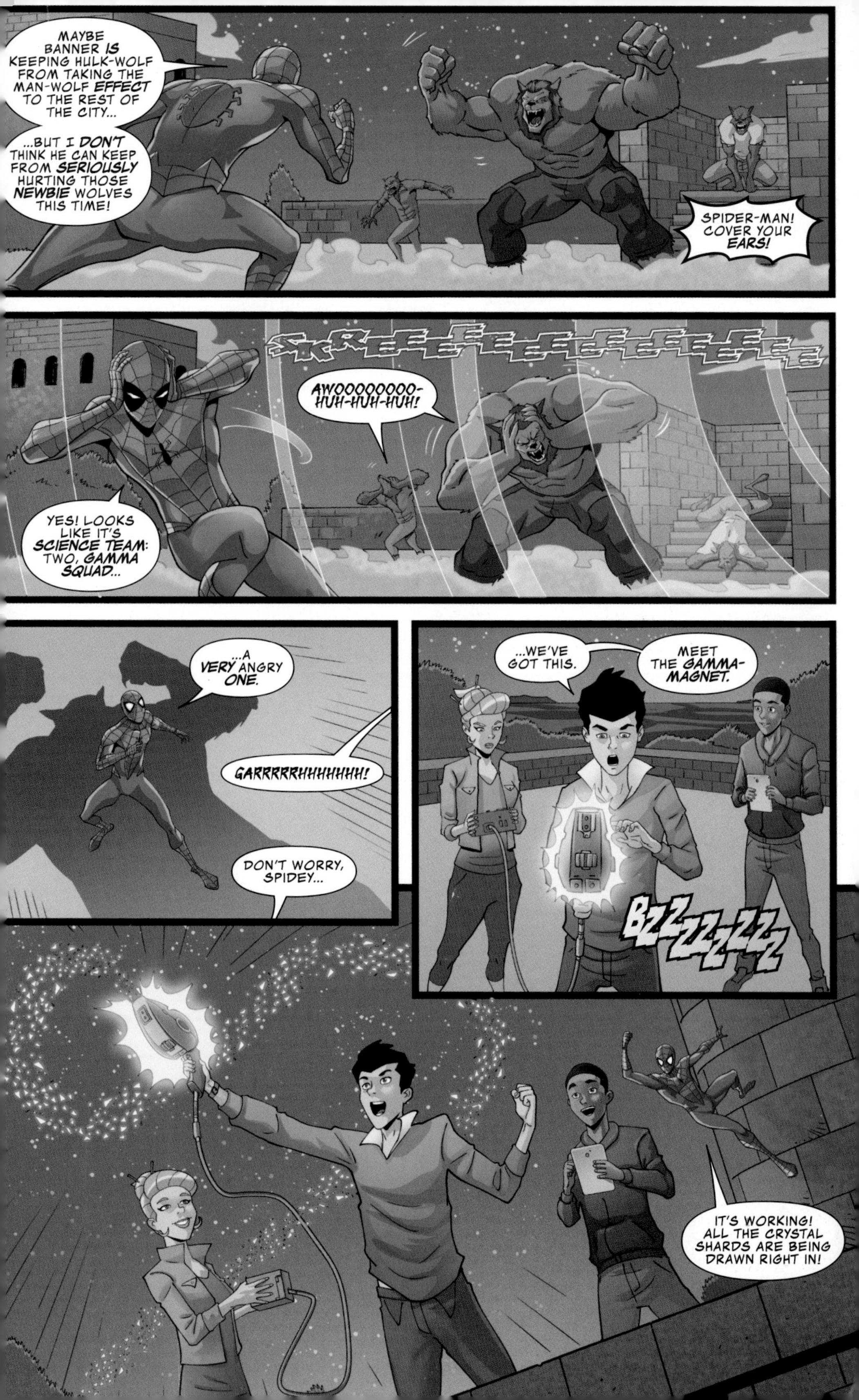
MAYBE BANNER IS KEEPING HULK-WOLF FROM TAKING THE MAN-WOLF EFFECT TO THE REST OF THE CITY...
...BUT I DON'T THINK HE CAN KEEP FROM SERIOUSLY HURTING THOSE NEWBIE WOLVES THIS TIME!
SPIDER-MAN! COVER YOUR EARS!
SKREEEEEEEEEEEEEEEEEE
AWOOOOOOOO-HUH-HUH-HUH!
YES! LOOKS LIKE IT'S SCIENCE TEAM: TWO, GAMMA SQUAD...
...A VERY ANGRY ONE.
GARRRRRHHHHHHH!
DON'T WORRY, SPIDEY...
...WE'VE GOT THIS.
MEET THE GAMMA-MAGNET.
BZZZZZZZZ
IT'S WORKING! ALL THE CRYSTAL SHARDS ARE BEING DRAWN RIGHT IN!

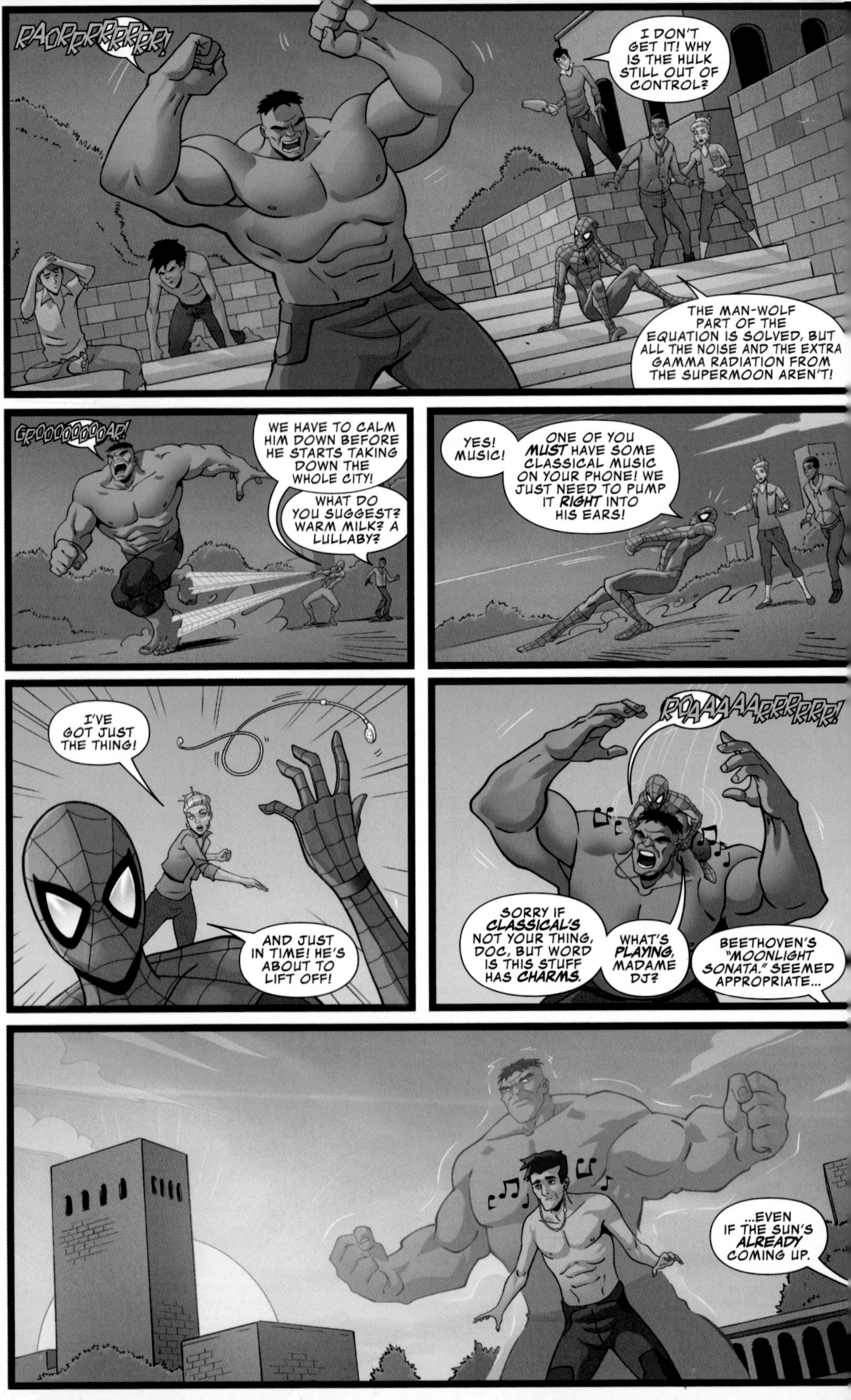
RAORRRRRRRR!
I DON'T GET IT! WHY IS THE HULK STILL OUT OF CONTROL?
THE MAN-WOLF PART OF THE EQUATION IS SOLVED, BUT ALL THE NOISE AND THE EXTRA GAMMA RADIATION FROM THE SUPERMOON AREN'T!
GROOOOOOOOAR!
WE HAVE TO CALM HIM DOWN BEFORE HE STARTS TAKING DOWN THE WHOLE CITY!
WHAT DO YOU SUGGEST? WARM MILK? A LULLABY?
YES! MUSIC!
ONE OF YOU MUST HAVE SOME CLASSICAL MUSIC ON YOUR PHONE! WE JUST NEED TO PUMP IT RIGHT INTO HIS EARS!
I'VE GOT JUST THE THING!
AND JUST IN TIME! HE'S ABOUT TO LIFT OFF!
ROAAAAARRRRR!
SORRY IF CLASSICAL'S NOT YOUR THING, DOC, BUT WORD IS THIS STUFF HAS CHARMS.
WHAT'S PLAYING, MADAME DJ?
BEETHOVEN'S "MOONLIGHT SONATA." SEEMED APPROPRIATE...
...EVEN IF THE SUN'S ALREADY COMING UP.

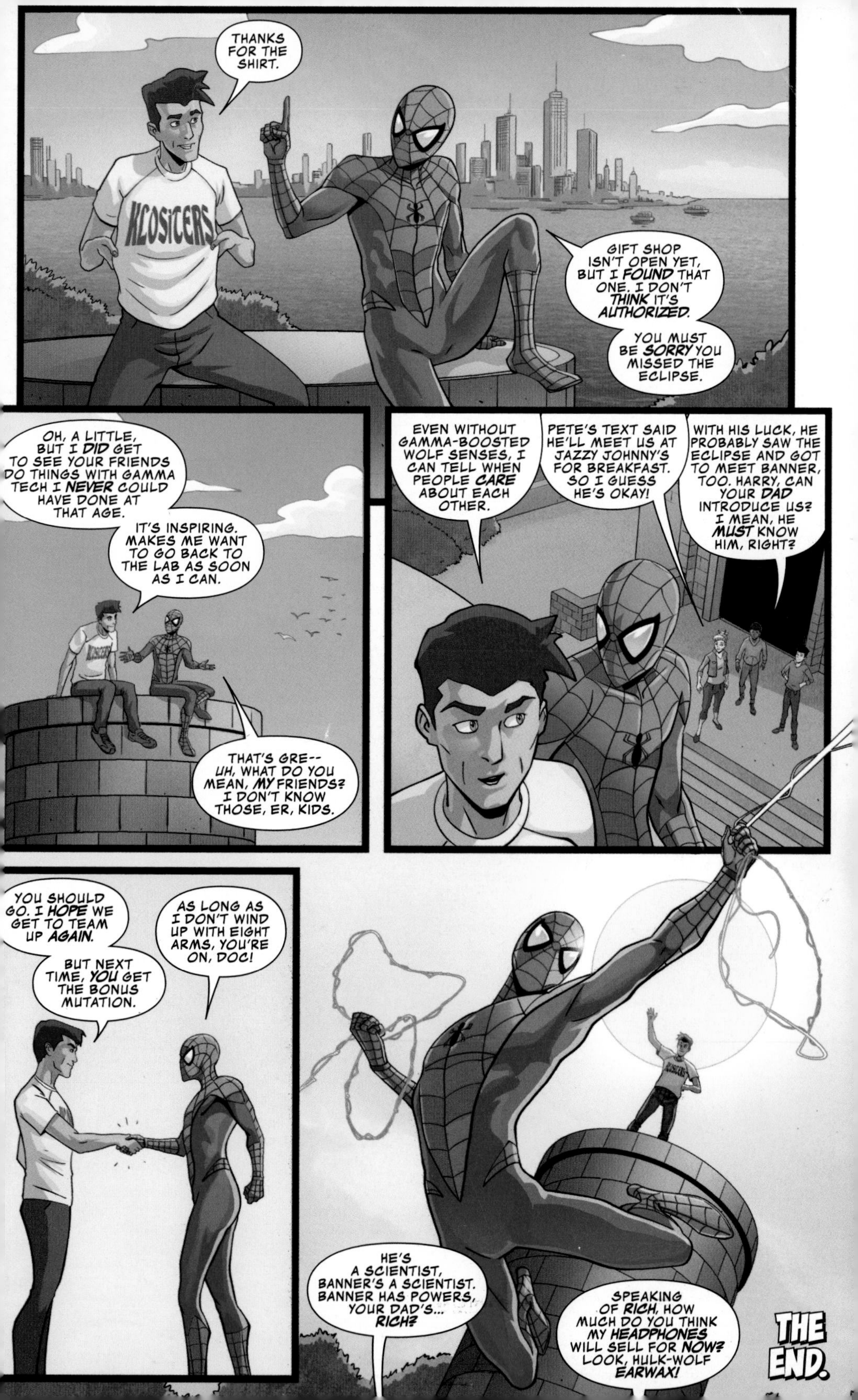
THANKS FOR THE SHIRT.
KLOSTERS
GIFT SHOP ISN'T OPEN YET, BUT I FOUND THAT ONE. I DON'T THINK IT'S AUTHORIZED.
YOU MUST BE SORRY YOU MISSED THE ECLIPSE.
OH, A LITTLE, BUT I DID GET TO SEE YOUR FRIENDS DO THINGS WITH GAMMA TECH I NEVER COULD HAVE DONE AT THAT AGE.
IT'S INSPIRING. MAKES ME WANT TO GO BACK TO THE LAB AS SOON AS I CAN.
THAT'S GRE-- UH, WHAT DO YOU MEAN, MY FRIENDS? I DON'T KNOW THOSE, ER, KIDS.
EVEN WITHOUT GAMMA-BOOSTED WOLF SENSES, I CAN TELL WHEN PEOPLE CARE ABOUT EACH OTHER.
PETE'S TEXT SAID HE'LL MEET US AT JAZZY JOHNNY'S FOR BREAKFAST. SO I GUESS HE'S OKAY!
WITH HIS LUCK, HE PROBABLY SAW THE ECLIPSE AND GOT TO MEET BANNER, TOO. HARRY, CAN YOUR DAD INTRODUCE US? I MEAN, HE MUST KNOW HIM, RIGHT?
YOU SHOULD GO. I HOPE WE GET TO TEAM UP AGAIN.
BUT NEXT TIME, YOU GET THE BONUS MUTATION.
AS LONG AS I DON'T WIND UP WITH EIGHT ARMS, YOU'RE ON, DOC!
HE'S A SCIENTIST, BANNER'S A SCIENTIST. BANNER HAS POWERS, YOUR DAD'S... RICH?
SPEAKING OF RICH, HOW MUCH DO YOU THINK MY HEADPHONES WILL SELL FOR NOW? LOOK, HULK-WOLF EARWAX!
THE END.

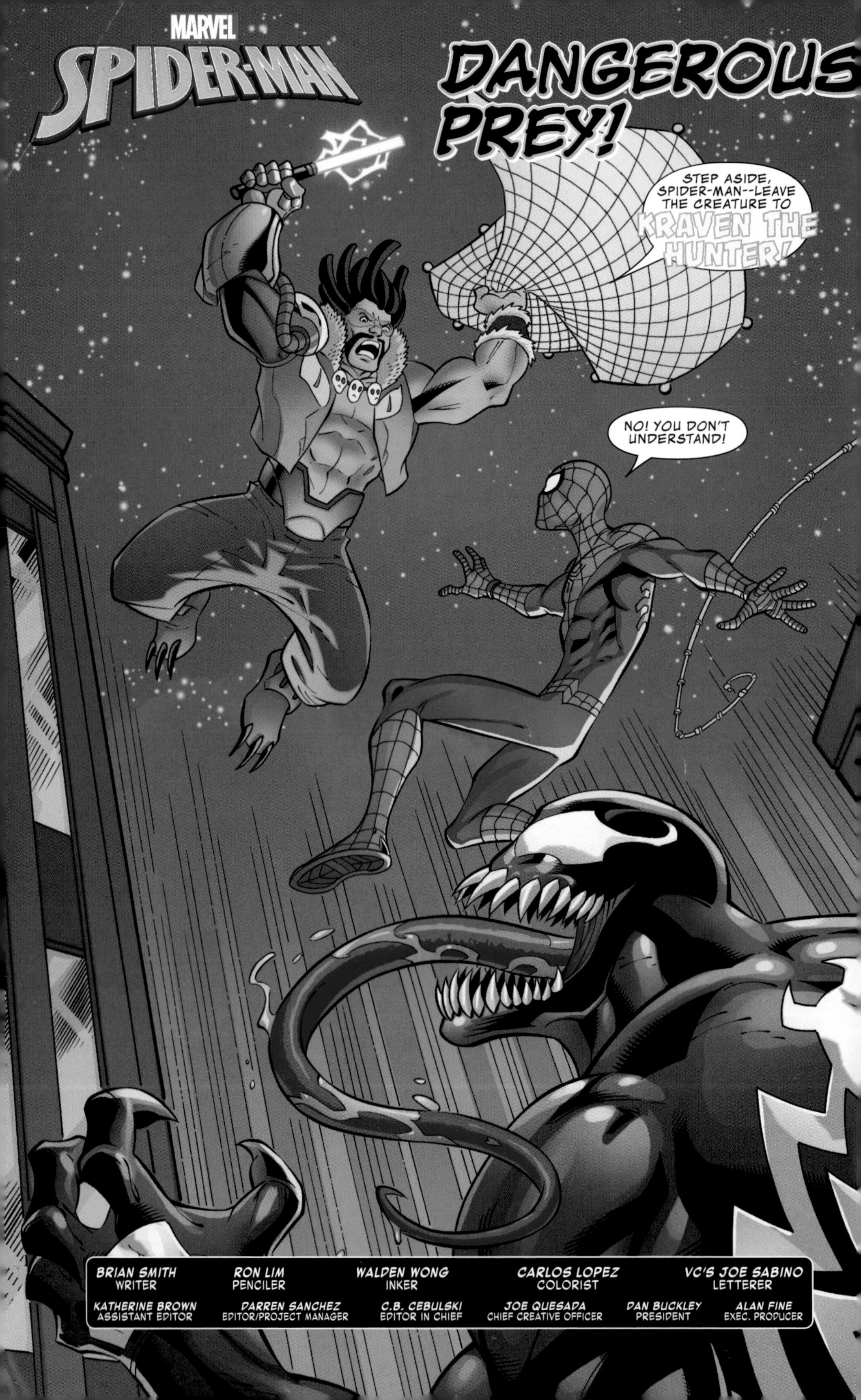
MARVEL
SPIDER-MAN
DANGEROUS PREY!
STEP ASIDE, SPIDER-MAN--LEAVE THE CREATURE TO KRAVEN THE HUNTER!
NO! YOU DON'T UNDERSTAND!
BRIAN SMITH WRITER
RON LIM PENCILER
WALDEN WONG INKER
CARLOS LOPEZ COLORIST
VC'S JOE SABINO LETTERER
KATHERINE BROWN ASSISTANT EDITOR
DARREN SANCHEZ EDITOR/PROJECT MANAGER
C.B. CEBULSKI EDITOR IN CHIEF
JOE QUESADA CHIEF CREATIVE OFFICER
DAN BUCKLEY PRESIDENT
ALAN FINE EXEC. PRODUCER

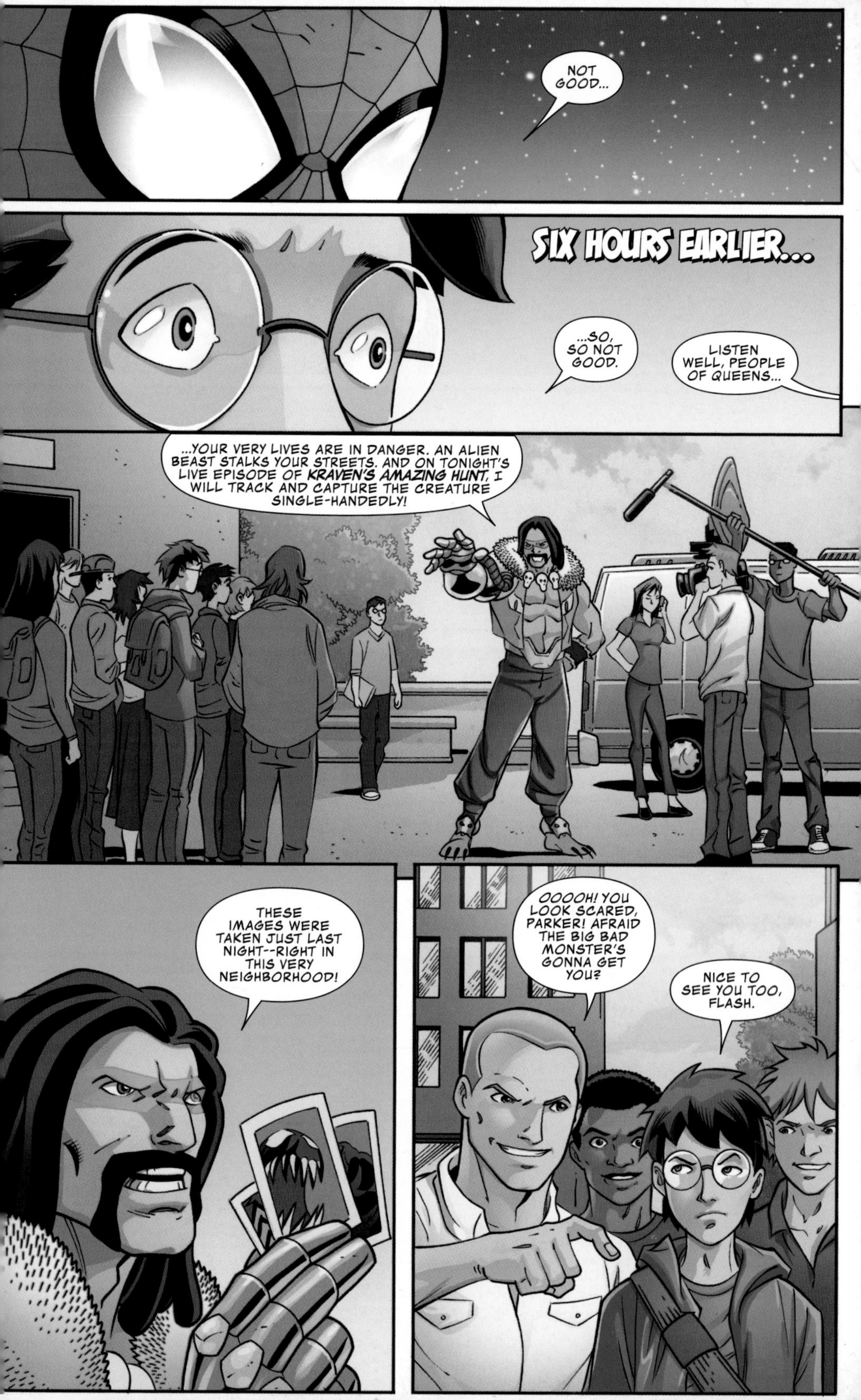
NOT GOOD...
SIX HOURS EARLIER...
...SO, SO NOT GOOD.
LISTEN WELL, PEOPLE OF QUEENS...
...YOUR VERY LIVES ARE IN DANGER. AN ALIEN BEAST STALKS YOUR STREETS. AND ON TONIGHT'S LIVE EPISODE OF KRAVEN'S AMAZING HUNT, I WILL TRACK AND CAPTURE THE CREATURE SINGLE-HANDEDLY!
THESE IMAGES WERE TAKEN JUST LAST NIGHT--RIGHT IN THIS VERY NEIGHBORHOOD!
OOOOH! YOU LOOK SCARED, PARKER! AFRAID THE BIG BAD MONSTER'S GONNA GET YOU?
NICE TO SEE YOU TOO, FLASH.

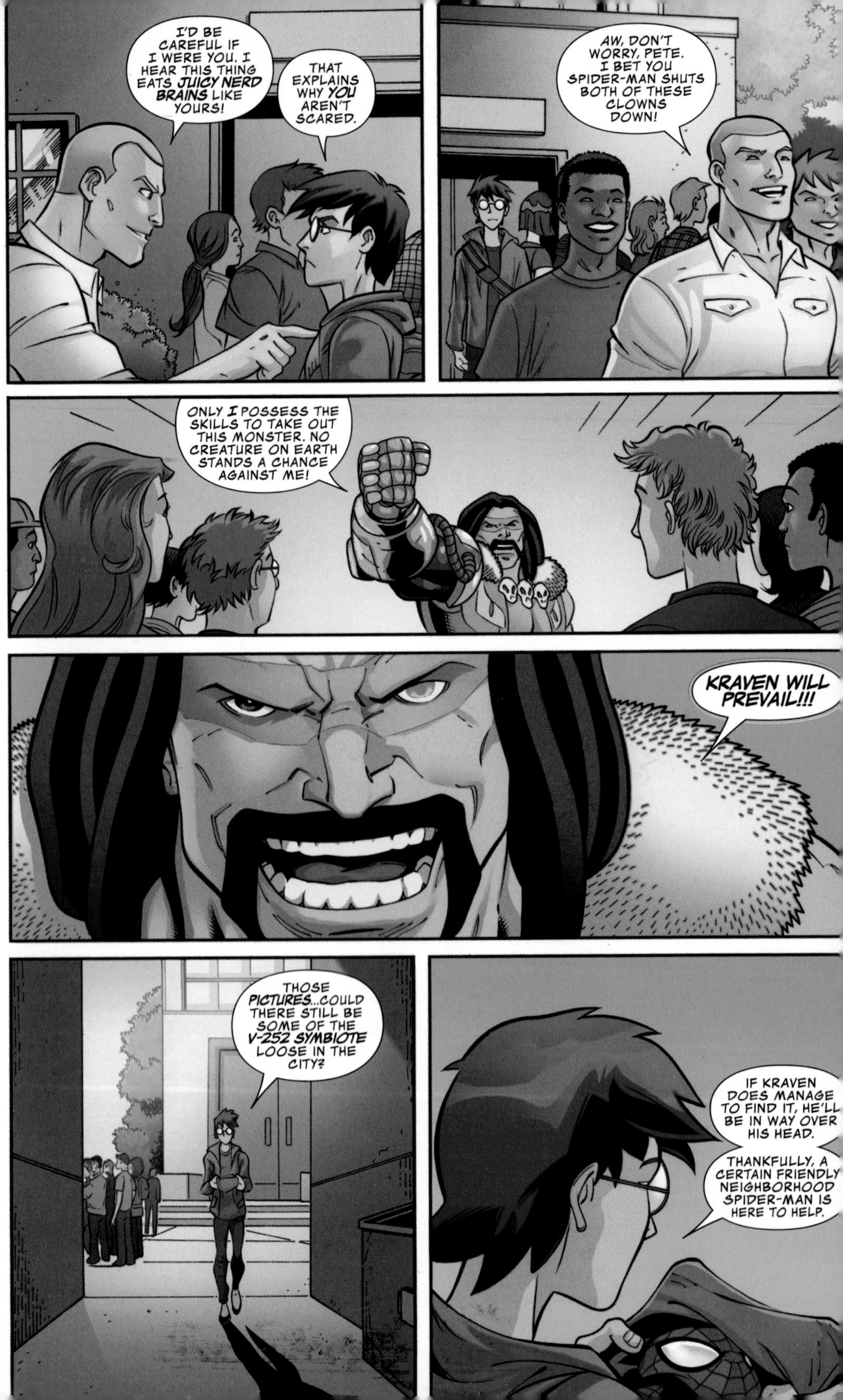
I'D BE CAREFUL IF I WERE YOU. I HEAR THIS THING EATS JUICY NERD BRAINS LIKE YOURS!
THAT EXPLAINS WHY YOU AREN'T SCARED.
AW, DON'T WORRY, PETE. I BET YOU SPIDER-MAN SHUTS BOTH OF THESE CLOWNS DOWN!
ONLY I POSSESS THE SKILLS TO TAKE OUT THIS MONSTER. NO CREATURE ON EARTH STANDS A CHANCE AGAINST ME!
KRAVEN WILL PREVAIL!!!
THOSE PICTURES...COULD THERE STILL BE SOME OF THE V-252 SYMBIOTE LOOSE IN THE CITY?
IF KRAVEN DOES MANAGE TO FIND IT, HE'LL BE IN WAY OVER HIS HEAD.
THANKFULLY, A CERTAIN FRIENDLY NEIGHBORHOOD SPIDER-MAN IS HERE TO HELP.

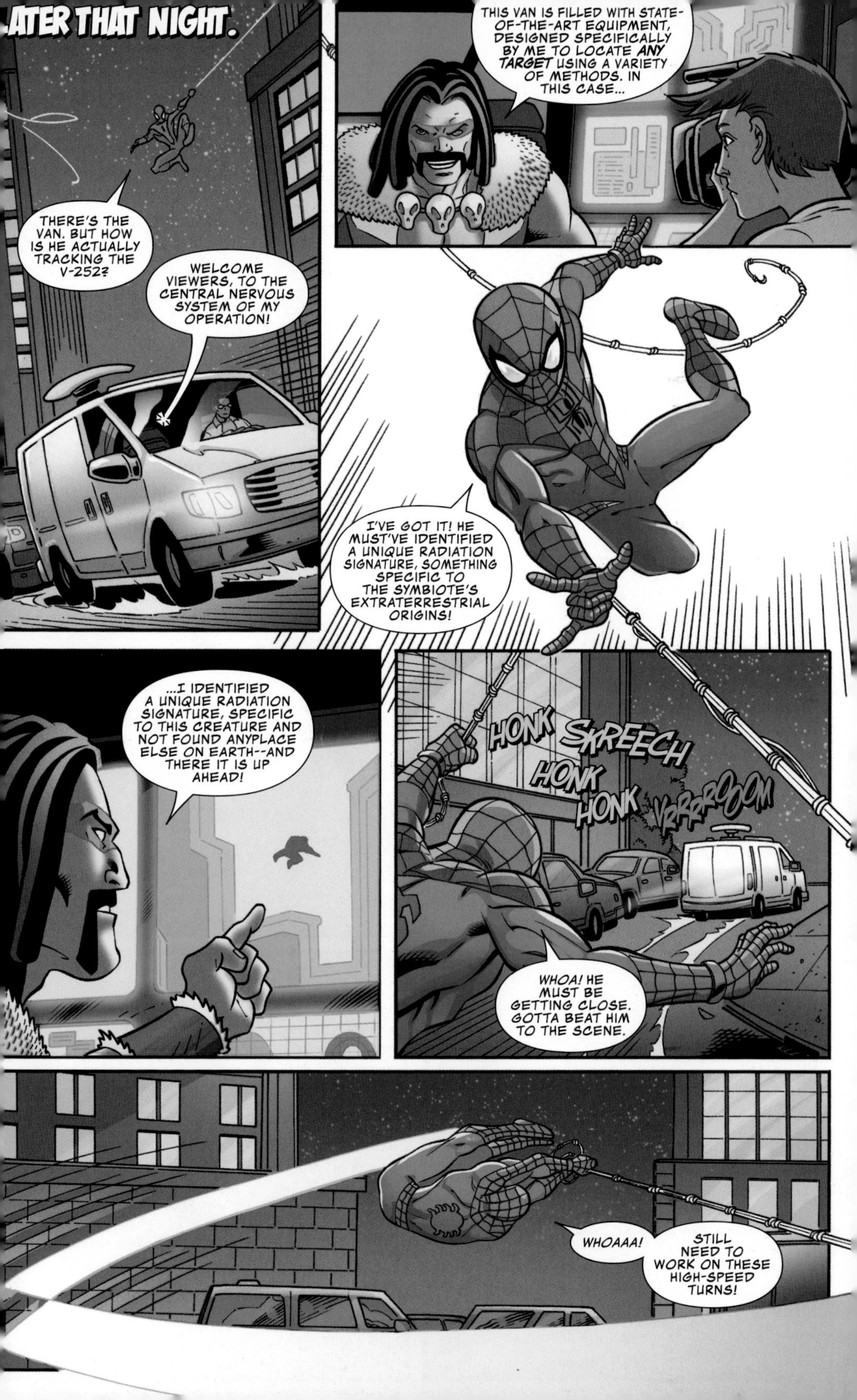

LATER THAT NIGHT.
THERE'S THE VAN. BUT HOW IS HE ACTUALLY TRACKING THE V-252?
WELCOME VIEWERS, TO THE CENTRAL NERVOUS SYSTEM OF MY OPERATION!
THIS VAN IS FILLED WITH STATE-OF-THE-ART EQUIPMENT, DESIGNED SPECIFICALLY BY ME TO LOCATE ANY TARGET USING A VARIETY OF METHODS. IN THIS CASE...
I'VE GOT IT! HE MUST'VE IDENTIFIED A UNIQUE RADIATION SIGNATURE, SOMETHING SPECIFIC TO THE SYMBIOTE'S EXTRATERRESTRIAL ORIGINS!
...I IDENTIFIED A UNIQUE RADIATION SIGNATURE, SPECIFIC TO THIS CREATURE AND NOT FOUND ANYPLACE ELSE ON EARTH--AND THERE IT IS UP AHEAD!
HONK SKREECH
HONK
HONK VRRRROOOM
WHOA! HE MUST BE GETTING CLOSE. GOTTA BEAT HIM TO THE SCENE.
WHOAAA!
STILL NEED TO WORK ON THESE HIGH-SPEED TURNS!

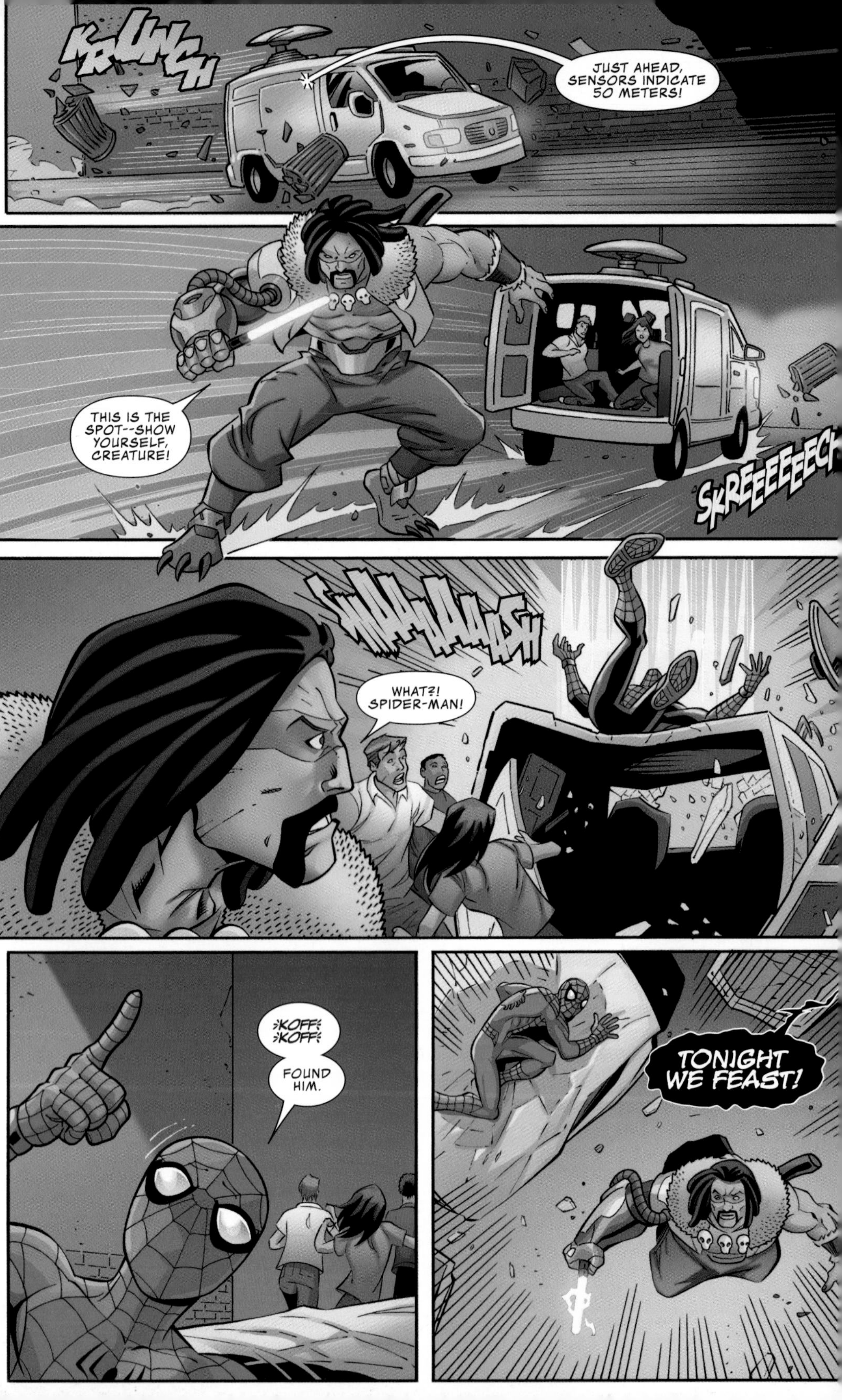
KRUNCH
JUST AHEAD, SENSORS INDICATE 50 METERS!
THIS IS THE SPOT--SHOW YOURSELF, CREATURE!
SKREEEEEEECH
WHAAAAAASH
WHAT?! SPIDER-MAN!
KOFF KOFF
FOUND HIM.
TONIGHT WE FEAST!

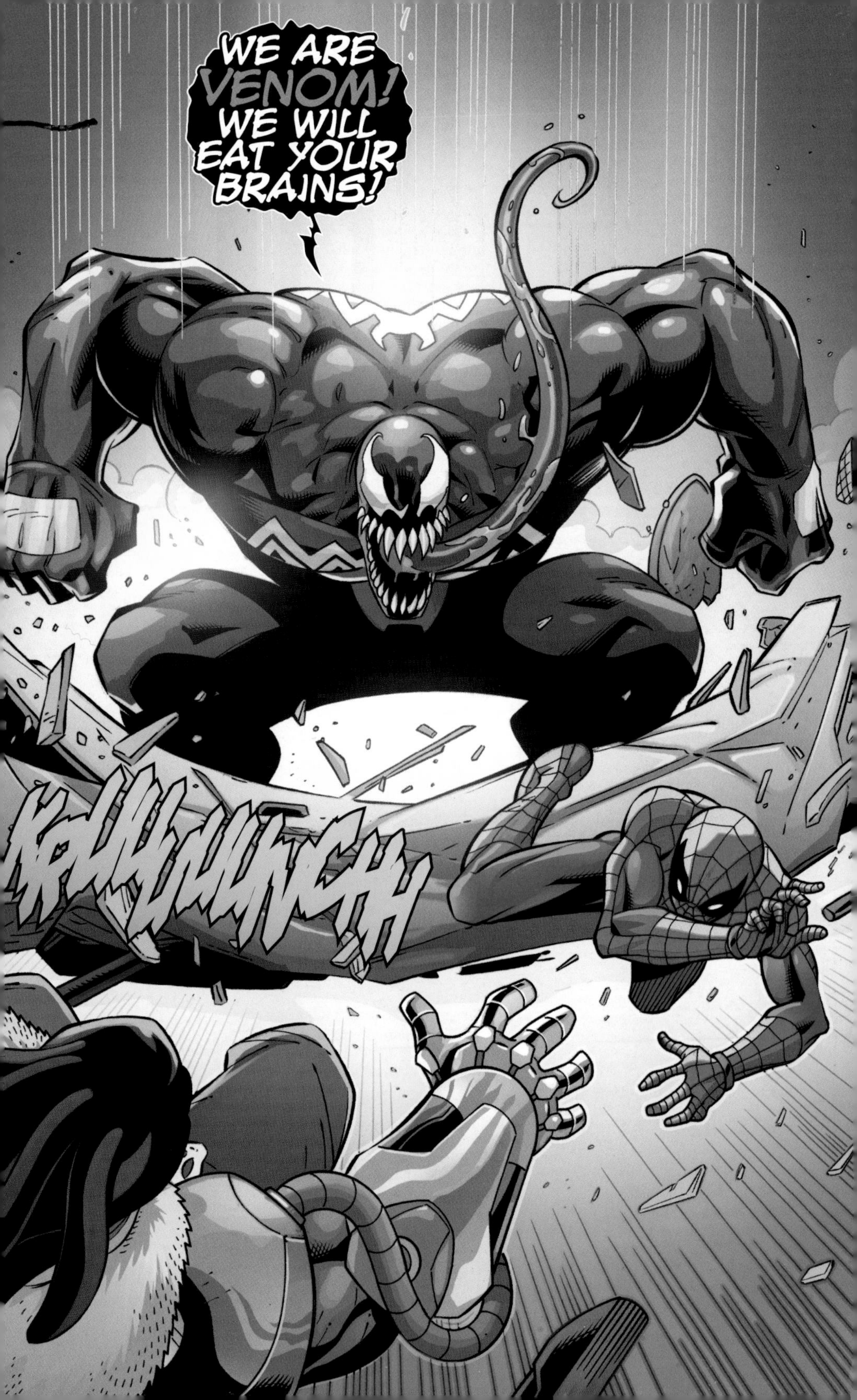
WE ARE VENOM! WE WILL EAT YOUR BRAINS!
KRUUUNCH

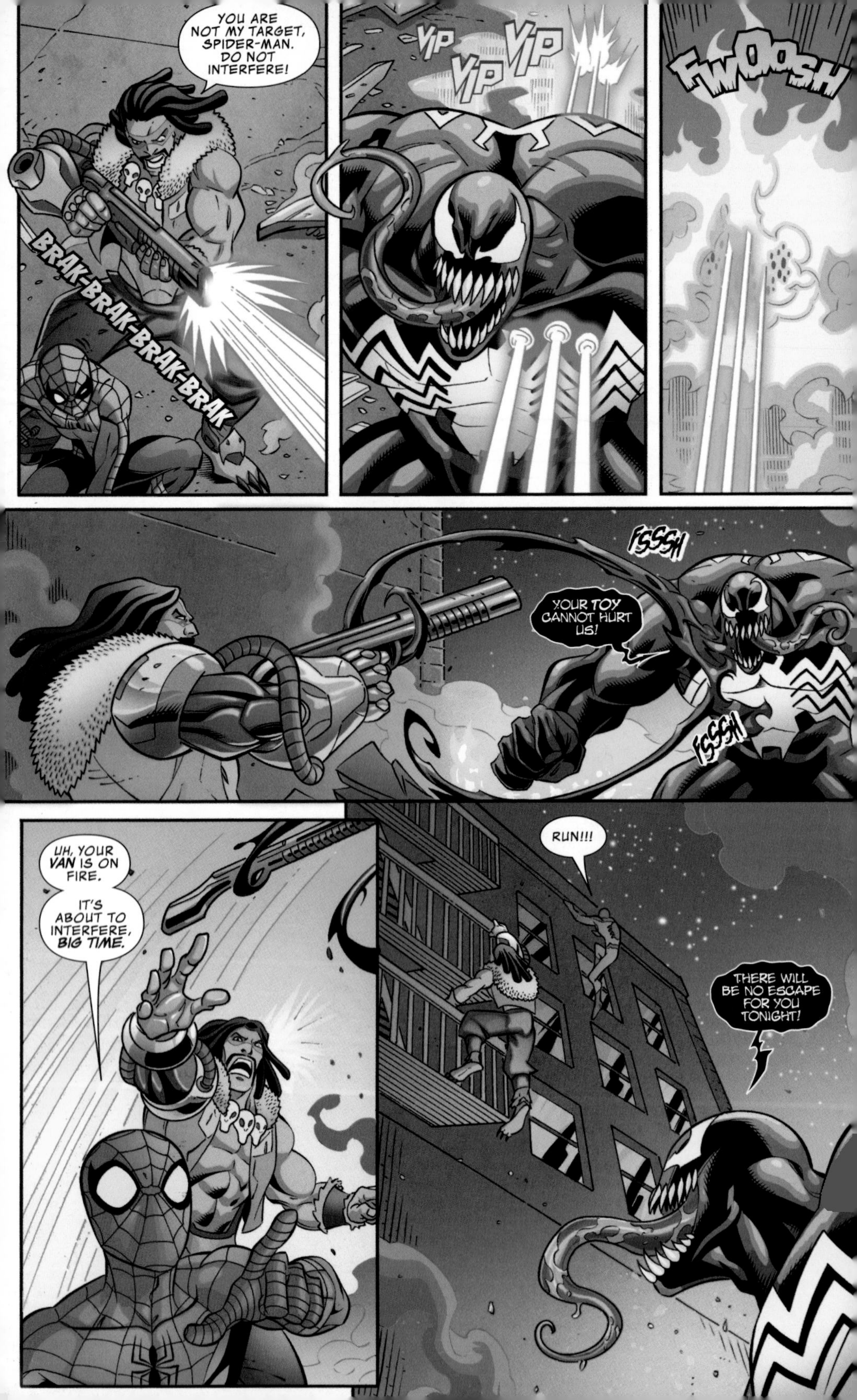
YOU ARE NOT MY TARGET, SPIDER-MAN. DO NOT INTERFERE!
BRAK-BRAK-BRAK-BRAK-BRAK
VIP VIP VIP
FWOOSH
FSSSH
YOUR TOY CANNOT HURT US!
FSSSH
UH, YOUR VAN IS ON FIRE.
IT'S ABOUT TO INTERFERE, BIG TIME.
RUN!!!
THERE WILL BE NO ESCAPE FOR YOU TONIGHT!

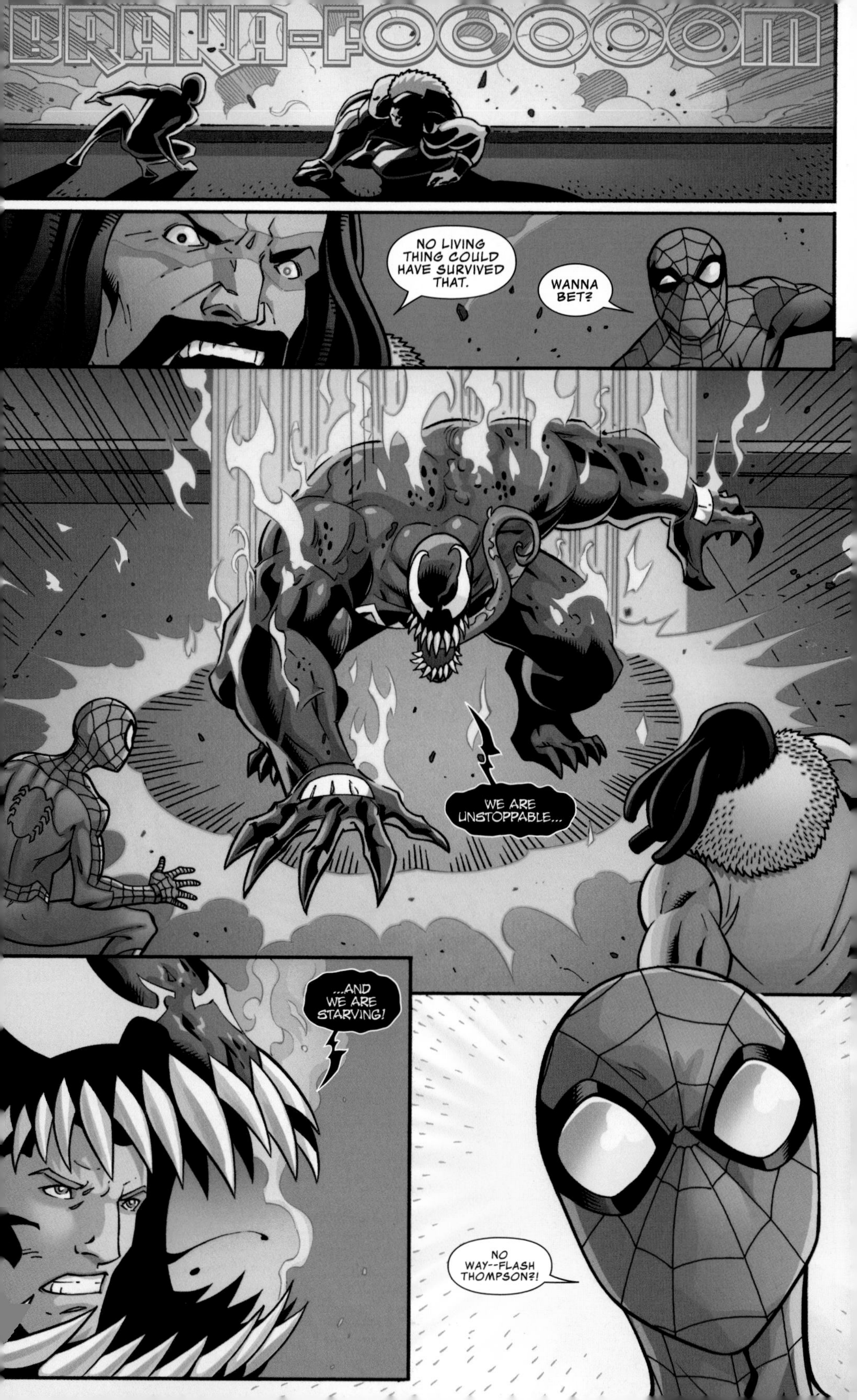
BRAKA-FOOOOOM
NO LIVING THING COULD HAVE SURVIVED THAT.
WANNA BET?
WE ARE UNSTOPPABLE...
...AND WE ARE STARVING!
NO WAY--FLASH THOMPSON?!

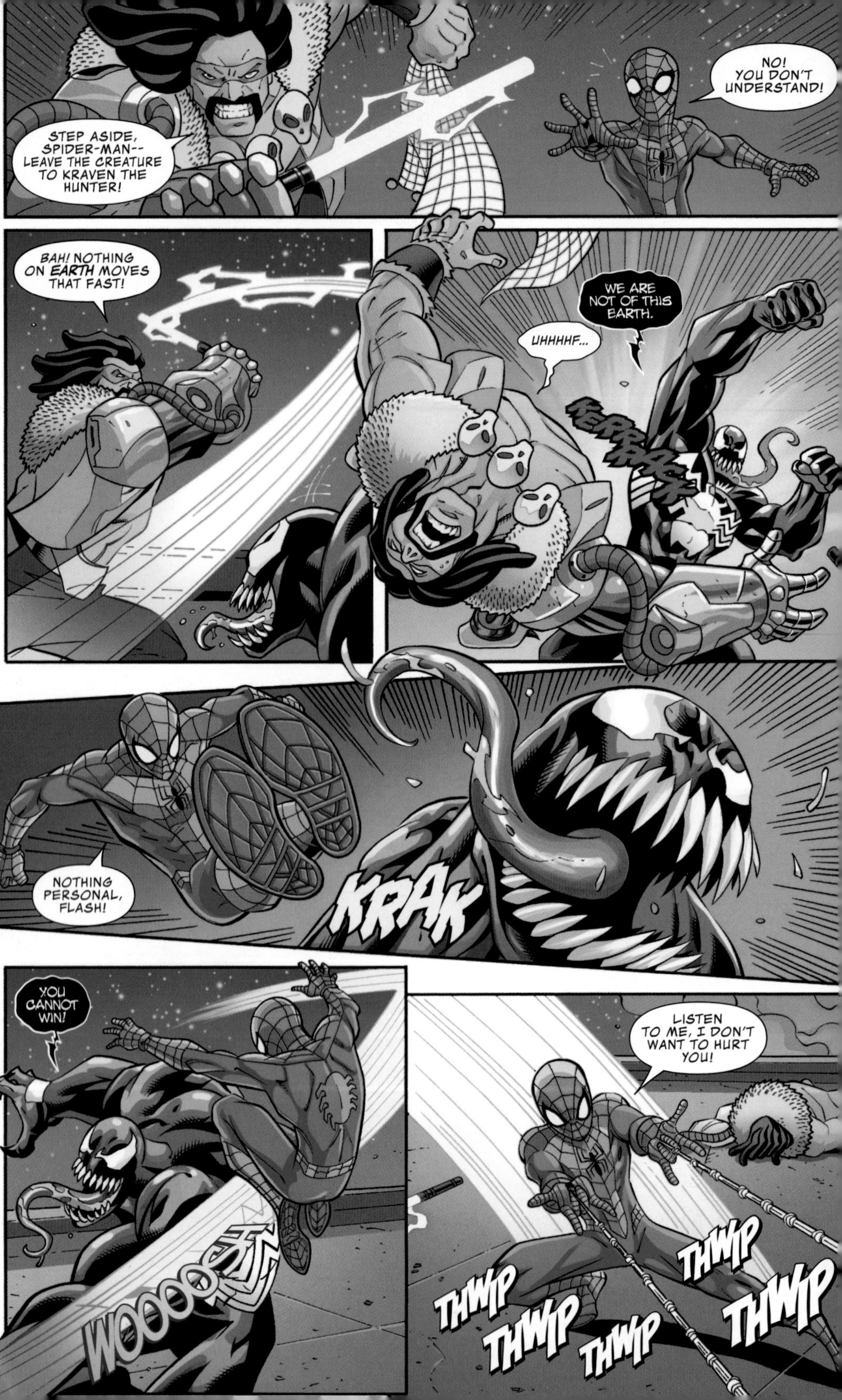
STEP ASIDE, SPIDER-MAN-- LEAVE THE CREATURE TO KRAVEN THE HUNTER!
NO! YOU DON'T UNDERSTAND!
BAH! NOTHING ON EARTH MOVES THAT FAST!
UHHHHF...
WE ARE NOT OF THIS EARTH.
KERRACK
NOTHING PERSONAL, FLASH!
KRAK
YOU CANNOT WIN!
WOOOOSH
LISTEN TO ME, I DON'T WANT TO HURT YOU!
THWIP
THWIP
THWIP
THWIP
THWIP
THWIP

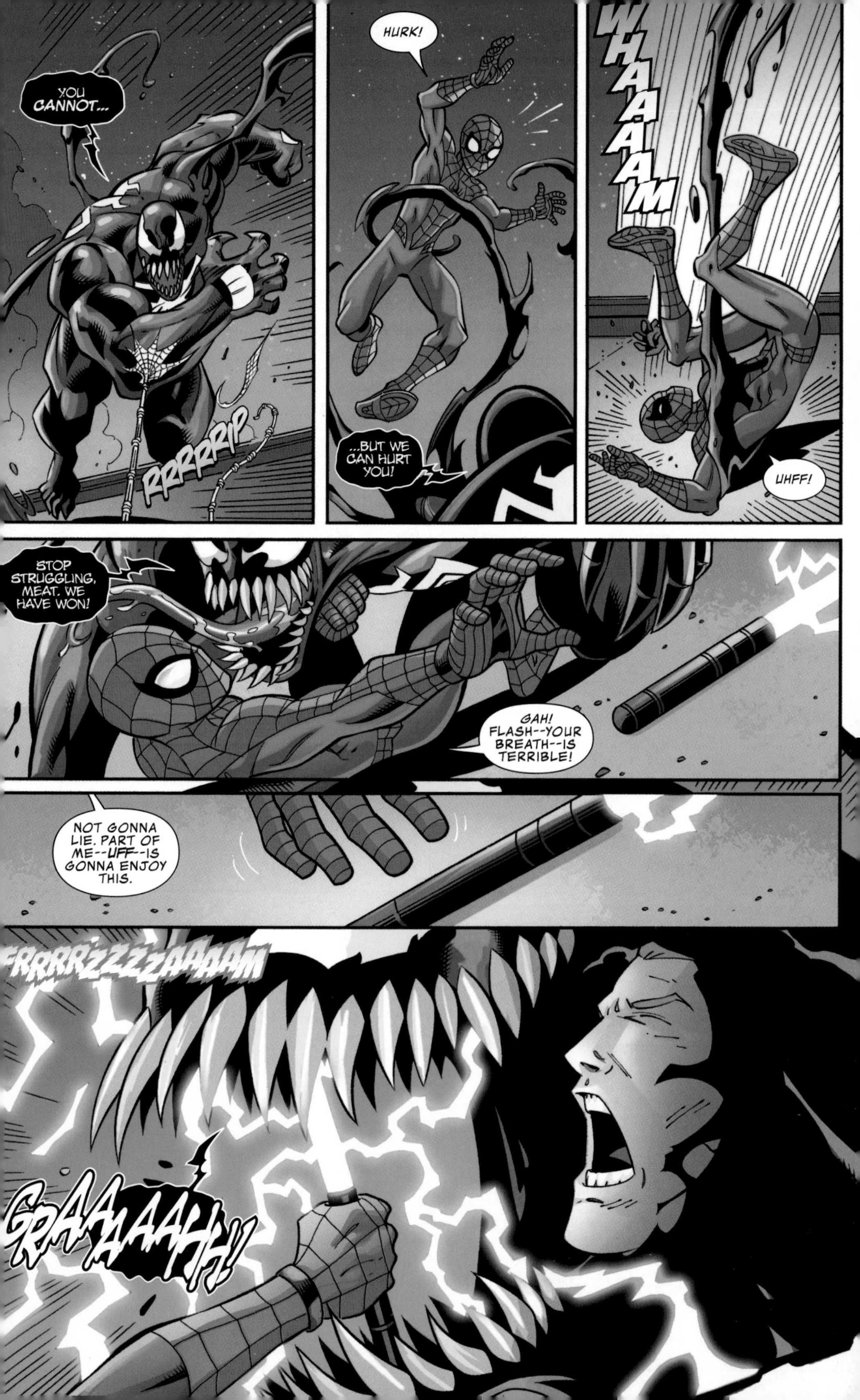
YOU CANNOT...
RRRRRIP
HURK!
...BUT WE CAN HURT YOU!
WHAAAAAM
UHFF!
STOP STRUGGLING, MEAT. WE HAVE WON!
GAH! FLASH--YOUR BREATH--IS TERRIBLE!
NOT GONNA LIE. PART OF ME--UFF--IS GONNA ENJOY THIS.
FRRRRZZZZAAAAM
GRAAAAAAHH!

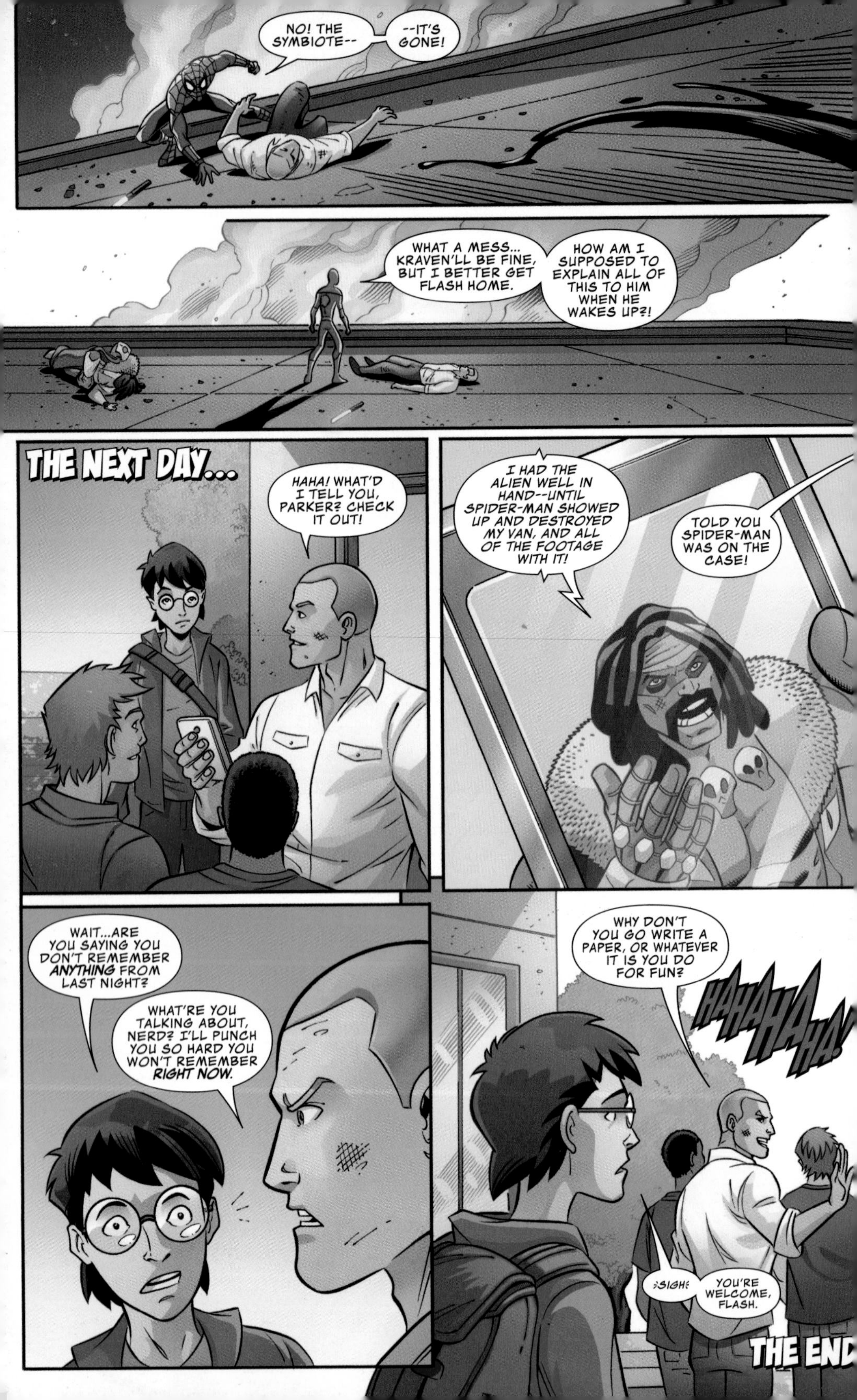
NO! THE SYMBIOTE--
--IT'S GONE!
WHAT A MESS... KRAVEN'LL BE FINE, BUT I BETTER GET FLASH HOME.
HOW AM I SUPPOSED TO EXPLAIN ALL OF THIS TO HIM WHEN HE WAKES UP?!
THE NEXT DAY...
HAHA! WHAT'D I TELL YOU, PARKER? CHECK IT OUT!
I HAD THE ALIEN WELL IN HAND--UNTIL SPIDER-MAN SHOWED UP AND DESTROYED MY VAN, AND ALL OF THE FOOTAGE WITH IT!
TOLD YOU SPIDER-MAN WAS ON THE CASE!
WAIT...ARE YOU SAYING YOU DON'T REMEMBER ANYTHING FROM LAST NIGHT?
WHAT'RE YOU TALKING ABOUT, NERD? I'LL PUNCH YOU SO HARD YOU WON'T REMEMBER RIGHT NOW.
WHY DON'T YOU GO WRITE A PAPER, OR WHATEVER IT IS YOU DO FOR FUN?
HAHAHAHA!
SIGH
YOU'RE WELCOME, FLASH.
THE END

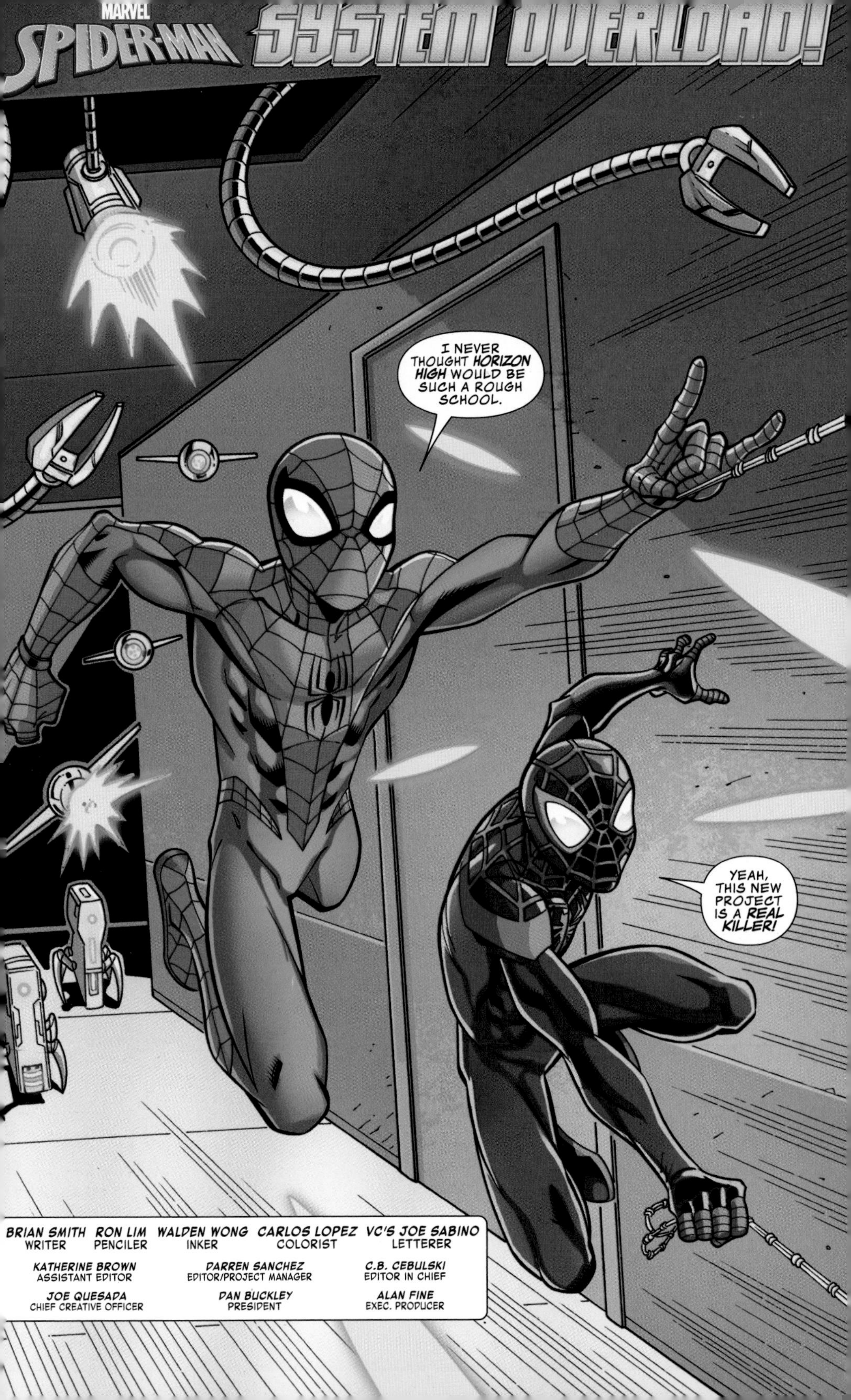
MARVEL
SPIDER-MAN
SYSTEM OVERLOAD!
I NEVER THOUGHT HORIZON HIGH WOULD BE SUCH A ROUGH SCHOOL.
YEAH, THIS NEW PROJECT IS A REAL KILLER!
BRIAN SMITH WRITER
RON LIM PENCILER
WALDEN WONG INKER
CARLOS LOPEZ COLORIST
VC'S JOE SABINO LETTERER
KATHERINE BROWN ASSISTANT EDITOR
DARREN SANCHEZ EDITOR/PROJECT MANAGER
C.B. CEBULSKI EDITOR IN CHIEF
JOE QUESADA CHIEF CREATIVE OFFICER
DAN BUCKLEY PRESIDENT
ALAN FINE EXEC. PRODUCER

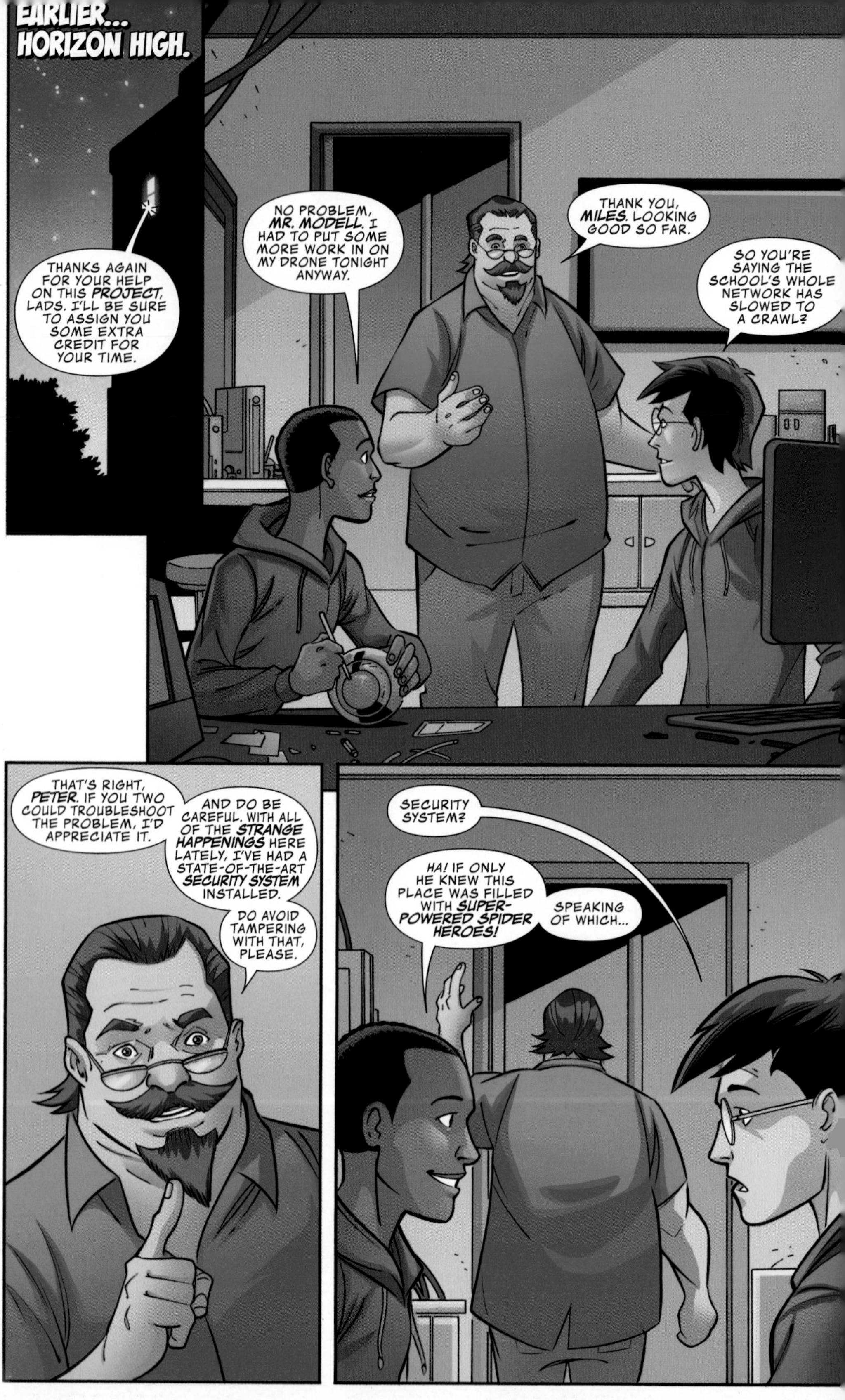
EARLIER... HORIZON HIGH.
THANKS AGAIN FOR YOUR HELP ON THIS PROJECT, LADS. I'LL BE SURE TO ASSIGN YOU SOME EXTRA CREDIT FOR YOUR TIME.
NO PROBLEM, MR. MODELL. I HAD TO PUT SOME MORE WORK IN ON MY DRONE TONIGHT ANYWAY.
THANK YOU, MILES. LOOKING GOOD SO FAR.
SO YOU'RE SAYING THE SCHOOL'S WHOLE NETWORK HAS SLOWED TO A CRAWL?
THAT'S RIGHT, PETER. IF YOU TWO COULD TROUBLESHOOT THE PROBLEM, I'D APPRECIATE IT.
AND DO BE CAREFUL. WITH ALL OF THE STRANGE HAPPENINGS HERE LATELY, I'VE HAD A STATE-OF-THE-ART SECURITY SYSTEM INSTALLED.
DO AVOID TAMPERING WITH THAT, PLEASE.
SECURITY SYSTEM?
HA! IF ONLY HE KNEW THIS PLACE WAS FILLED WITH SUPER-POWERED SPIDER HEROES!
SPEAKING OF WHICH...

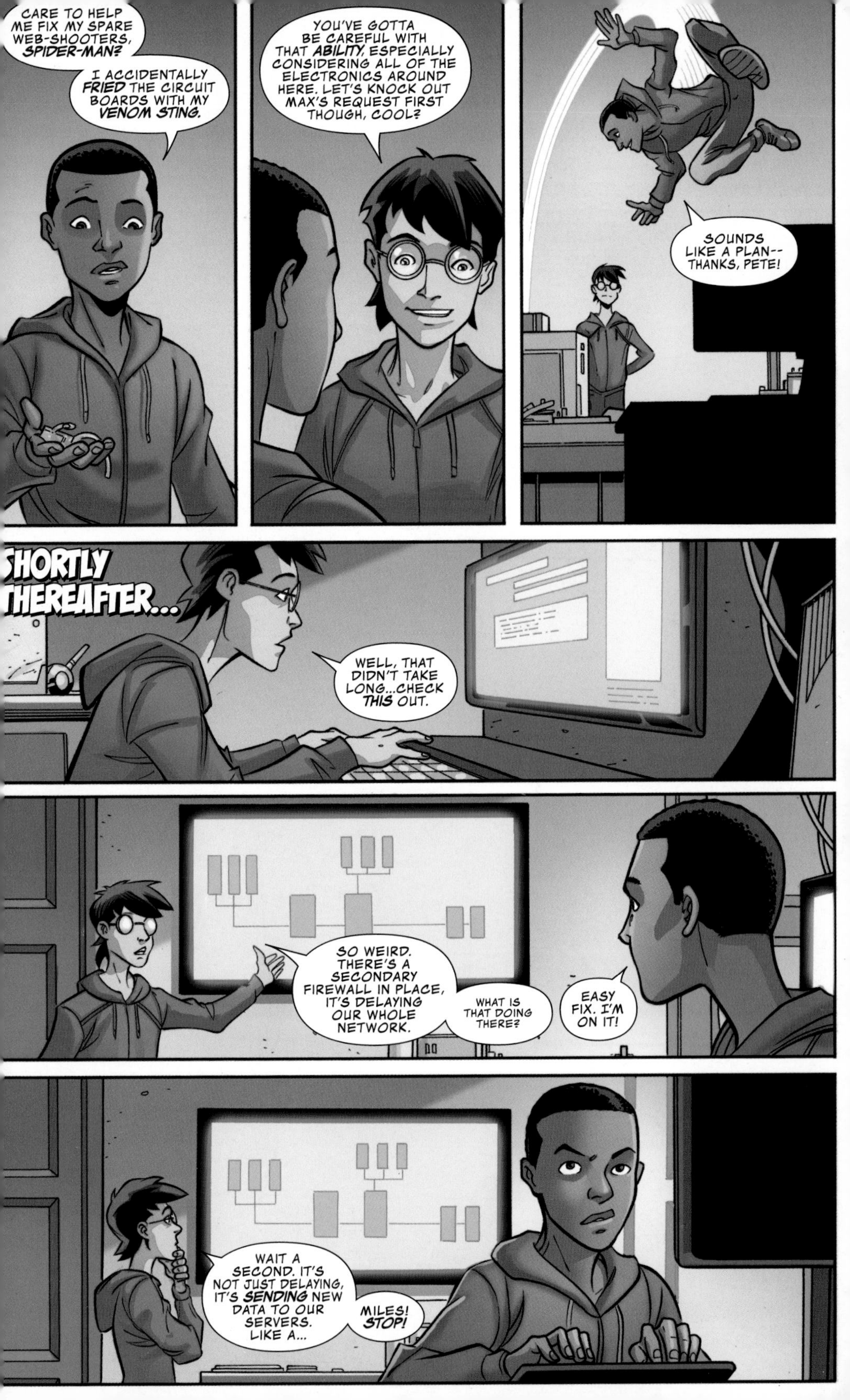
CARE TO HELP ME FIX MY SPARE WEB-SHOOTERS, SPIDER-MAN?
I ACCIDENTALLY FRIED THE CIRCUIT BOARDS WITH MY VENOM STING.
YOU'VE GOTTA BE CAREFUL WITH THAT ABILITY, ESPECIALLY CONSIDERING ALL OF THE ELECTRONICS AROUND HERE. LET'S KNOCK OUT MAX'S REQUEST FIRST THOUGH, COOL?
SOUNDS LIKE A PLAN-- THANKS, PETE!
SHORTLY THEREAFTER...
WELL, THAT DIDN'T TAKE LONG...CHECK THIS OUT.
SO WEIRD. THERE'S A SECONDARY FIREWALL IN PLACE, IT'S DELAYING OUR WHOLE NETWORK.
WHAT IS THAT DOING THERE?
EASY FIX. I'M ON IT!
WAIT A SECOND. IT'S NOT JUST DELAYING, IT'S SENDING NEW DATA TO OUR SERVERS. LIKE A...
MILES! STOP!

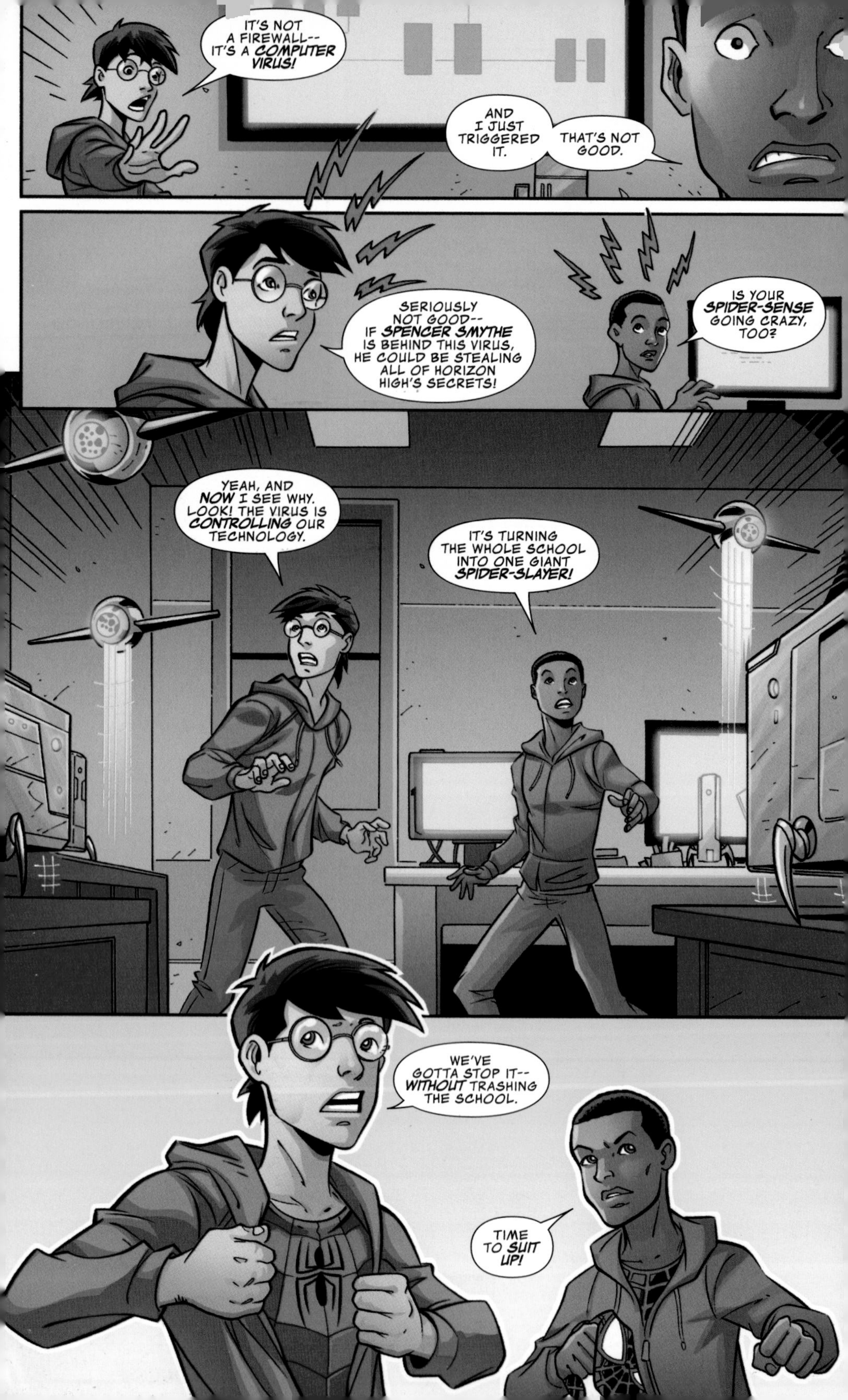

IT'S NOT A FIREWALL-- IT'S A COMPUTER VIRUS!
AND I JUST TRIGGERED IT.
THAT'S NOT GOOD.
SERIOUSLY NOT GOOD-- IF SPENCER SMYTHE IS BEHIND THIS VIRUS, HE COULD BE STEALING ALL OF HORIZON HIGH'S SECRETS!
IS YOUR SPIDER-SENSE GOING CRAZY, TOO?
YEAH, AND NOW I SEE WHY. LOOK! THE VIRUS IS CONTROLLING OUR TECHNOLOGY.
IT'S TURNING THE WHOLE SCHOOL INTO ONE GIANT SPIDER-SLAYER!
WE'VE GOTTA STOP IT-- WITHOUT TRASHING THE SCHOOL.
TIME TO SUIT UP!

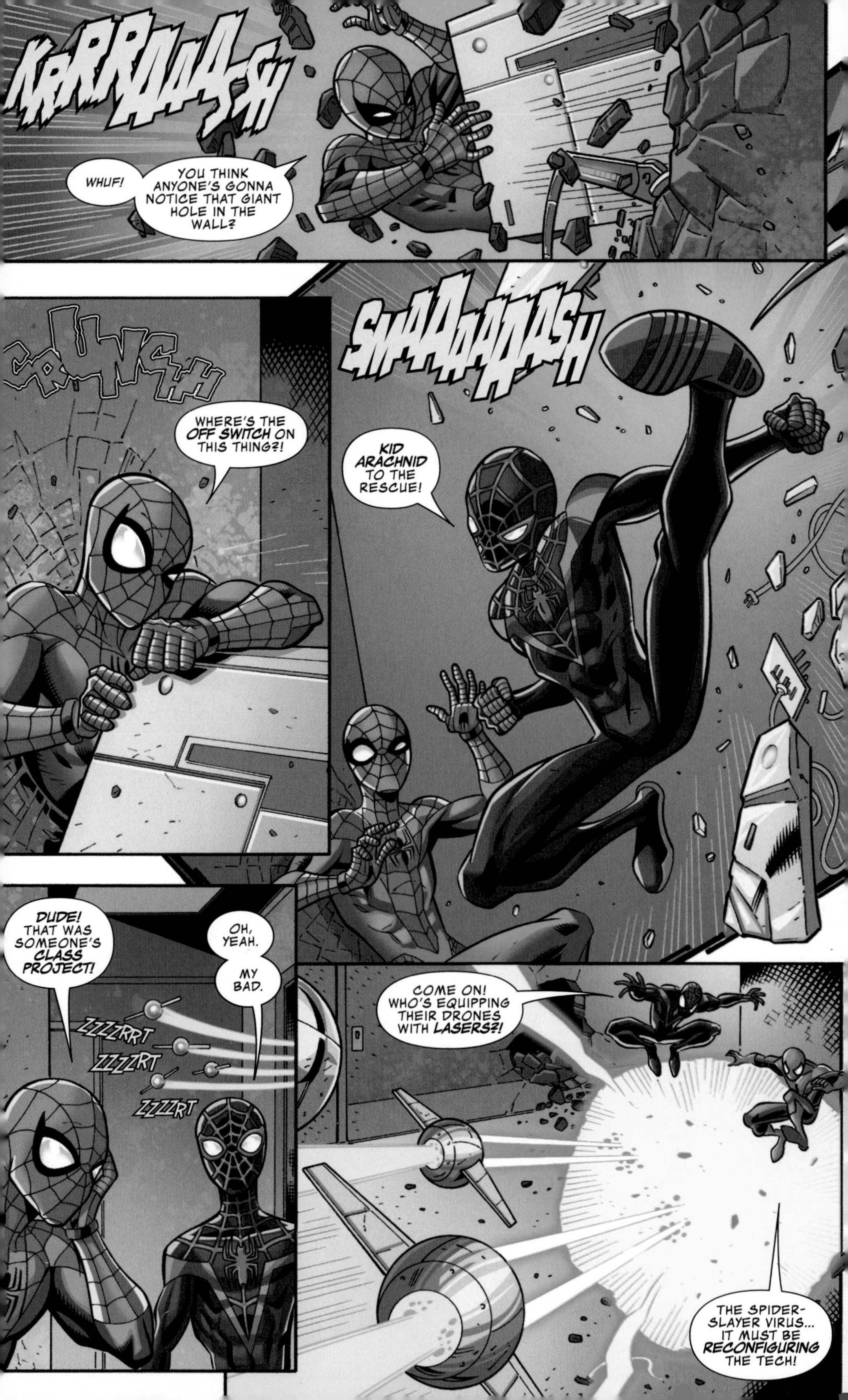
KRRRAAAASH
WHUF!
YOU THINK ANYONE'S GONNA NOTICE THAT GIANT HOLE IN THE WALL?
CRUNCH
WHERE'S THE OFF SWITCH ON THIS THING?!
SMAAAAAASH
KID ARACHNID TO THE RESCUE!
DUDE! THAT WAS SOMEONE'S CLASS PROJECT!
OH, YEAH.
MY BAD.
ZZZZRRT
ZZZZRT
ZZZZRT
COME ON! WHO'S EQUIPPING THEIR DRONES WITH LASERS?!
THE SPIDER-SLAYER VIRUS... IT MUST BE RECONFIGURING THE TECH!

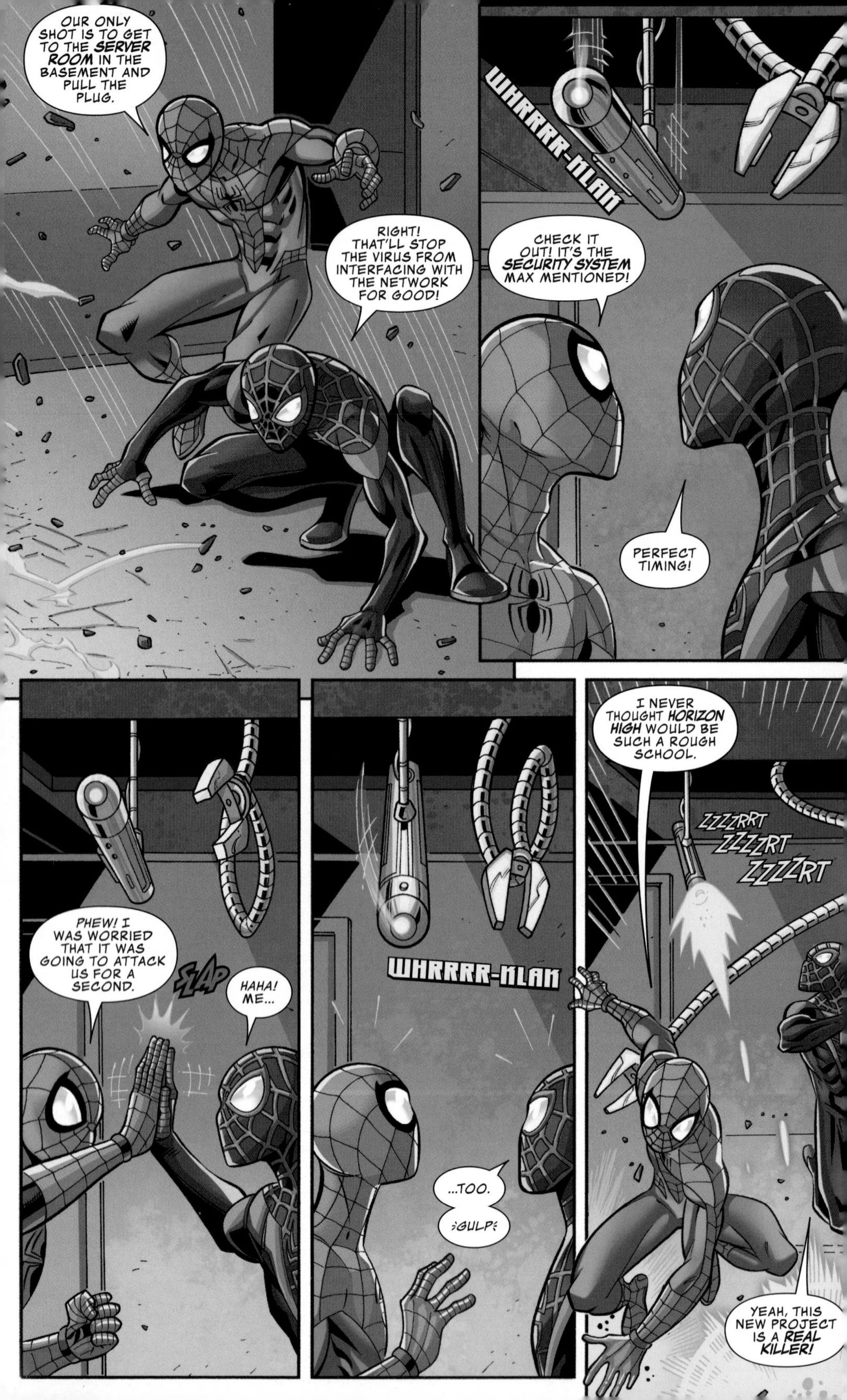
OUR ONLY SHOT IS TO GET TO THE SERVER ROOM IN THE BASEMENT AND PULL THE PLUG.
RIGHT! THAT'LL STOP THE VIRUS FROM INTERFACING WITH THE NETWORK FOR GOOD!
WHRRRR-KLAK
CHECK IT OUT! IT'S THE SECURITY SYSTEM MAX MENTIONED!
PERFECT TIMING!
PHEW! I WAS WORRIED THAT IT WAS GOING TO ATTACK US FOR A SECOND.
SLAP
HAHA! ME...
WHRRRR-KLAK
...TOO.
GULP
I NEVER THOUGHT HORIZON HIGH WOULD BE SUCH A ROUGH SCHOOL.
ZZZZRRT
ZZZZRT
ZZZZRT
YEAH, THIS NEW PROJECT IS A REAL KILLER!

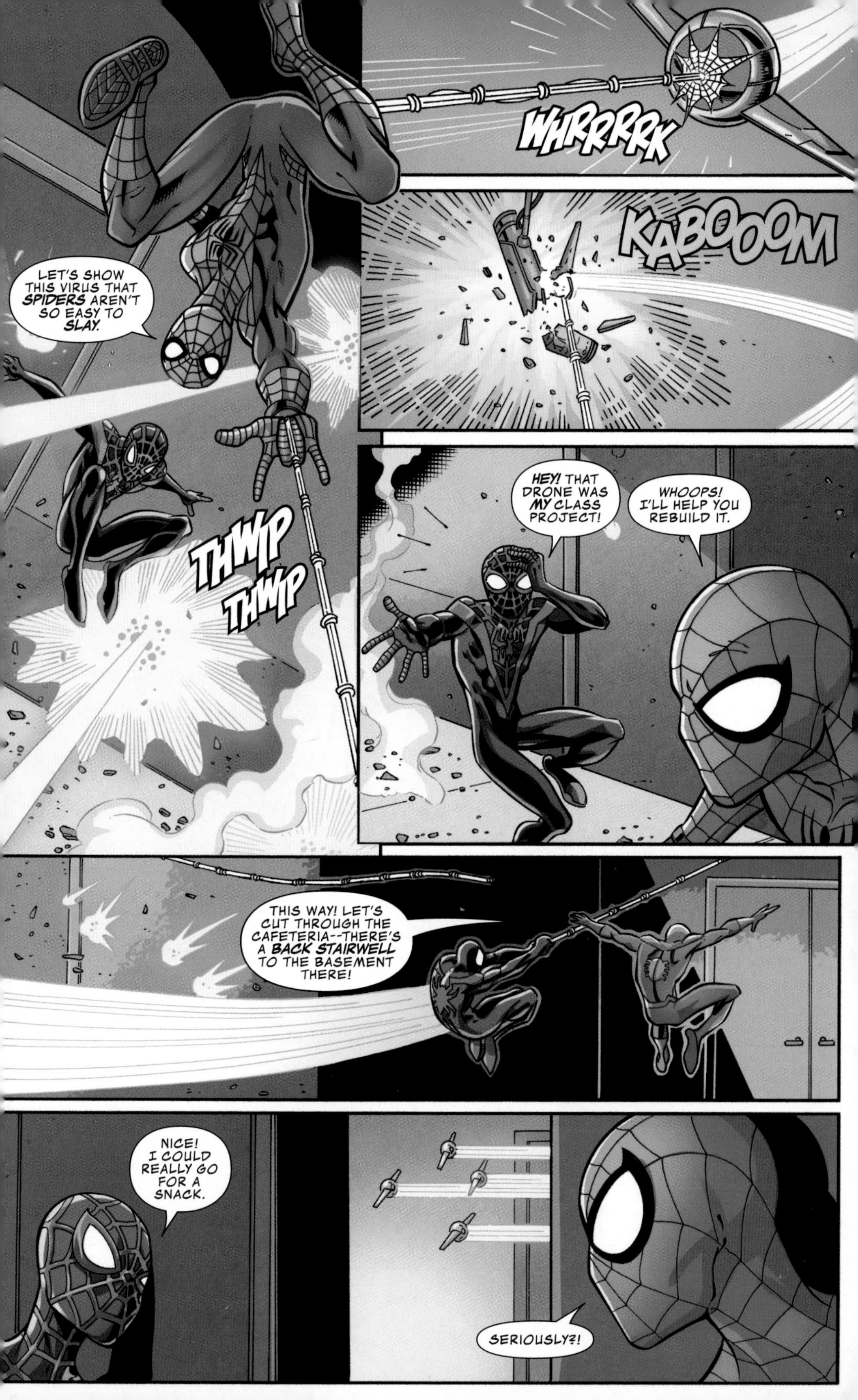
WHRRRRK
KABOOOM
LET'S SHOW THIS VIRUS THAT SPIDERS AREN'T SO EASY TO SLAY.
THWIP THWIP
HEY! THAT DRONE WAS MY CLASS PROJECT!
WHOOPS! I'LL HELP YOU REBUILD IT.
THIS WAY! LET'S CUT THROUGH THE CAFETERIA--THERE'S A BACK STAIRWELL TO THE BASEMENT THERE!
NICE! I COULD REALLY GO FOR A SNACK.
SERIOUSLY?!

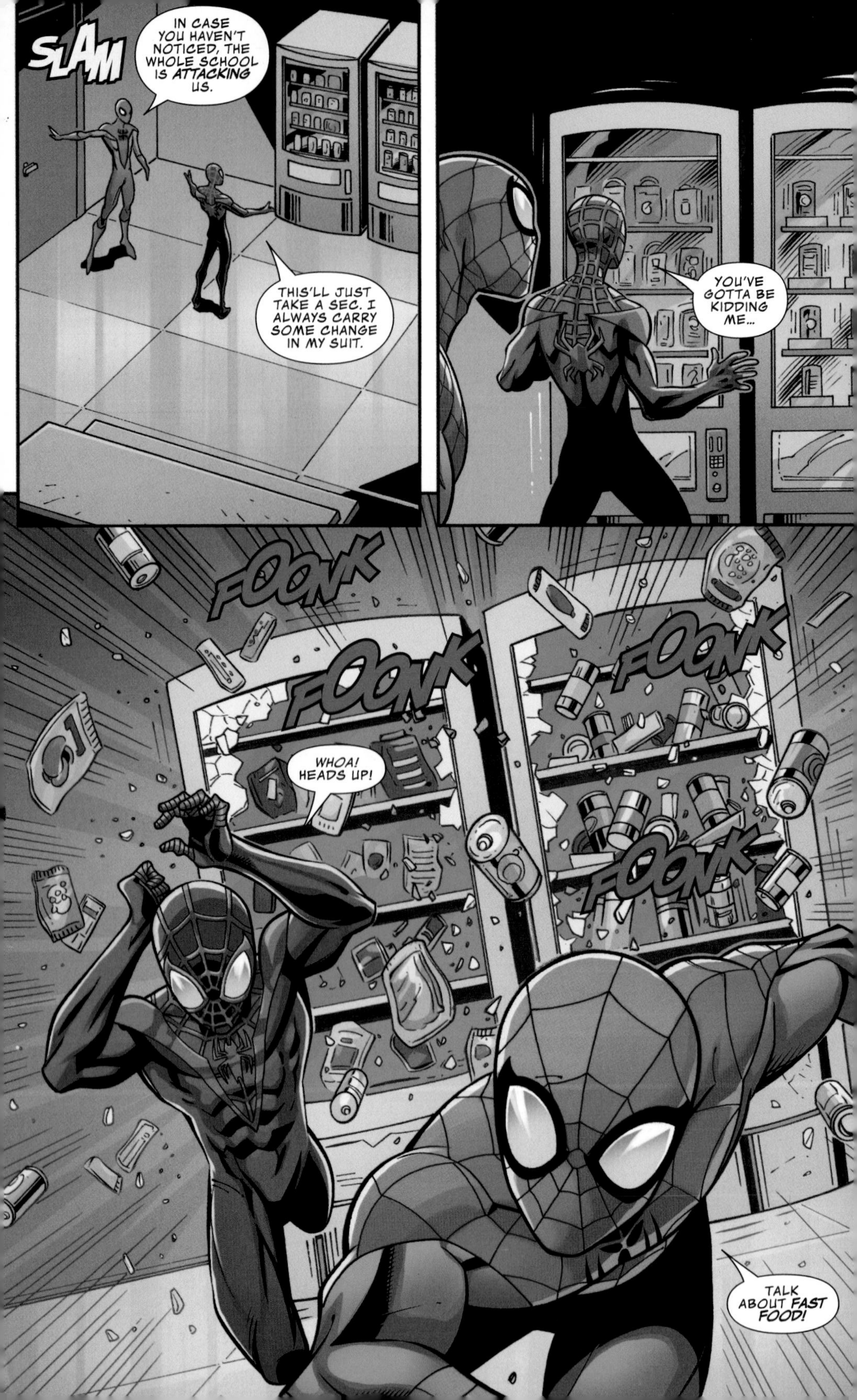
SLAM
IN CASE YOU HAVEN'T NOTICED, THE WHOLE SCHOOL IS ATTACKING US.
THIS'LL JUST TAKE A SEC. I ALWAYS CARRY SOME CHANGE IN MY SUIT.
YOU'VE GOTTA BE KIDDING ME...
FOONK
FOONK
FOONK
FOONK
WHOA! HEADS UP!
TALK ABOUT FAST FOOD!

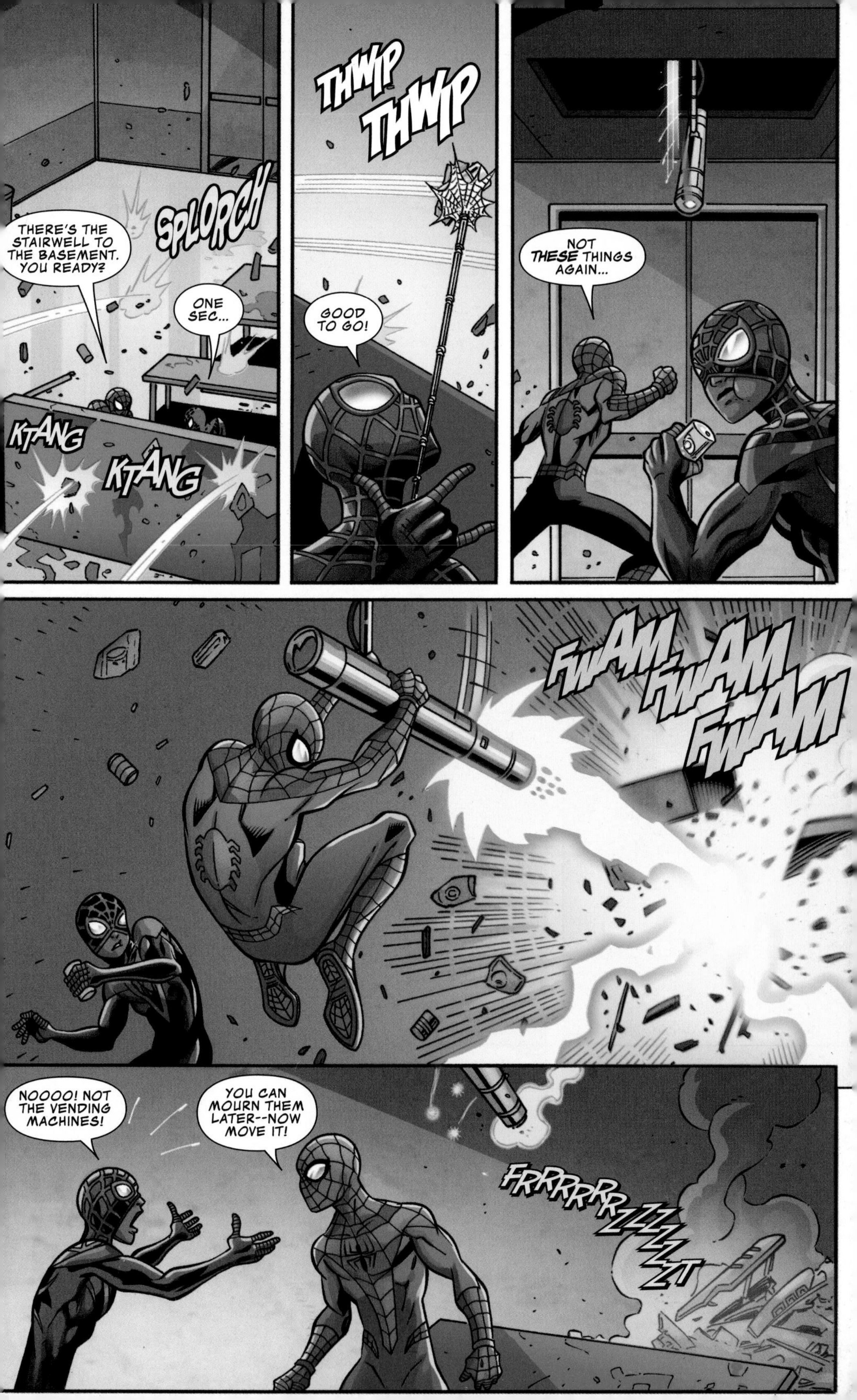

THERE'S THE STAIRWELL TO THE BASEMENT. YOU READY?
SPLORCH
ONE SEC...
KTANG
KTANG
THWIP
THWIP
GOOD TO GO!
NOT *THESE* THINGS AGAIN...
FWAM
FWAM
FWAM
NOOOO! NOT THE VENDING MACHINES!
YOU CAN MOURN THEM LATER--NOW MOVE IT!
FRRRRRRZZZZZZT

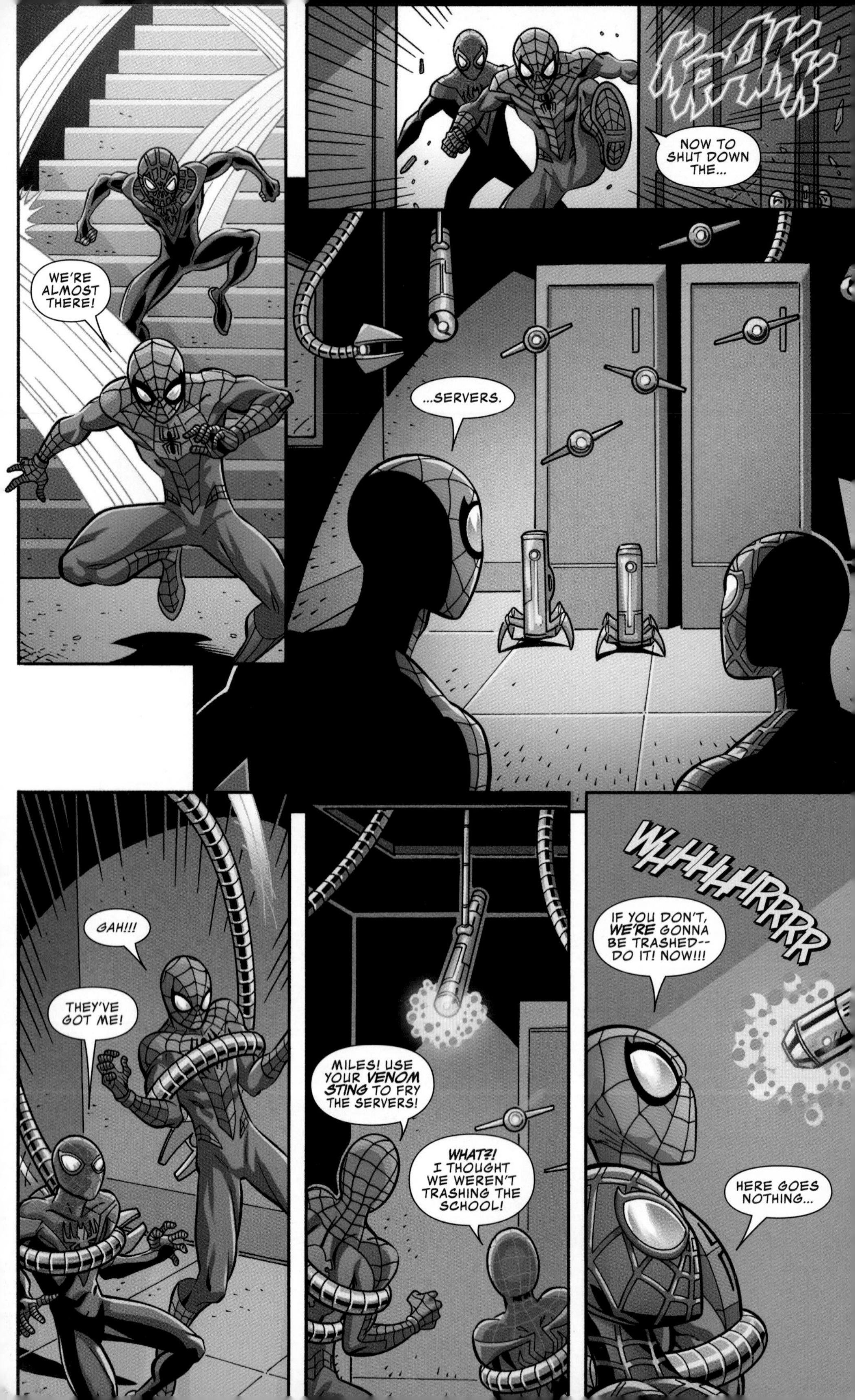
WE'RE ALMOST THERE!
KRAK
NOW TO SHUT DOWN THE...
...SERVERS.
GAH!!!
THEY'VE GOT ME!
MILES! USE YOUR VENOM STING TO FRY THE SERVERS!
WHAT?! I THOUGHT WE WEREN'T TRASHING THE SCHOOL!
WHHHHRRRRR
IF YOU DON'T, WE'RE GONNA BE TRASHED-- DO IT! NOW!!!
HERE GOES NOTHING...

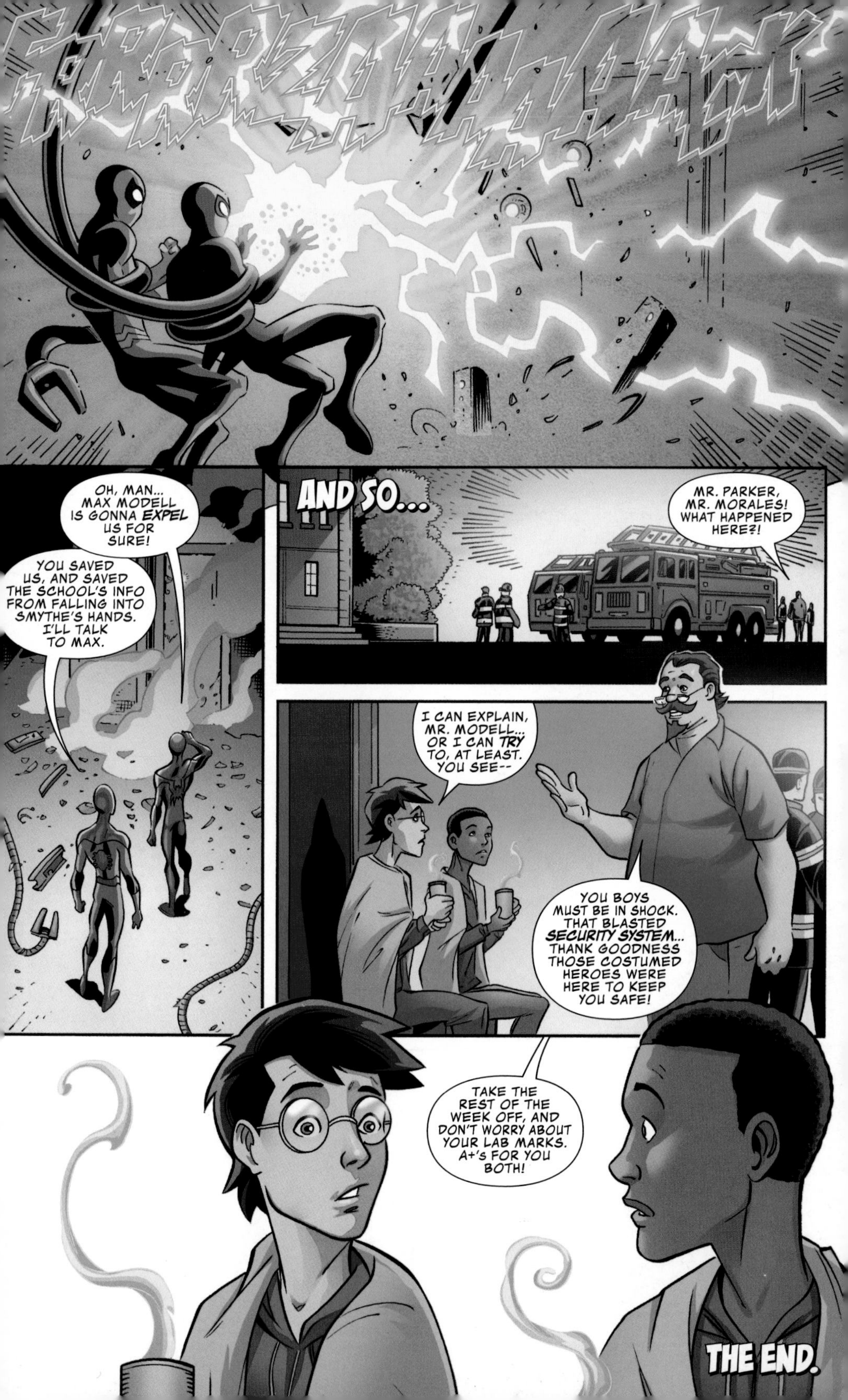
OH, MAN... MAX MODELL IS GONNA EXPEL US FOR SURE!
YOU SAVED US, AND SAVED THE SCHOOL'S INFO FROM FALLING INTO SMYTHE'S HANDS. I'LL TALK TO MAX.
AND SO...
MR. PARKER, MR. MORALES! WHAT HAPPENED HERE?!
I CAN EXPLAIN, MR. MODELL... OR I CAN TRY TO, AT LEAST. YOU SEE--
YOU BOYS MUST BE IN SHOCK. THAT BLASTED SECURITY SYSTEM... THANK GOODNESS THOSE COSTUMED HEROES WERE HERE TO KEEP YOU SAFE!
TAKE THE REST OF THE WEEK OFF, AND DON'T WORRY ABOUT YOUR LAB MARKS. A+'S FOR YOU BOTH!
THE END.

Here's a special sneak peek of
Marvel Super Hero Adventures: To Wakanda and Beyond!

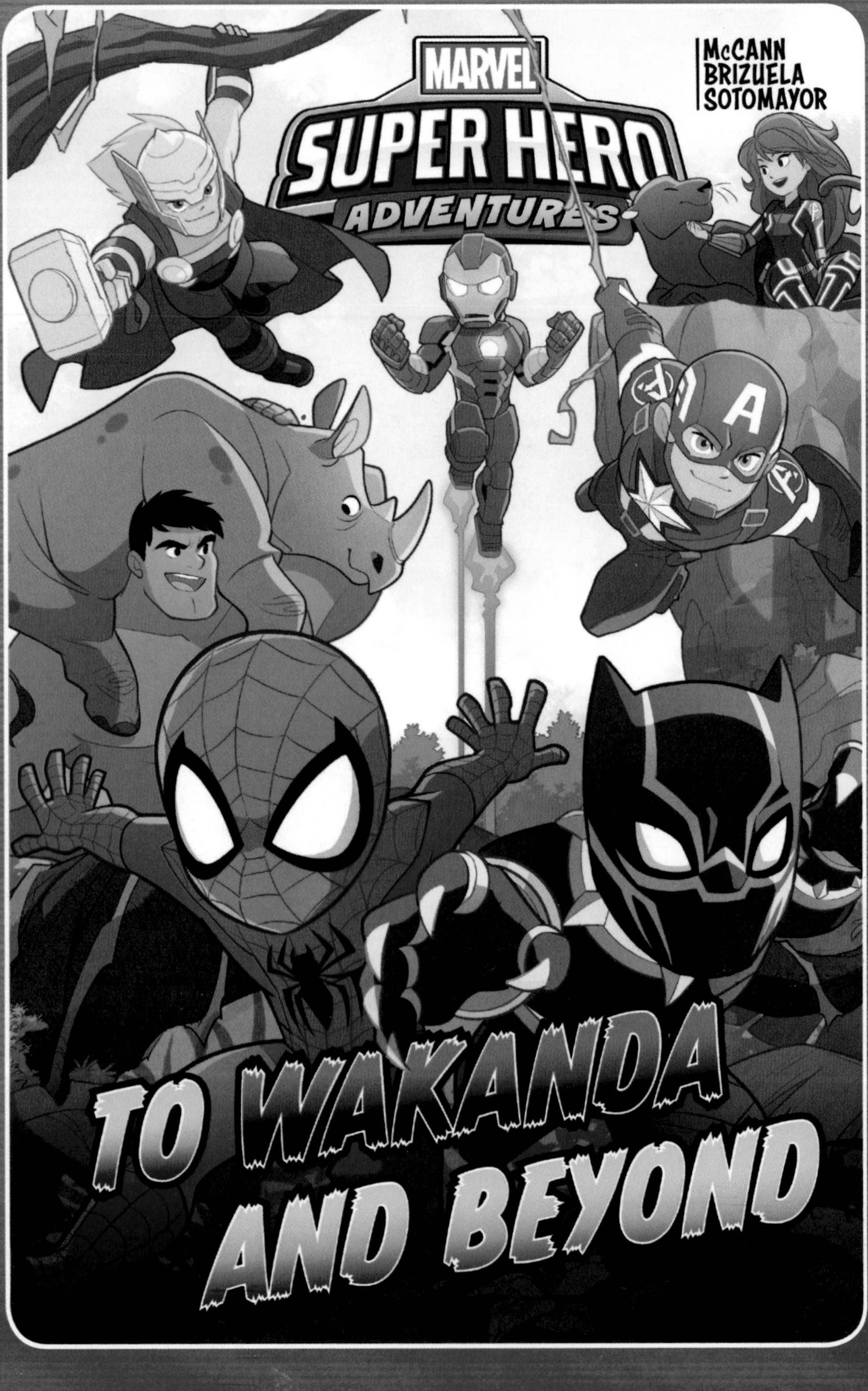
MARVEL
SUPER HERO
ADVENTURES
McCANN
BRIZUELA
SOTOMAYOR
TO WAKANDA AND BEYOND

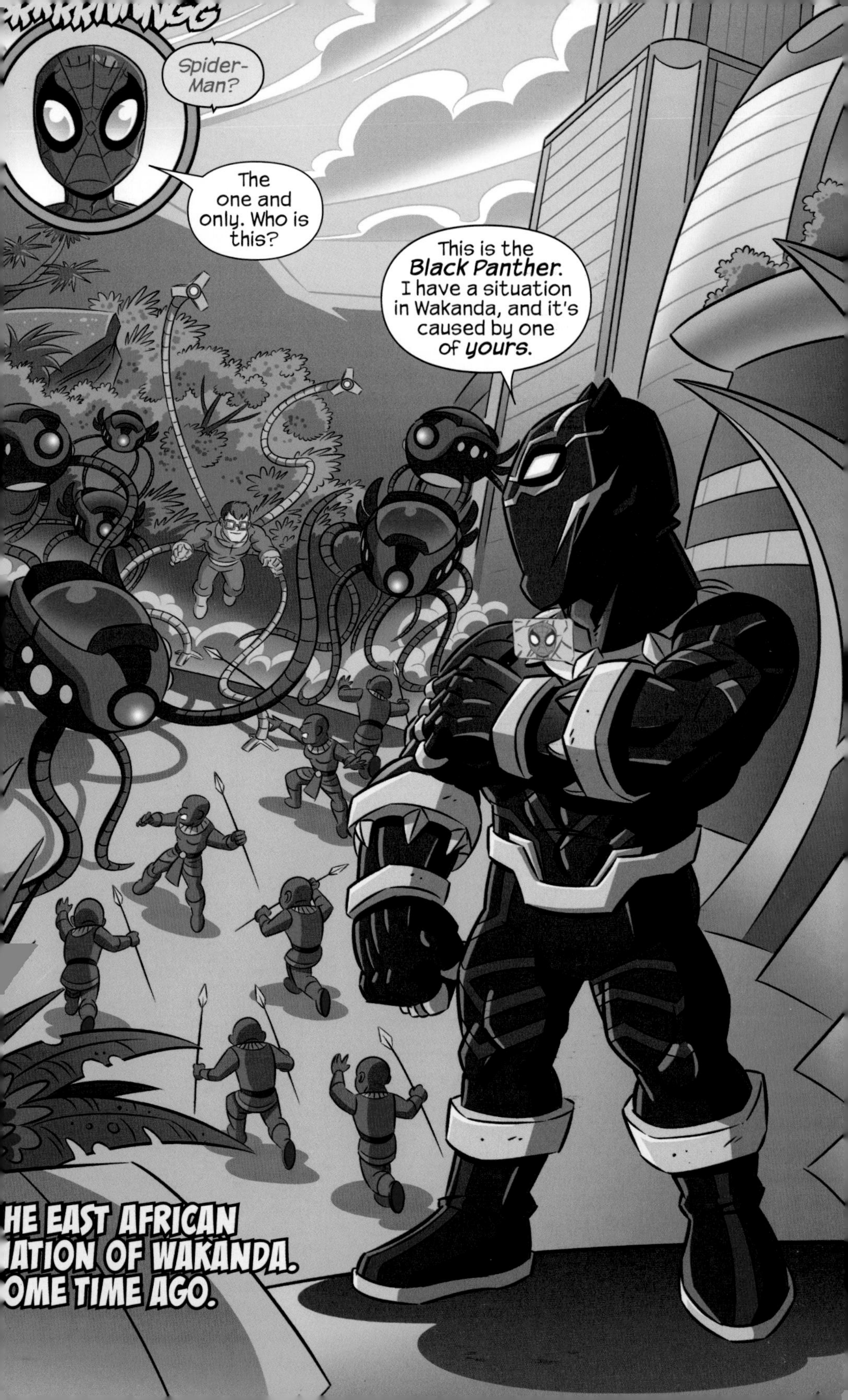

RKKRIIINGG
Spider-Man?
The one and only. Who is this?
This is the Black Panther. I have a situation in Wakanda, and it's caused by one of yours.
HE EAST AFRICAN
ATION OF WAKANDA.
OME TIME AGO.

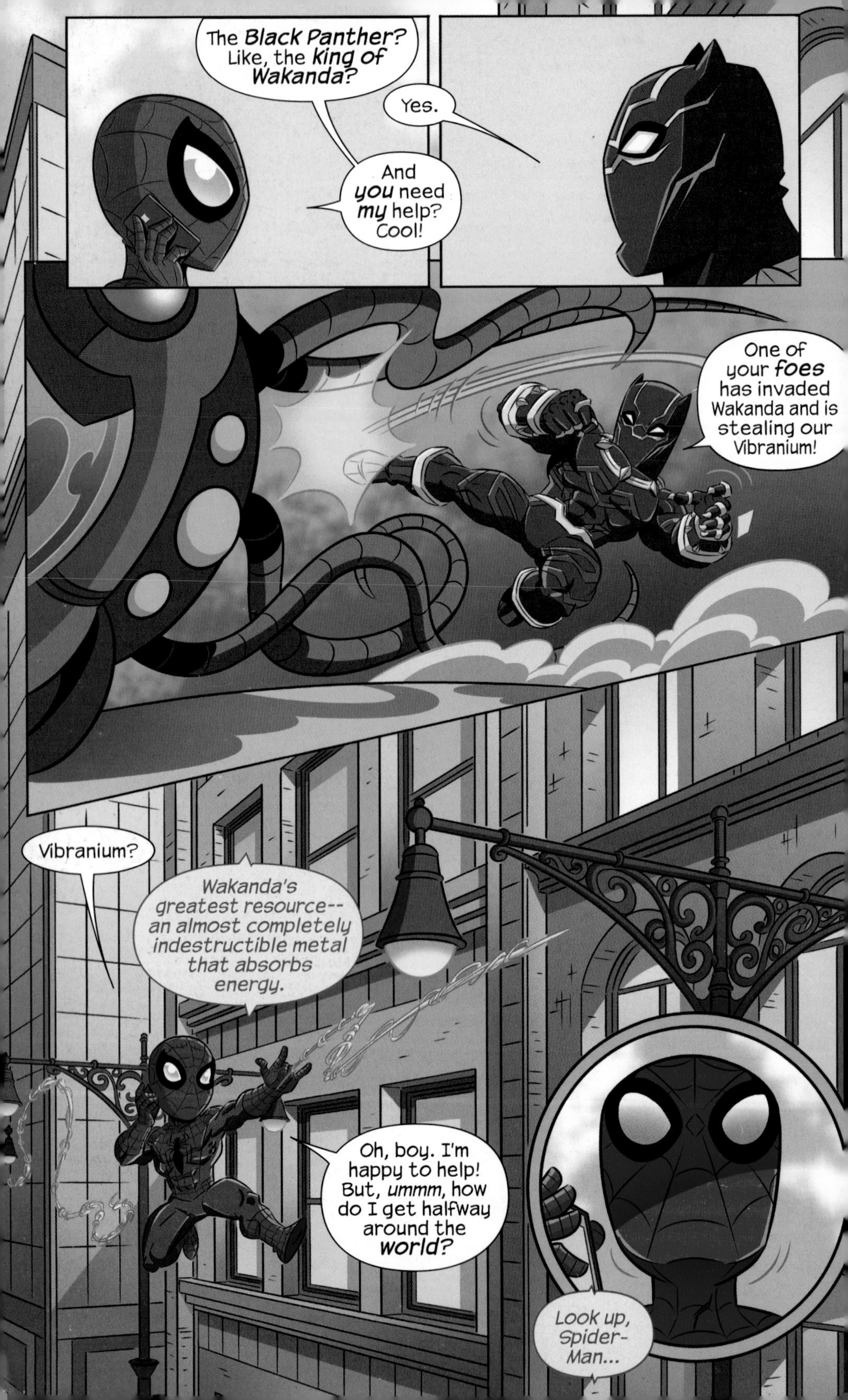

The Black Panther? Like, the king of Wakanda?
Yes.
And you need my help? Cool!
One of your foes has invaded Wakanda and is stealing our Vibranium!
Vibranium?
Wakanda's greatest resource-- an almost completely indestructible metal that absorbs energy.
Oh, boy. I'm happy to help! But, ummm, how do I get halfway around the world?
Look up, Spider-Man...

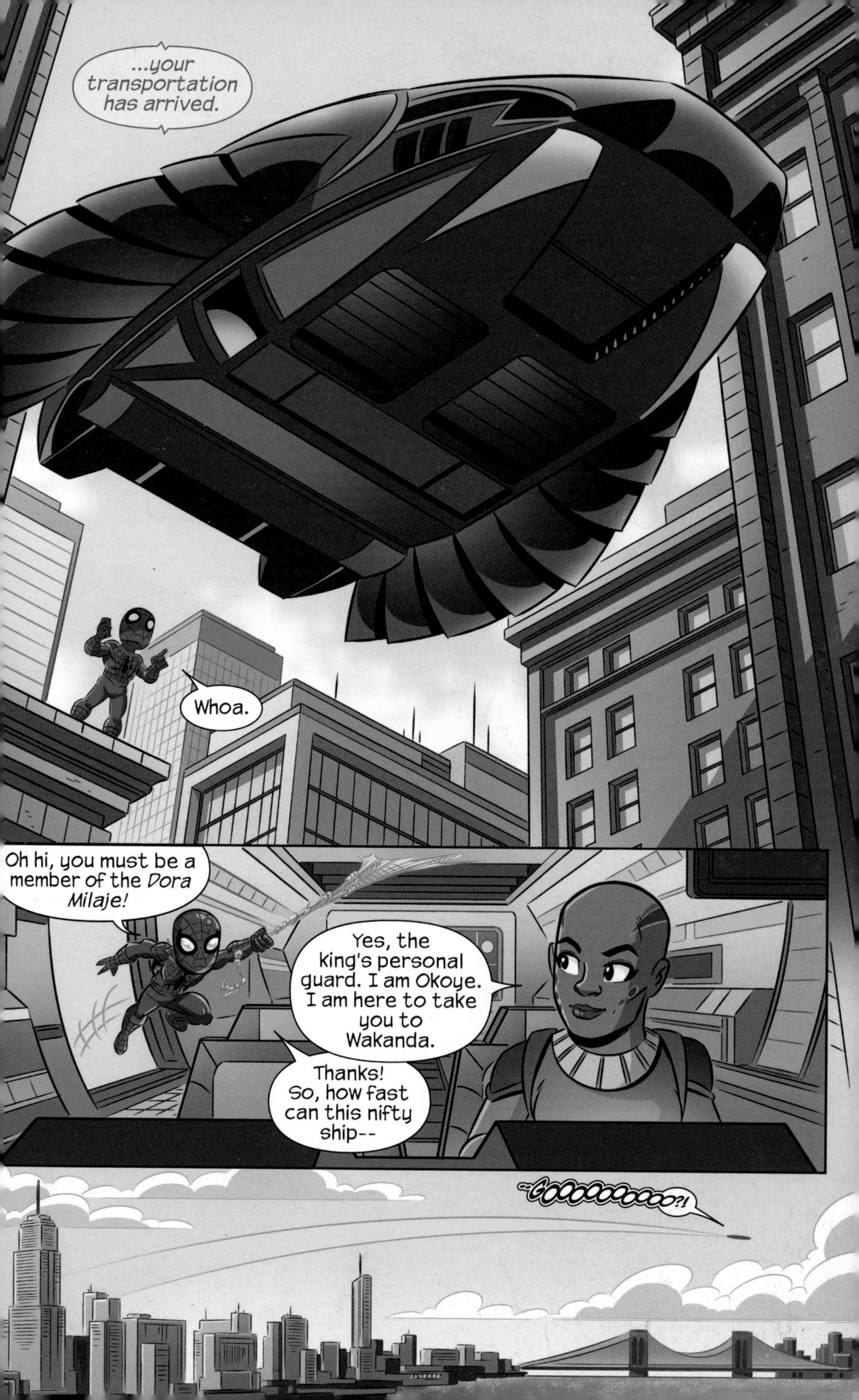
...your transportation has arrived.
Whoa.
Oh hi, you must be a member of the *Dora Milaje!*
Yes, the king's personal guard. I am Okoye. I am here to take you to Wakanda.
Thanks! So, how fast can this nifty ship--
--GOOOOOOOOOO?!

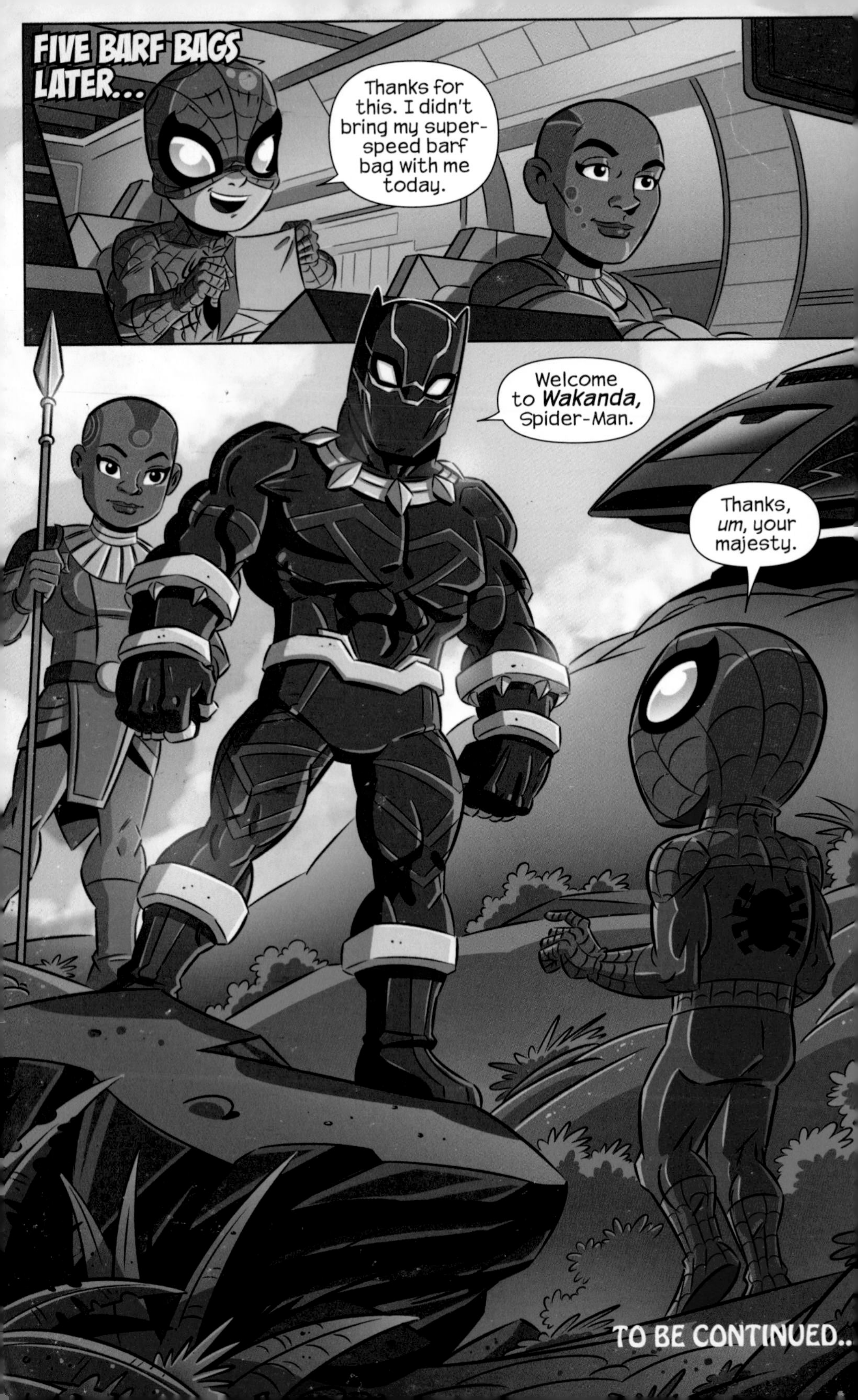
FIVE BARF BAGS LATER...
Thanks for this. I didn't bring my super-speed barf bag with me today.
Welcome to *Wakanda,* Spider-Man.
Thanks, *um,* your majesty.
TO BE CONTINUED...